TOUCHING THE DARK

Recent Titles by Jane Adams

ANGEL EYES
THE ANGEL GATEWAY
BIRD
CAST THE FIRST STONE
FADE TO GREY
FINAL FRAME
THE GREENWAY
LIKE ANGELS FALLING
MOURNING THE LITTLE DEAD *

* *available from Severn House*

TOUCHING THE DARK

Jane A. Adams

Severn House

This first world edition published in Great Britain 2003 by
SEVERN HOUSE PUBLISHERS LTD of
9–15 High Street, Sutton, Surrey SM1 1DF.
This first world edition published in the USA 2003 by
SEVERN HOUSE PUBLISHERS INC of
595 Madison Avenue, New York, N.Y. 10022.

British Library Cataloguing in Publication Data

Adams, Jane
Touching the dark
1. Obsessive compulsive disorder - Fiction
2. Detective and mystery stories
I. Title
823.9'14 [F]

ISBN 0-7278-5937-4

Typeset by Palimpsest Book Production Ltd.,
Polmont, Stirlingshire, Scotland.
Printed and bound in Great Britain by
MPG Books Ltd., Bodmin, Cornwall.

Prologue

Champagne stings when it hits you in the eyes.

Simon had never much thought about it before, but now he knew, and as he strode out of the gallery, wiping at his face with the palms of his hands, he was glad of the fact that his eyes were watering. It saved him making up excuses about grown men not crying in public.

Behind him, he was aware of the stunned silence. The tangible sense of expectation, just waiting for him to leave before the buzz of gossip started. Already a couple of the guest journos reached indiscreetly for their mobiles and were only distracted from following him by the screams of their hostess cutting through the silence.

'It was never me,' Tally yelled at Simon's back. 'It wasn't me, Simon. It was Jack. It was always Jack.'

'Always bloody Jack,' Simon muttered to himself. He allowed the heavy glass doors to swing shut behind him, cutting him off from Tally's world and Tally's people and Tally's judgements.

But at the same time, he wanted to turn back, to look . . . to see Tally, surrounded now by 'interested' friends. Maybe she'd be fending them away, maybe standing numbly allowing them to gather about her and press their sympathy against her stillness. Maybe . . . maybe see her coming after him, begging him not to leave.

He found himself asking, would he want to see Tally beg?

Just now? Damned right he would!

And would he go back if she did?

Yeah, that too. Damned right he would that too.

Simon crossed the road, quiet at this time of the night, and turned right, not sure where he intended to go. There were parked cars closely wedged on both sides of the street, left there by guests at the exhibition or patrons at the fashionable wine bars that now crammed into what had, in Simon's childhood, been tidy rows of grocers' shops and scrubbed-stepped terraced houses. Families like his own, who played in the little park across the street.

He'd not intended to fight with her. He'd gone, uninvited, but he hoped not unwelcome, to the opening night of Tally Palmer's Homecoming show. A coup for the local gallery, her choosing to launch her retrospective here before it went off to London. He'd wanted so much to see her, to tell her he was sorry and that he still wanted . . .

Wanted what, Simon? Wanted her back again and everything to be the way it was?

He laughed harshly. Fat chance of that after all they'd said to one another. Bitter, angry words when Tally had told him that he didn't understand and Simon had been too annoyed to even try. But, for a brief time, when he'd slipped quietly into the gallery, and Tally had noticed him from across the room, he had been certain he had seen her smile. Certain that the opening had been there for either one of them to make a move and everything to be all right.

Then he'd said the wrong thing and she'd replied with another wrong thing and before they knew it, they'd been fighting about the same old thing again.

'Always Jack,' Simon muttered angrily to himself, almost spitting the name of his enemy. His biggest rival in Tally's life. 'Too right it was always bloody Jack.'

He'd reached the park gates. He remembered them being locked at dusk, but they stood open now and to his surprise the main path leading through the park was brightly lit. He dredged the memory of this being done a few years back. Streetlights installed and the thoroughfare opened up from the university – what, in his school days had been the second rate Ingham Polytechnic – to the centre of town. He turned that way now, intending to head for home. It was around a two- or three-mile walk if he cut through the park; long enough to cool down, time enough to think. Not that he needed to think about Tally any more, he reflected angrily. Not after the hours and days and weeks he'd spent in Tally Palmer-related reverie, but she was not an easy image to erase once you let her into your mind.

And now, his mind so full of Tally, he noticed nothing else. Not the man following from the gallery or the quiet footsteps that dogged his own. He walked a well-lit path and his mind was so occupied with familiar if unwelcome thoughts that Simon sensed no danger. His first thought at the impact of a body barging against his was that some drunk had stumbled against him.

And then he knew different as he felt the pain of the knife driven into his back and, as Simon turned instinctively, the knife plunged deep again and he fell down into the dark.

One

April

Naomi Blake was familiar with the sound and the smell of hospitals. Once, she had been familiar with the sight of them too, but since the accident that had left her blind, she had to rely upon her other senses to confirm what she remembered.

First, there was the smell of disinfectant that clung to your skin for hours. Disinfectant and a particular brand of floor polish, faint now so late in the day but there in the background, ready to be resurrected with the dawn cleaners. And a faint stickiness to everything you touched in the waiting room, as though a lifetime of relatives spilling coffee from plastic cups was something even the cleaning staff could not erase.

Then the sounds: hushed voices, as though even in this separate waiting area, the sick might be disturbed and, conversely, the creak-crash of swing doors, now distant and accompanied by the metallic rattle of a trolley being pushed along a corridor. Then closer, the quick slap of leather shoes as the doctor came back to speak to Lillian and Samuel, telling them about their son. Napoleon, lying patiently by her feet, lifted his head, his tail twitching in expectation that this new intrusion might mean that it was time to go. Sorry mate, Naomi thought. It's going to be a while yet.

'Stable,' Naomi heard the doctor say, and she squeezed

gently on the cold, limp hand she held in both her own. Lillian had not let go of her since they'd heard the news. Seated on the other side of his wife, Samuel had possession of her other hand. Beyond Samuel, sitting close but emotionally so much apart, the woman police officer assigned as their liaison.

'Will he . . . ?' Lillian could not complete her sentence.

'Is he out of danger?' Naomi tried to keep her voice steady, knowing that both Lillian and Samuel needed her strength, required her to be their voice.

She felt the hesitation. Knew from long experience just how unready medics were to commit themselves; to raise false hope. 'We believe . . . I hope he'll come through,' the doctor said. He reached out and touched their hands, Lillian's and Naomi's. 'He's come this far,' he said, more certain of his ground and, Naomi thought, wanting so much to give them reassurance even while he feared to get it wrong. 'He was found so soon after the attack. The ambulance was there in minutes. Your son was lucky. I believe his luck will hold, Mrs Emmet. I really do.'

Naomi heard Lillian murmur thanks and the doctor rise to his feet and felt his tangible relief that he could go, get on with the practicalities of doing and leave them to the time-dragging, soul-eating task of waiting.

'Has he said anything more?' This from the police officer seated on their other side.

'Not since he was first brought in,' the doctor told her. 'Your colleague's waiting by the bedside and, Mrs Emmett, Mr Emmett, if you want to go in, just for a minute or two, then you can. But be prepared, there are tubes and drips and . . .'

'I know.' Lillian was on her feet. She pulled gently from Naomi's grasp. 'I want to see. To make sure he's . . .' She broke down and Naomi heard Samuel gently hushing her and then their soft, careful footfalls as they moved away, following the doctor through the swing doors, the crash as they passed through startling Naomi even though she'd been expecting it. Grumbling, Napoleon lowered his head again.

'You were with them when they found out?'

'Yeah, they've been friends for ages. I'd gone round to dinner. Alec was supposed to join us but he got called back to work.'

'Some flap or other,' the officer confirmed. 'You might not remember me, I was just a probationer when you . . . when you left.'

Naomi smiled. People, especially ex-colleagues, never quite knew what to say.

'I recognize the voice,' she said. 'June, you said, June Pritchard?'

'Yeah, that's right. Never done one of these before. I mean, I've done the deed, you know, told the parents their kid's been in an accident, been attacked, but I've never done the waiting bit.'

Naomi's smile broadened. 'How'd you manage to escape this long?' she asked. 'It's OK, no one finds it easy. I hated it. Still do.'

'You think he'll make it?'

'I hope so. God, I hope so.' She imagined Lillian and Samuel losing one of their beloved boys and found she couldn't even deal with the possibility. They were a lovely family, close, supportive, always laughing . . . or had been until Simon got involved with Tally Palmer.

'What he said, the victim, I mean, when he was brought in. That mean anything?'

'Oh yes, could mean a whole lot.'

She felt the other woman shrug. 'Well, at least they've got a suspect,' she said. 'Better than nothing.'

'Maybe,' Naomi half agreed. Privately, she really wasn't so sure. 'Always Jack,' Simon had been muttering when the dog walker and his girlfriend had found him, losing blood and going into shock. That's what they said, anyway. He kept murmuring that it was always Jack.

Footsteps and the crash of doors. Running feet this time, running feet in heels. Then the second crash of doors. Naomi knew who it was even before the woman spoke, her voice filled with tears and edging on hysteria. 'I want to see him. They said at the desk he was in ITU. I've got to see him.'

Naomi rose and reached out towards the newcomer. June was speaking, trying to placate this unknown woman, but it was Naomi, slipping automatically back into her old role, who took over now. 'Tally, it's all right. He's going to make it. His mum and dad are with him now. It's going to be all right.'

'You know her?'

Naomi nodded briefly, but said nothing. Instead she reached out and gathered a distraught Talitha Palmer into her arms, holding her tightly. 'It will be all right.'

Tally sobbed, her whole body shaking in Naomi's embrace and Naomi wondered what to do next. Simon's parents could be back at any time and just now she didn't feel that a meeting between them and Tally would be a useful thing. Too late, she heard the opening doors again, signalling Lillian and Samuel's return.

'What's she doing here?' Lillian almost screamed.

Tally pulled away from Naomi.

'I want to see Simon.'

'*You*! You want to see my son? Don't you think you've done enough? *You* get out of my sight.'

'Lillian, please.' Samuel sounded weary, but calm at least, Naomi noted. 'I think you'd better go,' he added. 'Miss Palmer, you have no place here just now.'

'Miss Palmer? Samuel, you used to call me Tally. We used to be—'

'Tally, please,' Naomi intervened. 'Come on. Take me downstairs. I'll get you some tea.'

'I don't want—'

'It would be best, Miss Palmer,' June intervened, somewhat belatedly. 'Please, go with . . . with Naomi.'

She'd been going to call her DI Blake, Naomi realized. It was an odd feeling. She took Tally by the arm and led her towards the door. Napoleon, taking his cue and pressing gently against her leg to guide her through. 'Lillian, Samuel. I'll be back soon.'

Samuel patted her gently on the arm, but Lillian did not acknowledge her and suddenly Naomi felt so much like the enemy. She sighed deeply, wondering how much of a betrayal Lillian would see this as. Her 'siding' with Tally Palmer while Simon lay there, in ITU, still not far enough from dying. She decided that there was nothing she could do for the moment. June's brief had been to stay with the family, and there was no one else to deal with Tally, though Naomi did feel, with a sudden pang of irritation, that she was doing much of the officer's job for her. She reminded herself impatiently that June Pritchard was only just out of her probationary year and that she, Naomi, had something like a decade of knowledge to fall back on, but it still rankled.

'You'll have to direct us,' she told Tally, trying to keep the annoyance from her voice. 'I can't remember the way to the café and Napoleon doesn't know this hospital. I think it's this way to the stairs.'

She heard Tally sniff, trying to control her tears, and fished in her pocket for the remains of the pack of tissues she had been given for Lillian. 'Here,' Naomi said. 'Wipe your eyes. We'll find the Ladies, so you can wash your face and comb your hair. Then we'll go and get some decent tea. Those machines are bloody awful. Then I'll tell you what I know about Simon and you can fill me in on what the hell went on tonight.'

*   *   *

'We fought, argued, I mean,' Tally said slowly.

'About Jack?'

Tally sighed. 'What do you think? You know, I didn't invite Simon. But I hoped he'd come. I wanted . . . wanted to try and patch things up between us.'

'Seems he had the same idea.'

'Yeah, and we both blew it. If I hadn't . . . If he'd just listened to me, he wouldn't have gone out there and it wouldn't have happened.'

'Wouldn't it?'

Tally's cup clattered back on to the saucer. 'What do you mean?'

'Tally, I don't know what the police have told you . . .'

'Nothing. I mean they said he'd been mugged. Stabbed walking through the park. I only heard because someone noticed the party at the gallery and thought we might have seen something. Then when they realized he'd come from the reception they started to ask a lot of questions and . . .' She began to cry again, deep, throaty sobs that Naomi knew would not cease in any hurry.

She tried to find it in her to be sympathetic, but for the moment her sympathies were with Lillian and Samuel and her instincts were to press this home and see what Tally came out with.

'Simon managed to speak to the couple that found him,' she told the younger woman. 'Tally, it wasn't a mugging. Nothing random about this. Tally, Jack stabbed Simon in the back. Simon told them so.'

'Jack?' The sobbing ceased abruptly. 'No. You're lying. It was just some thief. No, it wasn't Jack.'

'Some thief that leaves his wallet behind,' Naomi objected. 'Street crime might be bad, Tally, but petty thieves don't usually attack first then run off empty-handed. Threaten, yes, but most have no intention of adding murder to their CV.'

Tally moaned as though in pain. 'Nooo, not this. Not this.'

'Yes, this. Tally, you said you loved Simon and I believe you. I believe you when you said you hoped he'd be there tonight, that maybe you could patch things up and if that's true then you've got to go to the police. Talk to Alec even, but you've got to tell them about Jack, about the threats, and all the things he's put you through. He's a violent man, Tally. He was almost a murderer tonight. Jack wanted Simon to die.'

'You don't know that. Simon might have thought—'

'You don't believe that any more than I do!' Naomi took a deep breath and lowered her voice. 'Tally. How can you protect him? This man is a killer.'

'Simon will live. You told me.'

'The intent was to kill. In my book that adds up to practically the same thing. And what's to stop him trying again? What's to stop him harming you or the next man who gets too close to you? Damn it, Tally, the man's a bloody psycho.'

Not very professional, Naomi thought, regretting the violence of her words as soon as they were out, but it was too late by then.

'I'm going now,' Tally told her and Naomi could hear that she was regaining some of her usual icy control. 'I'll come back later . . . later this morning. They'll have to let me see him then. He'll ask for me, I know he will.'

'I wouldn't count on it,' Naomi told her. 'Please, Tally. Tell them where to find Jack.'

'I don't know where to find Jack,' Tally said softly. 'You don't understand, do you. I never did. I never do.'

Naomi heard her walk away and leaned back in her chair with a deep sigh. Somewhere in the distance the hum of a buffing machine announced the start of another hospital day and Naomi felt for the time on her watch. Six a.m. Of course it was. Her own days in hospital had been punctuated by such routine. Tea and floor polish at six ten sharp.

And two floors above her in ITU, Lillian and Samuel would still be waiting.

Two

The night Simon told Tally that he loved her she took him back to her apartment at the edge of town. They had driven in silence, the windscreen wipers sussing across the glass and something bluesy that he couldn't place playing softly on the radio.

He was certain that he'd lost it. That saying to Talitha Palmer that he loved her was the worst thing he could have done. She must have heard it so many times before and learnt to treat such casual adoration with the contempt that it deserved. But this time it was true. For weeks now Simon had lived and breathed in Tally's shadow and he loved her with an intensity he had not felt since he'd been seventeen and been possessed by those feelings for the first time.

He tried to speak as they pulled into the parking space in front of the converted warehouse where Tally lived on the top floor.

'Tally, I . . .'

'Shh.' She waved him into silence and was out of the car before he could manage another word.

He followed her, not certain that she wanted him to but reluctant just to walk away. She waited for him at her front door and held it open for him to go inside.

He glanced around. 'It's big,' he said. 'Spacious. It's . . .' He was lost for words. Minimal and empty was what it was. The longest wall was of unplastered brick, while the two end walls were a matt, unbroken white that continued on to the doors. A line of windows ran along the outer wall and Tally walked along the row, closing the blinds and shutting out the night. He had expected to see her pictures mounted on the walls, but the space that he would have used for display was empty. Even the blinds were plain and unadorned.

'It's . . .'

'Simple,' she said. 'I like it that way. When I need a place to think I can come here and know there'll be no distractions. Nothing to break my focus.'

'Right,' he said. Then: 'Can I sit down?' It was the kind of room that made him feel he had to ask her first.

'Sure.'

He perched himself on the edge of one of the plain white chairs. There were two of them, and a large sofa facing the windows. No sign of a television or a hi-fi, or of books or any kind of clutter.

Below the windows was a solid line of cupboards. They were light wood, maple, he guessed, with doors that fitted flush merging cleverly into the rolled edge of the top. Tiny curved notches cut into the upper edge of each door served as handles. The one Tally opened held glasses and bottles. She poured, offered him the drink. He took it without asking what it was and sipped slowly, savouring the smoothness of the bourbon he liked so much.

'Have you lived here long?'

'Two years.'

'Do you always have it so bright?'

The lighting was strong, almost industrial. Tally picked up a small box that lay on the arm of her chair and pressed something. The lights dimmed and their colour softened. She came over and bent down. Her lips on his tasted of the wine she had been drinking. She took his hand. 'Come to bed with me,' she said. 'It's what you came here for.'

'Not just that . . .'

But she silenced his protests. 'It's all right.'

The bedroom was through a door in one of the plain white walls, the open door a dark wound in the once unbroken surface. She left the bedroom lights switched off, pale illumination from the room beyond casting deeper shadows, accentuating the whiteness of her naked skin.

'I can hardly see you,' she whispered. Black skin in shadow. White skin in faint light. She kissed him and he pulled her to him, afraid to tell her again how much he loved her.

Afterwards, they lay close, bodies wrapped together in a tangle of limbs. 'I want to know you,' Simon whispered. 'Everything there is to know. Everything.'

'I doubt that,' she told him, and though she still lay beside him, he sensed her pull away. Nothing physical, but the shift was there and it brought emptiness.

Finally, Tally got up and crossed to the window. She lifted the edge of the blind and looked outside at the night sky, starless and still thick with rain. Simon studied her body outlined faintly in the uncertain light and wondered what to do. The sudden withdrawal of intimacy hurt and confused him.

'You should go,' she told him. 'You've a long journey tomorrow.'

There was nothing he could say. He picked up his clothes and dressed in the main room, feeling stupid and used. He didn't even say goodbye.

Tally watched him from the window, the tall, slim figure running across the car park and back towards the main road. Running from patch of light to rain-filled shadow and back to patch of yellow light.

'I want to know you,' she whispered, echoing Simon's words. 'Everything there is to know.'

Three

April

'You're thinking about your friend,' Harry said. 'Naomi, did you get any sleep when you came home?'

'Not a lot, no. I tried, but by that time it was eight in the morning and I couldn't settle. Too much going through my head, I suppose. But I'm sorry, Harry, you asked me something and I don't know what it was.'

'It's all right, it was nothing urgent.' He got up and came over to sit beside her on the sofa. A rare and intimate act for Harry. 'I just keep talking for the sake of it, I suppose. You know me, Naomi, I'm never good at this sort of thing. I don't know what to say.'

'I'm just glad of the company,' she told him. 'I don't really want to be alone.'

He patted her hand. 'Tea, I think,' he said. 'I'll do the honours, shall I?'

He got up and crossed to Naomi's little kitchen, Napoleon following hopefully in his wake. Harry wasn't such a good bet as Alec when it came to begging snacks, but was still worth a try. Alec, Naomi's ex-colleague and now close friend and lover, often stayed at her flat and Napoleon knew him well. 'Patrick wanted to know if you were still on for tomorrow,' Harry said, 'but I told him, under the circumstances . . .'

'No, I'll still go,' Naomi told him. 'I promised and frankly, I can't do any good sitting around here. Lillian and Samuel will be at the hospital and I'm still not sure how Lillian feels about me at the moment.'

'She'll get over it.'

'I hope so. I couldn't believe Tally arriving like that last night. I didn't know what to do for the best. Look, tell Patrick I'd love to see the film with him. Sure you don't want to come?'

'No, thank you. I hate anything science fictional. I don't much like the cinema, as you well know.'

Naomi laughed. 'Are you still on for dogsitting, though?'

'I surely am. Mam and I are looking forward to it. Frankly, I think we've got the better part of the deal.'

Harry's family and Naomi had been friends since Naomi's childhood when Harry's sister, Helen, had been her best friend. Harry, now a single parent with a teenage son, had come back to the area to be closer to his mother – and to Naomi – and the friendship between them had grown. Patrick, Harry's son, was fifteen and Naomi got along well with the sometimes too grown-up boy. Visits to the cinema had become a regular feature of their friendship. It was an activity Naomi had loved before she had lost her sight and even now it had kept its appeal.

'I can't believe she means to go on protecting this man,' Harry commented.

Naomi shook her head. 'Maybe she'll change her mind. Maybe she's right and Simon was confused. After all, he was badly hurt. We don't know for certain he even saw his attacker.'

'You don't believe that,' Harry told her.

'No. No I don't, but I don't see what we can do about it either.'

The kettle had boiled and she could hear tea-making noises coming from the kitchen. Naomi leaned her head back against the sofa cushions and closed her eyes. 'I'll talk to Alec later,' she told Harry. 'See what else the police know. That's if he's heard anything more.' She shrugged. 'I don't know, Harry. I believe she does care for Simon, what I can't make out is what a hold this Jack has over her.'

'Fear, I suppose,' Harry said. 'This man's obviously violent. Maybe she's quite simply scared of him.'

'Then tell the police. Get him convicted. Get him out of her life and out of Simon's.'

'For how long?' Harry questioned. 'Naomi, I've known women who . . . I worked with this one. I'd worked with her for years and never knew . . . Then it all came out one day. He'd been abusing her since they were first married, but always, he was sorry. He wanted her to forgive him and she said he'd be fine for weeks then. Before it all started up again.'

'What made her tell?'

'Oh, that was the strangest part. The saddest too, I suppose. He left her for a younger woman. Told her he didn't find her attractive any more. And after she'd put up with all that for years.'

'You think she stayed with him through fear?'

'No. I think she stayed with him because of love,' Harry said simply. 'Or a version of it anyway, what she . . . and he too, I think . . . took to be love. Fear too, but I don't have to tell you how much more complicated than that these things can get.'

He brought her tea. Naomi folded her hands around the bright red mug. It had an odd texture to it, some kind of slip glaze technique that made the outside feel like a part melted candle, the trails running down and ending in satisfying bumps like frozen wax. Alec told her it was the ugliest thing he'd ever seen and that it went with nothing else she owned, but Naomi didn't care.

'You know,' she said. 'That's what I don't get. Usually abusive relationships are like the one you described. There's an element of, I don't know, possessiveness about them in the sense that the couple usually live together or . . . ? But Tally dated Simon for months before Jack began to interfere again. It was as if he didn't care until . . . I don't know. Until some particular point. Until Simon fell in love?'

'Until Tally fell in love with him, more like,' Harry suggested.

'Hmm,' Naomi mused. 'Maybe this Jack can handle all the other stuff. Maybe Tally just told him straight. She wasn't coming back to him this time. She wanted Simon. Simon himself said she kept warning him off because of Jack. Harry, it seems like we've been chasing the Tally-Jack-Simon triangle around for months.'

'That's because you have,' Harry observed.

'True.' She sipped her tea. 'I don't know, Harry, I don't think any of us could have foreseen anything like this.'

'Of course you couldn't,' Harry declared warmly. 'Ex-boyfriends don't generally go around knifing their rivals in the back.'

'It happens,' Naomi sighed. 'One of those things that happen to other people in other places. Not to the likes of Simon.'

Harry had taken himself off, having shopping to do for Mari, and once left alone Naomi found that sleep at last began to threaten. But she couldn't go to bed. Somehow, that was too much like giving in and she'd never been good at sleeping in the afternoon. Instead, she dragged the soft blue blanket from her bed, put some music on the stereo, a Dinah Washington compilation that reminded her of her gran and always managed to soothe her nerves. She curled up on the sofa, the blanket wrapped tightly around her, and with Napoleon snoring contentedly on the rug she let her mind drift back to the first time she had heard about the

Jack presence some three months before, right back at the beginning of the year.

Visits to the Emmets were always things to look forward to, Naomi thought. Lillian was a fantastic cook and they ate informally in the big kitchen that stretched the length of the back of the house, Lillian putting last minute touches to Caribbean dishes while her guests chatted to her.

The Emmets had been Alec's friends for longer than he could remember. His parents had lived next door to them and Alec had played big brother to their two sons. When the Emmets had moved, it had been Alec that had made an extra effort to keep in touch with them, while their relationship with his parents had drifted into the occasional phone call and cards at Christmas and birthdays. Three years ago, he had first introduced Naomi to them and the friendship had been an instant and lasting one.

This time though, on a bitter January day, despite the usual banter and easy conversation, Naomi had felt that something was wrong. There had been moments of silence, looks that she had sensed exchanged between Lillian and Samuel that had spoken of a problem one or other was on the verge of revealing.

Lillian's kitchen was a bright place with a stripped wooden floor and primrose yellow walls. Naomi could no longer see the vibrant strings of chillies hanging from wooden pegs and the blue glass proudly displayed on open shelves, or the Mexican bowls filled with fruit standing on the sideboard, but in her mind's eye she could still visualize this scene which reflected so much of Lillian's character. The Emmets were happy, lively people, with a strong sense of their own worth and their ability to truly welcome others into the warmth of their home. It hurt Naomi that whatever it was that troubled them was strong enough that it seemed to strip the colour even from her memory of the room.

'More wine?' Samuel asked her.

'Thank you.' She heard the deep red liquid glug into her glass and reached forward cautiously to pick it up. 'What are you feeding that dog, Alec?' she asked as the slight shift of black Labrador and the thump of tail told her that Alec had slipped some titbit to Napoleon, who lay on the floor beside her chair.

'She's caught us out again, old son,' Alec told him.

'He'll get fat.'

'Fat? No way. Built like a runner is our Napoleon.' He reached out and clasped her hand beneath the table, squeezing gently as he said in reply to Samuel's enquiring gesture, 'No thanks Samuel, if you've something in the soft drink line that would be great, but I've got to drive home.'

'You can always stay. There's Simon's old room. The bed is almost double.'

'I've got an early start tomorrow. But another time we'll take you up on that.' He paused and Naomi felt him squeeze her fingers once again before letting go. 'How is Simon these days?' he said. 'I've not seen him in months and you've spent the entire evening trying not to mention him.'

'Oh, he's well,' Samuel began. Then: 'No, he's not, Alec, and I should know better than to hide things from the two of you. The fact is, Lillian and I agreed we should talk to you about him, then when it came to it, I didn't know how to even begin.'

'Is he still seeing Tally Palmer?' Naomi asked, breaking the awkward silence that followed.

'No, no he's not,' Lillian told her and Naomi was alarmed to hear tears in the woman's voice.

'Lillian? Have I said something wrong?'

'No, no, of course not dear. But that's the problem, you see. She broke it off with him and nothing . . . nothing's been the same since then.'

'I'm sorry to hear that,' Alec said, 'but these things

happen, I suppose. It must be difficult for someone like Tally Palmer, travelling all the time . . .'

'Oh, that's what we told him,' Lillian said. 'But no, *that's* not what he thinks at all. He thinks that someone's taken her from him. He won't have it that sometimes relationships just came to an end. As far as he's concerned, he was in love with that girl and we thought she loved him too, and as far as he's concerned neither thing has changed.'

'If she still loved him, why stop seeing him?' Naomi questioned. 'When was this, Lillian?'

'Oh, Lord, it must be a couple of months ago now. She broke things off and then got angry when he wouldn't take her word that things were over. Simon swears she never told him why. We put it to him: this is a famous woman with an international reputation, with a life all over the world. It was foolishness to even think that such a thing should last between them.'

'I thought they were getting on so well,' Alec commented.

'Oh, they were,' Samuel told him. 'And she is such a *nice* young woman. Honest, genuine. She helped Darien with his pictures and called us a couple of times a week just to say hello. Then suddenly, all over. I tried calling her, but after the first few times, all I got was her machine.'

'Maybe she thought it was best to break cleanly?' Naomi said.

'That's what I thought, then I found out that Darien had seen her, spoken to her several times. She promised him some information on a course and that she would talk to him about his latest photographs. She kept her promise, but asked him not to tell, and Darien would have kept his word too, but we don't like secrets in this house. You know that, Naomi. Darien is no better at keeping them than the rest of us, and finally he told.'

'Simon was furious,' Lillian took up the tale. 'He

threatened never to speak to his brother again, then of course, Samuel had words with him and he calmed down.'

'I can't imagine Simon being angry at anyone for long,' Naomi commented.

'Not in general, no,' Lillian agreed. 'Though lately, he's not been himself. Not himself at all.'

Naomi could imagine the worried frown creasing Lillian's broad forehead. She was a handsome woman and in her youth, Naomi knew, she had been beautiful. When Naomi had first met the Emmets, she had still been able to see, still been a police officer, still had a career working alongside Alec Friedman. When Alec had first introduced them all, Naomi had been regaled with stories of how Lillian and Samuel had met. She had admired the family photo albums and particularly the framed wedding picture of Samuel and Lillian taken thirty years before in front of the local Baptist church.

Samuel's skin was very dark. Black skin that almost glowed it was so intense a colour. He was a tall, slim man with the most wonderful brown eyes and a smile that twitched almost constantly at the corner of his mouth.

Lillian was small and had been slim. In later years she had gained a little weight, but lost nothing of her prettiness, though her features had matured and her gaze carried a confidence and determination that had been lacking in the girl she had been when she married Samuel Emmet.

Simon was, Naomi recalled, the image of his father as a young man. Tall and strongly built, with that same smile, whereas Darien, the younger by a half-dozen years, favoured his mother's side, small and lightly made and almost too pretty for a boy.

'You want me to talk to him,' Alec said. It wasn't a question.

Across the table, Naomi sensed that Lillian nodded. It filled a moment's silence before Samuel said, 'We didn't like to ask you, but Alec, you two have been close since

Simon was a child. He *might* listen to you. He *has* to listen to someone.'

'I'm not sure I know what to say,' Alec commented. 'Samuel, what do you *want* me to say to him?'

Samuel shrugged. 'I don't know. That we love him. Care about him.'

'Oh, Samuel, I'm sure he knows that,' Naomi told him.

'But sometimes those who really love are not the ones to remind,' Lillian said. 'Alec, Naomi, try to talk to him, please. Tell him he can't go on like this. So miserable, so depressed, so . . . He'll lose his job, Alec. I talked to his editor. He's been refusing assignments and those he's produced are not good enough to print. And you know how much that job meant to him. A journalist was always what he wanted to be.'

Naomi felt Alec shift in his chair and the dog lifted his head to see if anything interesting might be on offer.

'If you think it will help, then I'll give it a go,' he told Samuel, though Naomi could hear in his voice that he felt, given time, the young man would come out of it himself. 'We'll both go,' he added. 'Simon always got on well with Naomi and maybe . . . I don't know, maybe she can give him the woman's angle.'

Naomi laughed. 'And what *is* the woman's angle?' she asked.

'You're asking *him*?' Lillian said. '*He's* only a man!'

Naomi could feel and hear the relief in Lillian's voice. She felt guilty, suddenly, that they might be making light of something that the Emmets plainly saw as deadly serious and that Lillian's relief might be far from justified. But she laughed anyway, feeling that was what Lillian expected and needed from her.

'He might not listen, you know,' Naomi said.

'Maybe not,' Samuel replied, 'but if you see him, talk to him, then at least you'll see what worries us. You'll see we're not overreacting. Simon is . . . sick with this, Nomi,' he told her, the diminutive of her name slipping affectionately from his lips. 'He is sick and he's getting worse, and Lillian and I, we don't know what to do.'

Four

The first time Simon saw Tally Palmer was in the Crash wine bar, the place of the moment for the arty scene. Dressed in his designer jeans and soft leather jacket, he felt he looked the part, but, he reminded himself, he was here to observe and not to socialize.

She wasn't difficult to find. Her face had been in the paper the night before in one of those 'local girl makes good' reports the daily rag was so fond of running. And anyway, she was surrounded by a crowd too big to miss. She had come back to open a new Arts Wing at her old college, a project she had been fund-raising for, a sort of thank you to her home town. He tried to keep the details of his assignment in his mind, but his attention was too much taken by the sight of long tanned legs and a very short black skirt that rode up even further as she perched, like a clichéd heroine, on a red leather stool.

Her hair was close-cropped, razor cut in a style so severe few women could have worn it and not looked naked. Her lips and nails were painted a rich blood red that exactly matched the shadowed wine in her glass.

She was circled by admirers. Students and young advertising bucks, whose self-assurance and practised, casual poise made him conscious of his flimsy cover, reminded him that his jeans were pirate copies and his jacket the one expensive thing he owned. And he was aware, as she glanced at him, that she saw him exactly for what he was.

Tally Palmer. Cover girls and rock musicians. Avant-garde writers after immortality and artists seeking a way to impress the buying public all flocked to her. Fêted her, paid extortionate amounts to be given the Tally Palmer look, and greater even than those whose images she made famous, Tally Palmer had herself become a star.

It was her smile that really blew him away. That smile and the slight tilt of her chin as she raised her glass like a question and he found himself moving through the parting crowd towards her.

'What are you drinking?' she asked him, and he was aware of the disapproval and disappointment, drifting like a sigh through the surrounding throng.

'Er, whatever you are. I mean, let me get these.'

She smiled at him again. This time it was a childlike grin that tweaked the corners of her mouth and made her eyes dance. He tried to say more, but he seemed to have lost the power of words.

As his drink arrived, she slipped from the bar stool, displaying as she did, the rest of her thigh and a tiny glimpse of red silk, edged with lace.

'My dinner date,' she announced to the waiting herd of confident young men. 'Don't forget your drink.'

Then she led him through the tight packed bar and into the quiet of the restaurant beyond, and he went after her, suddenly much too hot in his soft leather jacket and too conspicuous following in Tally Palmer's gently swaying wake.

Five

Back in January, when Naomi and Alec had first taken on the Tally-Simon problem, they had gone to visit Simon, intending to pay a duty visit and then leave him to sort himself out.

Simon still lived in the tiny flat he had first moved to on leaving his parents' home. It was on the attic floor of an Edwardian house, up several flights of stairs from a communal hall. It had once been student accommodation, the house divided into cramped bedsits with shared bathrooms and kitchens, but since then the landlord had changed twice and the new owner had attempted to go upmarket, the house itself being on the fringes of the up-and-coming developments closer to the canal. Simon now occupied the entire top floor, had his own bathroom and a sort of cupboard space that he called a kitchen – and almost double the rent. The lower storeys now housed just a tenant each.

The front door opened to a buzzer system; in theory, each tenant having to buzz their visitors through, but neither Alec nor Naomi could recall a time when the heavy oak door, its paint still peeling despite the renovations, had not been propped ajar by a large grey stone.

Naomi had visited Simon only once since the new landlord and Simon's spatial promotion, but as far as she could tell from the smell of the musty hallway, any changes were superficial ones. The hall still stank of stale cigarettes and boiled cabbage and, oddly, school plimsolls. The gritty feel beneath her feet as she crossed the tiled space between door and stairs called to memory just how grubby the floor had always been, no matter who or how many of them lived there.

Napoleon halted as they reached the stairs, waiting for her to take hold of the rail and tell him to move on. He pressed comfortably against her leg, his tail whacking damply at the skirt of her raincoat leaving the wet and hairy imprints of his pleasure at being inside once more. Alec had been forced to park some way down the road and it was pouring with rain. Napoleon had never much liked the rain. He shook himself, showing remarkable restraint, Naomi noted, but still managing to shower the rest of her coat and her bare hands with odour of wet dog.

'Are you OK?' Alec asked her. 'Or would you like me to take your arm?'

'No, I'm fine, thanks. You go on ahead and give dog and me some room for manoeuvre. Tell Simon to get the kettle on.'

Alec laughed. He paused to kiss her as he squeezed by, his damp hair dripping on to her face. 'Mmm,' he said. 'Eau de canine. Lovely.'

Naomi wrinkled her nose and bent to pat the dog's still damp coat. 'Don't you take any notice,' she told him. 'Mind you, he's right. You do stink. What did you find up there on Harry's allotment?' Harry had just acquired an allotment and that morning, Naomi and Napoleon had been called upon to admire the squelchy plot of land and free mountain of well-rotted manure that was allowed for in the rent.

Napoleon arfed happily and wriggled even more closely to her side, then, when she began to move, began carefully to climb the stairs, his pace slow and cautious as a child's.

To her surprise, Alec was still hammering on the door when they arrived.

'Maybe he isn't in?'

'No, he's there. I can hear his music.' He banged again. 'Simon. Come on, open up or I'll go and arrest your neighbours.'

Napoleon whined and dropped his head to sniff beneath the door as the sound of faint shuffling came from the other side and the music abruptly switched to silence.

'Ignoring us?' she ventured.

'Oh, I don't like to be ignored. Not used to it, you know, are we, old man?'

Napoleon whined again and the beating of his tail increased.

'Come on, Simon,' Alec called again. 'Open up. I'm not leaving 'til you . . .'

The door opened with a creak and Simon stood in the doorway.

'Alec?' he said. He made it sound like a question, as though he wasn't sure. 'Naomi?'

'Last time we checked. You going to invite us in?'

Naomi heard him hesitate before he stepped aside. 'Sure,' he said. She heard his footsteps falling first on wood and then muffled by carpet as he crossed back into the room, followed by the faint scratching of Napoleon's claws as he led her in. Alec brought up the rear.

'Your cleaning lady abandoned you?' Alec questioned as he closed the door behind them.

'What? Oh . . . oh yeah. I just don't seem to have found the time . . . Been busy, you know.'

'Really? Your mum seen it this way?'

'What?' He took a deep breath and released it heavily. 'No, she hasn't and I know what you're saying. It's a mess. I'll get on to it. Anyway, I'm not a kid any more. This is my place and she doesn't have to check to see I've tidied my room.' He paused and Naomi felt his scrutiny. 'Don't mean to be rude, but what *are* you doing here anyway?'

'Came to see you, isn't that right, Nomi?'

'That's right. We thought, what should we do on this wet afternoon? I know, we'll visit Simon. He's always made us welcome.'

'You've seen my parents,' Simon said flatly. 'And they've sent you round.'

He sighed again and Naomi heard him drop into the old fake leather chair that usually stood in front of the window. It creaked beneath his weight.

She moved forward cautiously. There used to be a sofa at right angles to it. Red, covered with a mountain of cushions that Lillian had made. She found the arm of it with her fingertips and moved around, Napoleon guiding her now.

'All right to sit down? Nothing I'm going to regret? Only last time I didn't ask I found the dish of jelly Sam had left there.' Her nephew, Sam, was five years old.

Simon almost laughed. 'No,' he said. 'Nothing as terrible as that, despite Alec's description. Look, I don't mean to be rude, but . . . well, Mum and Dad, they worry too much. I'm fine. Really fine.'

She felt Alec move something from the seat beside her and plonk himself down. 'They don't seem to think you are,' he said, 'and I have to say, you don't look like it to me either.'

'I'm sorry to hear about you and Tally,' Naomi chimed in. 'I hear you were getting along really well.'

'But these things do happen,' Alec added. 'And when they do, it's no good just letting yourself go.'

'Letting myself . . . Alec, you make it sound like I'm some middle-aged frump. I'm not letting *anything* go . . .'

'Sounds like that's the trouble.' Alec paused and Naomi could feel the younger man's anger and frustration bristling from across the room.

'They're worried about you, Simon,' she told him softly.

'They've got a right to be from what your mum was saying,' Alec added. 'A break up of a relationship hurts for a long time, we all know that, but learning to let go of it and go on with your life is all part of being grown up.'

'What is this? Good cop, bad cop? Look, I've been a bit down, I'll admit to that, but since when has depression been a criminal offence? Stupid, just stupid them sending you round like this. Like I was ten or something and needed a big brother.'

He got up, the chair creaking again and the soft padding of his carpeted footsteps changing to the sound of hard soles on wood. 'I think you'd better go,' he told them. 'I've nothing to say about it and you've no right, either of you, to poke your noses in.'

'Being your friends gives us that right,' Alec told him firmly, 'and looking at the state of you, I think your mum and dad have every reason to be worried.'

'Why, 'cos I've not cleaned my flat? God's sake . . .' He took another deep and heavy breath. 'Look, I'll admit to being upset. I'll admit to behaving just a bit weird, but I was hurting, Alec. I love that girl.'

He sounded so mournful when he said this last statement that Naomi could not help but feel for him.

'And I know she still loves me,' he added softly. 'Whatever she may say.'

There was a moment's silence as they absorbed his words, then Alec rousted himself from the couch and took Naomi by the hand, pulling her after him.

'So you don't have her pictures plastered all over your bedroom walls,' he asked. 'Or files and tapes and all that rubbish your mum talked about. You're not stalking the girl . . .'

'Stalking her?' Simon was outraged. 'I'm not stalking her. What do you take me for, some bloody pervert?'

Simon's living room was not large. A few paces brought Alec to the bedroom door and before Simon could stop him he had swung it wide.

'A shrine to the great Miss Palmer,' Alec said. 'Simon, I think this is what your parents meant.'

'You have no right. Alec, you're treating me like some kind of suspect.'

Naomi heard him cross the room and slam the bedroom door. 'Pictures,' he said. 'Just some bloody pictures. Look, Alec, you might be capable of just switching yourself off. Refusing to feel anything, but I can't. I can't just chuck stuff away and pretend it never happened. I love her. I'm going to get her back.'

'What if she doesn't want to be taken back?'

The silence fell heavily between them and then Naomi heard the bedroom door being opened again. 'Look if you want to,' Simon said gruffly. 'Pictures, that's all, just bloody pictures. Look at them and then go back to Mum and tell her it's nothing to worry about.'

Alec stepped into the bedroom and Naomi could hear his footsteps, softer now on another carpeted floor.

'Photos,' Alec said. 'Newspaper clippings. Old pictures. Is this Tally as a child?'

Naomi shifted closer. Knowing that his commentary was for her benefit.

'And these are new,' Alec commented. 'What did you do, Simon, borrow a long lens from one of the guys at work? 'Cause if I'm not much mistaken, that's what you'd need to see in through her window like that.'

'It wasn't like that . . .'

'Stalking was the right word to use after all.' Alec sighed. 'Simon, to be truthful I thought Lillian and Samuel were making a big fuss over nothing—'

'That why did you come in here acting like a storm trooper, treating me like some common criminal?'

'If you took these without her knowledge, that's exactly what you are.' Alec paused, calmed himself. 'I know I came in mob-handed, but one look at you told me there was more to this than either your mum or dad had been letting on. I've never seen you like this, not even when you went through your scruffy stage as a teenager, and boy, were you a mess then. But look at yourself now. When did you last shave, or shower for that matter? You've not turned up for work looking like that?'

'I've been sick,' Simon said defensively. 'I took a few days off, that's all.'

'This isn't like you.'

'You don't know me.'

'Obviously not!'

'We only want to help you,' Naomi interceded quietly. 'And you're right, we did come down heavy. You're not a little kid.' She let go of Napoleon and took a few hesitant steps to where she guessed Simon was, reached out and touched him, finding his bare arm beneath her fingertips. Close to, his scent was as musty as the downstairs hall; Simon, who was always so careful about the way he looked, the way he smelt.

His other hand closed gently over hers and she felt him move, his head resting against hers. 'I just don't know how to handle this,' he told her softly. 'I've never felt like this before.'

She hugged him then, big sister-like, slipping her arms around him and drawing his head down on to her shoulder. It wasn't a comfortable position, he was a tall man. Naomi wasn't small, but Simon still had a good few inches on her, but it was a measure of how miserable he felt that he remained there, wordless and unhappy until finally she pulled away.

'Whatever we can do, we will,' she told him. 'You know that.'

She felt him shake his head. 'You meant that,' he said, 'then you'd help me to get her back.'

Six

After Naomi and Alec had gone, Simon spent the afternoon raging against the injustice they had done to him. Bursting into his home and making accusations that were . . . all too true. He had known it, admitted to himself just how difficult his behaviour had been, how probably reprehensible, but he had not wanted, still did not want, to let his anger go or put his pain aside.

He had been so certain of his feelings for Tally and of hers for him. Never more certain of anything in his entire life and to suddenly lose that had been more than he could bear.

He stood in his bedroom, the curtains open and the darkness gathering outside. Rain still falling but less noticeable now against the steel grey sky giving way to night. He stood cradling a glass in his hands, sipping occasionally, staring at his gallery, his encapsulation of the life of Tally Palmer, laid out in neat, straight rows against the pale blue walls.

Some of these he shouldn't even have; he knew that. He had taken them . . . stolen them, Alec would have said, as surely as he had stolen those images of Tally photographed with the aid of a long lens and a camera borrowed from a colleague. The fact that the colleague had been unaware of having lent the camera to Simon, he supposed, was also not so good. Further cause for blame.

Slowly, Simon perused the images and his gaze finally came to rest on the picture of a grave, unsmiling child, with long fair hair and bright blue eyes. She was dressed in a dark blue frock, the lace of a white petticoat peeping out from beneath the hem, and all around her bloomed flowers, trumpet-headed lilies standing tall and straight as though forming an honour guard on either side.

The child Tally gazed out at him with a quite unbending stare.

Seven

April

On the Sunday morning following the stabbing, Naomi and Alec returned to the hospital, more in the hope of seeing Lillian and Samuel than in any hope Simon might be well enough to have visitors. Neither Alec nor Naomi could bear to think that such a firm friendship should suffer because of a third party, or because of some preference Lillian might have perceived Naomi showing towards Tally.

Simon was still in ITU, but they were told he had shown some improvement, and Samuel, seeing them through the window, waved at them and came out. They wandered back to the waiting room together and bought machine coffee. Napoleon whined for attention until Samuel bent to say hello and fondle his ears.

'They say Simon's a bit better?' Naomi asked.

'He's going to make it,' Samuel told her. His voice was shaking and he sounded exhausted.

'Is Lillian still mad with me?' she asked.

Samuel reached out and took her hand. 'Never was, my love. Not really. She was hurt, you know. We both were and with Tally just bursting in like that . . .'

'I know. Samuel, I thought it better to get her out of here.'

'She came back. This morning. Wanted to see him. They wouldn't let her, of course, even if we'd been willing.'

'You'll have to let her in at some point,' Alec observed. 'Once Simon's back on an ordinary ward, you won't be able to stop her.'

'No,' Samuel sighed deeply. 'I know and . . . after all it's Simon's choice. Once he's strong enough to make his own choices, I'll not stand in his way if he wants the girl to visit him.'

'And Lillian?'

'Lillian might take a little more persuasion. We'll cross that bridge, as they say. Nothing more on Jack, I suppose?'

'Sorry. No,' Alec told him.

'Did she say anything last night, Nomi? Tally must be able to find him or at least give a clue as to where the man might go.'

Naomi hesitated. 'She said she didn't know, Samuel. I told you last night, she got very defensive when I accused her of lying. She just up and left in the end.'

'But you'll be asking her again, won't you, Alec? You won't be just leaving it there?'

'Of course we won't. And I agree, Samuel, she's probably our key to finding Jack.'

They left soon after, Samuel itching to get back to his son, but as they made their way across the car park, Naomi heard someone calling her name.

'Tally?' She turned.

Alec stiffened. 'What's she still doing here?' he muttered.

'I saw you go in,' Tally informed him as she came closer. 'How is he? When can I see him?'

'Not while he's still in intensive care,' Naomi reminded her. 'Nor after, if his parents request a block on you visiting.'

'Can they do that?' Tally sounded horrified.

'It's perfectly possible,' Naomi told her, hoping Tally wouldn't push too far. It *was* possible to block certain visitors, but in wards with open visiting time, like most at this hospital, it would be very difficult to enforce. 'They'd feel a lot better about you, Tally, if you'd help them find the man who almost killed their son.'

Tally was silent, then she said quietly, 'I made my statement. I don't know any more. I told the officer who interviewed me last night that Jack wasn't at the gallery. I don't believe Jack attacked Simon in the park. Even if I did, I can't tell you where to find him.'

'Can't? Or won't?' Naomi demanded. 'Tally, if you truly believe that Jack is innocent then let him come forward, call him, tell Alec where he can be found. Let him give himself an alibi for that night.'

'I don't know where he is.'

'You don't know?' Naomi repeated flatly. 'I don't believe you. Tally, you're on your way to facing an obstruction charge.'

'Then let Alec arrest me,' Tally replied. She turned away and Naomi heard her fast-retreating footsteps as she walked back to her car.

'She has to know more than she's saying.'

'OK, I agree, Detective Blake,' Alec told her, a wry note in his voice. 'I must say, I liked the bit about visiting. Applying the pressure in just the right way. Nice to know you haven't lost your touch.'

'Don't tease.' Naomi thumped his arm, half playful and half angry.

'I wasn't,' he defended. 'Are you assaulting me, Miss Blake?'

Naomi sighed and Alec hugged her to him. 'I wouldn't tease,' he said. 'I agree with everything you said. And we'll get to the bottom of it, Nomi. I promise you we will.'

Tally sat in her car, shaking with anger, frustration and unshed tears. She was too edgy to drive yet, she knew that and she knew also that Naomi had every reason to be angry. Jack had attacked Simon. There could not be any other explanation.

She closed her eyes and leaned back in her seat, trying to recall a time in her life when things had not been so painful or so complicated: a long time ago, she thought. A very long time and even further to go back to find a place in her memory that brought no pain.

When she was ten years old her aunt grew lilies in the garden. The scent of them filled the open space between the chicken house and the rabbit pens, a fragrant interlude between the stink of chickens and the warm straw, hot fur scent of lop-eared animals.

When they visited that summer, Tally's birthday had not long gone and her aunt had promised her a present. Tally had waited patiently all the afternoon while the women gossiped and the men drank beer, boredom and anticipation growing with the passing time. And finally she had laid down among the lilies, listening to the buzzing of the insects and the soft drone of men's voices as they set the world to rights, and she had fallen asleep in a shady perfumed bed heated by the summer sun.

In the late afternoon, when she woke to hear her mother calling, she realized that in her sleep she had broken one long stem of flowers. It had fallen across her lap and the pollen had stained her best blue dress with brilliant scars of yellow.

She picked up the stem of flowers and pulled the dress away from her body. Sun drunk, she was afraid that the stain would go right through and paint her skin. Pollen yellow marks, so bright she thought that they might burn. And when they saw it, the women fussed and flapped, her mother declaring that the stain was there forever and the aunt smiling and urging her to take off the dress so she could 'rub it through now' before the stain had time to set.

She remembered, she had stood there in the garden, just dressed in a clean white petticoat, still clutching the stem of flowers while the adults fussed and her head grew muzzy with the heat. Her uncle gave her lemonade and rubbed her cheek with his part grown whiskers, teasing and chatting until his wife came out again. In one hand she clutched the best blue dress, wet and tucked inside a plastic bag. In her other she held a box wrapped in birthday paper and tied with bright red cord.

'Open it in the car,' the aunt said smiling. 'Your mammy wants to go now.' Then she took the stem of lilies from Tally's hand. 'You don't want that, my darling. Not in the car, it's unlucky having lilies inside a house or in a car.'

'Why?' Tally wanted to know, and the aunt smiled at her again. A toothy smile that showed pink gums and the patches on her mouth where the lipstick had all worn away.

'They're angel's flowers, Tally dear. Their scent is like the breath of angels. You don't put angels in your car.'

And then she hugged her niece and kissed her goodbye and Tally did her best to turn her face so that the aunt kissed her cheek and not her mouth. The aunt had false white teeth that clacked and clattered when she kissed and breath that smelt, Tally thought, of rotting gums. She much preferred the scent of flowers.

Then the aunt let her go and she stepped back, watching as the others said goodbye, and gently rattling the birthday box trying to guess what might be inside. And while no one looked, she plucked a single flower from the lily stem and breathed it in. Inhaling deeply, the pollen filling her head like a sunlit drug, she breathed the scent of angels.

Eight

Back in January, when the Tally issue had first been broached, Naomi had expected Simon to tell them it was none of their business and that he could handle it. In his position, Naomi had mused, it would like as not be what she'd have done. She might not have meant it, but she'd have said it all the same and made certain everyone knew she was serious. Given this view, she had not expected to hear from Simon again for at least a week, maybe more, while he got used to the idea that his family and friends were in collusion, or a little longer, even, given that he then had to find a way of accepting they were right and that he could use some help, without losing face.

Given this reasoning, it was therefore something of a surprise to have him visit a scant two days after they had been to see him.

It was ten thirty p.m. one evening in the middle of January and threatening to snow when Naomi's doorbell rang and, frankly, the last thing she wanted was unexpected company. She had settled in for the evening watching a video with Alec: Alec watching and commentating, Naomi listening and asking far too many questions. They had split the best part of two bottles of red wine between them and were just contemplating bed. Answering the door to young men carrying large cardboard boxes had not been on their list of things to do.

Alec activated the intercom: Simon's voice, rather plaintively asking to be let in.

'I suppose we'd better,' Naomi said reluctantly.

'Oh, hell. He could choose a better time.'

'I know. Maybe it's revenge for us bursting in on him.' She grinned at Alec and sensed him grimace.

'He was alone,' Alec pointed out. 'And had nothing planned.'

Naomi giggled. Definitely too much wine, she told herself. She attempted to sober up in the time it took Simon to come upstairs, failing miserably as she knew she would.

'Erm . . . Am I interrupting?'

'Yes,' Alec told him, 'but never mind.' He paused. 'You look a bit tidier than last time we saw you.'

'Er, yes. I guess I do.'

Naomi heard the sound of something being placed on her dining table, two somethings in fact, placed and then slid across the polished surface.

'What have you brought?' she asked.

'Stuff,' Simon told her awkwardly. 'It's Tally's stuff, or at least some of it is. I mean, some of it is just *about* her.'

'Oh? And why do I get it?'

'Well, I just thought . . . Look, can I sit down? I mean, I won't take long but I need to tell you.'

'Sure,' Naomi told him. The mood of the evening had been broken now anyway. 'Alec, will you make some coffee. I think I need it.' She had the annoying feeling that despite what Simon had said, this was going to take some time.

Simon waited until he had his coffee and Alec had settled himself beside Naomi before he began. It was clear that he didn't know where to start, but slowly, with a little prompting, the story began to emerge.

'I did an assignment on her,' he told them. 'That was how we met.'

'I remember. Lillian was proud enough to burst.'

'Yeah, I know. It was my first break and boy was it a break and a half. I know people wait years to get the kind of coverage I did with that story. And we'd got involved too. Fallen in love, I thought. I know it happens, you report something and forget to keep your distance, but this was different. I just couldn't believe it, this fantastic woman, beautiful, talented . . .' He laughed. 'Rich too, I guess, and she wanted me. But I mean, who was I kidding. I shouldn't have been surprised that she dumped me, just that she bothered with me at all.'

'And this revelation,' Alec asked him. 'It emerged over the last two days, did it? I didn't think we'd done *that* good a job.'

Simon shook his head. 'No, it didn't. I guess I was coming round to it on my own but you guys kind of focussed it for me. I've been stupid, risking everything and I know I need to pull myself back on the horse, or whatever, and get on with my life.'

'For a wannabe journo, you sure mix your metaphors,' Naomi told him. She fell silent for a moment, suspicious of this sudden transformation from the scruffy, depressed young man they had visited only days before. Was this just another ploy to get everyone off his back? She didn't think so. She knew from her own bitter experience after the accident that blinded her that these dramatic mood swings were a normal way of dealing with grief. That from deepest despair one day, it was possible to swing back into some kind of euphoric state, only to plunge back down again. It was like being on a seesaw, and her therapist had taught her not to feel bad about it, just accept it as part of the process. Gradually, the highs became less high; the lows a little more manageable, and for most people some kind of equilibrium established itself.

She didn't think Simon was anywhere near that place yet.

'So, what's in the boxes?' she asked.

'Oh, stuff. Mostly the stuff Alec saw on my bedroom

walls, but some other things too. I thought . . . I suppose I thought that if I brought it here, got it out of the house and maybe told you why I was acting like such a jerk . . . it might get better.'

She could hear it in his voice, the bubble of confidence already thinning and the euphoria set to dump him once again.

'That's probably good thinking,' Alec said, but Naomi knew from his tone that he too recognized the pattern.

'Apart from not wanting to let go,' Naomi asked, 'what is your excuse for acting like a prat?' It was a rather blunt comment to make to such a fragile ego, but the wine had robbed her of a degree of subtlety.

He pushed himself to his feet and for a moment Naomi thought that she had gone too far and Simon was about to leave. Instead, she heard him walk over to the table and retrieve his packages, bringing them back to where she sat on the big blue sofa and dumping them and himself on the floor at her feet.

'I don't think she wanted to break up with me,' he stated. Naomi heard him shuffling amongst papers and found a small stack of cards that felt like photographs dumped into her lap. 'They belong to her,' Simon said. 'They're photos of when she was a kid and I've no right to have them. I want you to take them back. Please, Naomi.'

Alec took them from her and skimmed through. 'She was a pretty kid,' he commented. 'Is this her mother?'

'Yes,' Simon confirmed. 'That's Rose.'

'Why not just post them?' Naomi didn't think she liked the idea of taking these personal possessions back to a young woman she didn't even know.

'Because that seems so . . . cold. I thought about going round there, taking them myself but . . .'

'Not the best of ideas,' Alec confirmed. 'But I'm with Nomi. Stick them in the post with a note saying you're sorry for being such an idiot. If she's half as decent as your parents seem to think she is, she'll forgive you. She'll just be glad to get the pictures back.'

'I guess you're right,' Simon said reluctantly, 'but the thing is, Alec, I want to make sure she's all right. I've been so worried about her. You see, I don't think she wanted to break up any more than I did. I think someone made her.'

Naomi remembered Lillian mentioning this theory. She was tempted to take it with a large pinch of salt and suspected that Simon's real reason was that she, Naomi, might act as a kind of go-between, tasked with persuading Tally Palmer to take Simon back. She remembered doing something similar in her teens, when she'd broken up with a boyfriend, asking a friend to go round and return his records and such, hoping that the friend would be persuasive . . . She had been, Naomi thought wryly, but persuasive in totally the wrong way. A week later and the ex-boyfriend and now ex-friend had become an item and Naomi left to fume, knowing that she'd probably helped to set them up.

'She's a grown woman,' Naomi told him. 'And from all accounts not one that's easily pushed around. Simon, you've got to face up to the fact that she simply didn't want to be with you any more.'

There was silence, a long silence, broken only by the soothing tick of the pendulum clock and the half-hearted thump of Napoleon's tail, reminding her that it was way past his bedtime and he was already practically asleep.

'You don't know her,' Simon said at last. 'She might seem really strong, independent, all of those things, but where Jack's concerned she doesn't seem to have a mind of her own. She just does as he says.'

Beside her, Alec shifted position and she turned her head automatically in his direction, exchanging puzzled glances. Even though she could no longer see she still used her sighted body language.

'Who the hell is Jack?' Alec asked for both of them.

'He's this man. This friend she's had for years. I think . . . I suspect that Jack is more than a friend.'

'You think they might be lovers,' Alec said bluntly and even though he sat a couple of feet away from her, Naomi could feel that Simon flinched.

'I . . . don't know. I just know that when Jack says jump, Tally asks how high. He wanted rid of me, I'm sure of it. And that's when things went wrong between us.'

'So,' Alec said, 'you've got a rival. Simon, if anything, that should make you more willing to let go. If this chap's been around for a long time, then they probably have a long-standing thing going. Maybe they just wanted a break for a while and now they've decided that they're right together after all. Long-term couples can get bored, I suppose, want a little variety. But if they're meant for one another . . .'

'That's not the way it was!' Simon was growing more and more exasperated. 'Look, Tally loved me. I wasn't an entertainment or a try-out. She loved me. I really believed it was going somewhere, then he started to interfere.' He fell silent again and then he said, 'I think he has some kind of hold over her. That she's in trouble. I need to know.' He reached forward and took Naomi's hands. 'Look, I've begun to gather evidence. It's here, in these boxes. It's all right,' he added, 'I've got copies of everything, so I don't need to have them back.'

'I thought you said you were trying to get rid of these things. That you felt you'd get over it better if they were out of your flat,' Alec demanded.

'I did . . . I do. I mean the copies are at work. I left them there. See, I'm trying. But this isn't about me, it's about Tally.'

'What kind of evidence?' Naomi persevered.

'Oh, newspaper stuff. And I've interviewed some of her old school friends, her mum, that sort of thing. I've been trying to find out about Jack. Who he is, what hold he has over her. I've—'

'You've interviewed people?'

'Sure. There are copies of the tapes in the big box.'

'And this was when you did the assignment on her?' Naomi pushed.

'No, no, this was after. I mean, after we broke up. I just knew there had to be a reason, a real reason, I mean. So I started my investigation. Alec, there's stuff I can't get hold of, old accident reports and such. I expect they're archived somewhere and I thought that you—'

'No way, Simon. This isn't a legitimate investigation. As I said before, it's stalking this poor woman. Does she know what you're doing?'

'No, she's been away. Working abroad. It's OK, the friends I talked to don't keep in touch much and she doesn't see her mother all that often. I told them we were planning a follow-up to my original article, that maybe a TV company would be getting involved . . .' He laughed harshly. 'Amazing what people will tell you just to get their fifteen minutes of fame.'

'Simon, you must know this isn't right,' Naomi pressed. 'You're obsessing, big time. You've got to get some help.'

'Of course it's right,' he insisted. 'Look, Naomi, Alec. I'm not doing this for me. I'm doing it for Tally. And in the end I know she'll understand and we'll be together again.'

'And if she doesn't understand?'

Simon laughed as if the notion were impossibility. 'She'll understand,' he affirmed, sounding happier than he had since he'd first entered Naomi's flat. 'All I've got to do is to get rid of Jack.'

Nine

Reluctant though she had been, Naomi had given in to Simon and promised to return the pictures. Plus, she had to admit, her curiosity had been piqued. She could just recall Tally from their school days at Ingham Comprehensive. Tally had been three or so years behind her. Naomi couldn't remember exactly, but she could recall the young girl who'd been called on to take pictures of school productions and prizegiving. A shy little thing with long blonde hair, who seemed happiest hiding behind the camera that looked way too big for her slender hands.

'Oh, hi,' the younger woman said as she opened her apartment door. 'Are you collecting for something? Did one of the neighbours buzz you in?'

'I came in with one of them, I think,' Naomi told her. 'A man who said his name was Brad.' She had noticed, since losing her sight, just how much more information people volunteered when talking to her than they had before. It was an interesting phenomena.

'Oh, Brad. Yes, he lives on the next floor down.' She hesitated for the briefest of instants before asking, 'Don't I know you from somewhere?' She laughed. 'Sorry if this sounds odd, but didn't we go to the same school?'

Naomi was amazed she should remember. 'I was a good few years ahead of you,' she said.

'Yes, but you were . . . a prefect. Very tall and dead skinny. Lots of long dark hair. I was dead jealous.'

Naomi laughed. She hadn't expected the conversation to take this turn, but was kind of glad it had. 'That was me,' she said. 'And heavy, dark-rimmed glasses. I switched to contacts in my final year.'

It was Tally's turn to laugh. 'Lord *yes*, I do remember. But what can I do for you? I mean, I'm assuming that you're not collecting for anything.'

'No,' Naomi told her quietly. 'Actually, I've come to give something back.' She had the pictures in an envelope in the pocket of her raincoat. She took them out now and handed them to Tally. Tally ripped the envelope and riffled through the pictures before speaking. Then: 'Simon,' she said. 'You've come because of Simon.'

'His parents are friends, they asked me to talk to him, about you. About leaving you alone and getting on with his life.'

'And will he?' Her voice was suddenly chilly, but there was also genuine curiosity in the question.

'I don't know. I don't think that I was that persuasive. But he gave me these, asked me to bring them round. He also asked me to talk to you, but I can't think of a single reason why I should and I told him that.'

'So that's why he didn't just post them. He sent you to be his advocate.'

'Tough on Simon if he did,' Naomi told her. 'Frankly, I think he should be taking his family's advice and putting this behind him. They think you're a nice person, but they also think that not letting go of you is bad for Simon, and frankly, I agree, so if you want to do me the favour of telling me to go away now, I'm quite happy to do that. It'll save me having to go back to Simon with what he'll see as hope.'

She could feel Tally considering her words, the younger woman's eyes resting upon her face, considering both what she had said and something else that Naomi could not quite fathom.

'You'd be good to photograph,' Tally Palmer said. 'Sorry, but you get into a certain way of thinking in my business. Do you mind if I ask you something?'

'About Simon?'

'Simon? No. I don't have to ask about Simon.' She sounded sad, for a moment almost as lost as Simon did himself, but the moment passed, a soft footfall behind her distracting them both and breaking the mood. Tally was not alone. A man, Naomi guessed from the footsteps. A guess confirmed as he spoke.

'Hello,' he said. 'And who are you?'

It might have been an unfriendly greeting, but his tone made it merely curious. He was as direct as Tally, Naomi thought, and intuition told her that this must be Jack.

'Naomi Blake.' She introduced herself, extending her hand in the direction from which the voice had come.

'Jack Chalmers.' He took her hand. His grip was firm, but the contact brief and his hand cool almost to the point of coldness.

'Naomi's brought my pictures back,' Tally informed him.

'Oh?' The curiosity had gone to be replaced by wariness.

'Don't worry, Jack, she's not here to plead his case.' Again that slight sadness in her voice. 'As a matter of fact, we were at school together. Secondary, that is, though *I* never made prefect.'

'I don't remember you,' Jack said.

'No, you wouldn't,' Naomi told him. 'We were never friends. I was a few years ahead of Tally. Were you there? Simon mentioned that you were old friends, you and Tally.'

'Ah. Simon. No, I went to another school.'

Naomi waited for him to elaborate, but he did not. It felt awkward now, Naomi standing in the hallway, Jack guarding the door. Napoleon caught their mood and shifted uncertainly, leaning hard against Naomi's leg as he always did when a situation caused him some concern.

'I'd better go,' Naomi said.

'Maybe you had. Sorry if that sounds rude, but I think it might be best. Are you all right making your way downstairs?' Tally enquired.

Naomi smiled. 'Thanks, I'm fine. Napoleon will make sure of that.' She turned awkwardly in the narrow hall and the dog, taking his cue, began to lead her slowly back to the stairwell, sitting down at the top until she got her bearings, gripped the rail and then urged him on. Tally must have watched her for a moment from the open door because as Naomi began to descend, taking it slowly, feeling each step at a time, she heard Jack's voice sounding angrily from inside the apartment.

'He'll never leave you alone,' Jack said.

'Oh, leave it, Jack. Yes he will.'

Naomi paused, fairly sure that she was out of sight now. As Tally closed the door she caught Jack's voice again: 'And that woman. If she comes again, tell her to go away. There's something about her I don't like at all.'

Ten

Tally sat alone in her apartment a few days later and stared at the photographs that Naomi had returned. She'd liked her, Naomi. Appreciated her attitude and her loyalty to Simon. A loyalty Tally herself had been unable to give no matter how much she might have wished it otherwise.

She'd been glad to get them back, realizing belatedly that Simon must have taken them but uncertain how to ask for their return, and now she turned them between her hands reviewing those long ago images. Tally aged nine and ten; Tally in the Christmas nativity play; Tally lined up with her class mates for the official school photo; Tally riding on the carousel; Tally snatched at moments in her life. Snatched and stored and lodged in memory.

One she was especially glad to have retrieved was Tally at nine years old, taken in her Aunt Bee's garden, standing amid the lilies in her best blue dress on the day her aunt had given her that dreadful gift. Tally smiled, then laughed at her own childish outrage, remembering Tallulah Two Heads and that awful journey home.

The car had not even pulled away from her aunt's front door before she had the scarlet cord untied and the bright paper ripped away. Inside was a box covered in images of action women riding horses and driving fast sports cars. They wore glamorous clothes and sipped Lord knew what from fancy glasses trimmed with fruit and paper umbrellas.

'Fashion Charm' the legend on the box read. 'Your true life fashion girl.'

Tally already owned a Barbie. She stayed, unplayed with, in the bottom of the cupboard, her stylish outfits crammed into a plastic shopping bag and all but forgotten.

'It's a doll,' Tally said and her mother must have heard the disappointment because she laughed.

'Most little girls like dolls.' She twisted around in her seat and peered at Tally over the back of it. 'Well, you can at least open the box. You never know, this one might be nice.'

Tally wrestled with the sticky tape that held the lid in place. Pulling at it tore the picture of the smart young woman waiting to board a plane, slicing her body with a knife-sharp edge. She eased the tight lid from the box and glared at the doll that lay inside. Blonde hair, red suit, high-heeled shoes and a little bag clutched in its slender hand.

'She should fit your Barbie clothes,' Tally's mother said.

'I suppose.'

'You don't have to play with her, you know. Just get her out when Auntie Bee comes round to stay, and that isn't often, is it pet?'

Tally was about to replace the lid, imprison the unwanted woman doll again, when she noticed something else. What she had taken for just cardboard packaging at the end of the box had something more inside. Hopefully, she pulled the thing out, unwrapping the tissue paper with more eager fingers. Then she dropped it with a little cry of shock and disgust.

'What on earth?' her mother said, and reached between the seats to pick up the offending thing. 'She's got a spare head!' she announced, delighting in the thought. 'What an odd idea. One long-haired blonde one that

you can style and a short brunette for when you want a change.'

'It's horrid. I don't want it, Mummy.' But her mother only laughed again.

'Tallulah Two Heads,' she said, her voice singing with amusement. 'You can call her Tallulah Two Heads.' She gave Tally one of her conspiratorial 'we-can-make-it-better' looks. 'I'll just bet none of your friends have one of these.'

Then she grew bored, as adults do when they think they've solved it all and she turned back to look out through the windscreen, beginning to chat to Tally's father who was too busy driving the car to bother passing comment on the hated toy.

Tallulah Two Heads lay in her coffin box and stared with her two sets of quite unblinking eyes.

The journey home was longer than it had ever been. She had shut the doll inside its box and tied it tightly with the scarlet cord, but even so Tally could feel its eyes staring at her through the shield of coloured card and the remnants of birthday wrapping. Before she had known what lay inside, the doll had no capacity to harm. No influence and no effect upon Tally's ten years of chronically active imagination.

Once opened it was as though the switch had been thrown and the doll breathed the first breaths of life.

She had always hated dolls. Hated their staring eyes and their bland, calm faces, moulded with the specific purpose of reproaching her. Tally, who was neither bland nor calm, lived in a world where all experience, however good, was as intense as pain.

Outside, the summer day had broken and rain fell suddenly in a heavy curtain.

Her father switched on the headlights and set the wipers to full. They wagged across the glass, clearing a momentary gap in the falling rain.

'If it gets any worse,' he said, 'we'll have to pull over. That damned wiper blade's worked loose again.'

She sat still, listening to the rain and willing it to stop. She was longing to reach home. To be able to thrust this woman doll away with the rest in the bottom of the cupboard. The loose wiper blade began to scrape across the glass, squeaking where it pressed tight, rattling where it was dragged back loose. The sound of it ate into her brain. The aggressive yellow screech setting her teeth on edge and fraying her nerves. And, in her heart, she must have reproached Aunt Bee every mile of the way. She had not let Tally bring the lilies into the car and yet she had given as a gift this hideous thing.

What could be so wrong with taking the breath of angels on her journey when this horrific doll could be so right?

So she closed her eyes and sat back in the furthest corner of her seat, the doll box in the other, and listened as her parents talked. Their voices little more than a murmur above the noise of the engine and the screech of the windscreen wipers and the tyres spinning on the road, and she tried to recall as vividly as she could the scent of lilies in the summer garden. Their hot, golden breath, mingled with the smell of scorched earth and the stabbing blue odour of the sky.

Eleven

Patrick was supposed to be doing his homework, but as always he was finding everything and anything he could to act as a distraction. Since he and his father, Harry, had moved back to Ingham to be close to Patrick's grandmother, he had taken to calling at Naomi's at least a couple of times a week on pretence of getting help with his homework.

Not that Naomi minded. Patrick was fifteen going on far too adult, was shy and funny and astute beyond his years. He'd had a rough time: his parents' divorce and the background of a murder in the family that had only just been solved. Naomi had good reason to bless the boy's common sense and courage and enjoyed his company.

Tonight's homework was history. World War One: causes of. It was fair to say that it had not entirely captured Patrick's interest. Simon's boxes lay still packed on the floor beneath the dining table and Naomi had heard the odd surreptitious poke and shuffle as Patrick tried hard to see what was inside without actually prying. Finally, curiosity got the better of him.

'What is all this stuff?'

'It belongs to Simon,' Naomi told him. 'Photos and newspaper clippings mostly, I think. I don't know, I've not been through them.'

'Maybe we could—'

'History, Patrick. First World War, remember.'

She heard him sigh. 'It's not that I'm not interested,' he

said. 'I mean, I know it's important and I know how bad it must have been. We watched this film, it was taken in the trenches of all these soldiers blinded by mustard gas. Did you know that in winter the trenches were half-filled with water and soldiers' feet rotted in their boots because they never had a chance to dry out?'

Naomi nodded. 'Yeah, I knew that. So what's the problem with you writing it?'

'I can't exactly write that the causes of World War One were a lot of mad old men who just wanted the excuse to grab more land and get more power, can I?'

Naomi laughed. 'You might need to put it a bit differently.'

'Or that most men died fighting over a few inches of land. The front line moved less than a foot in about four years. It was nuts, Naomi. Just stupid.'

'Most wars are, I guess. But you've just got to knuckle down and write this, I'm afraid. That's the way school is.'

'School's stupid.'

He fell back into a sullen silence, but this time Naomi heard the sound of writing as his pen scraped across the page and the occasional muttered complaint as he tried to figure out exactly how a word was spelt. She'd bought him a pocket spellchecker a couple of weeks before and was glad to hear him using it, the keystrokes beeping softly as he typed in the awkward word. His father, Harry, was still worried about him. Patrick was bright but still had problems with his spelling and his writing and, for things that did not interest him, the concentration span of the average gnat. Having moved, Harry now had to commute back and forth to work each day and that added to the time he could not be with his son. Naomi knew he had come to count on her as surrogate where supervision regarding homework was concerned.

Naomi wandered back into the kitchen, filling the kettle

and scrubbing potatoes. She wasn't really surprised when Patrick followed her a few minutes later.

'What is this?' he demanded. 'It's weird. It must have fallen out of one of those boxes. I found it on the floor.'

'Fallen out?'

'Yes, honestly. I wouldn't take something without asking, would I?'

No, she had to agree, he probably wouldn't. He might poke things with the toe of his boot, just to get a better view of something particularly tantalizing, but actually removing an object from the box was something else again. Obviously, though, if something happened to have fallen out . . .

She dried her hands. 'What is it anyway?'

'It's a key ring. And a key. The main key ring looks like silver . . . yes, it has a hallmark and it's shaped like an S. Then there's this other thing, looks like a doll's head. Someone's cut the hair really short and shoved a piece of wire right through, between the ears.'

'Ugh, sounds a bit macabre.'

'It's pretty gross,' he admitted. 'But dolls are gross anyway. Here, take a look.' He handed it to her and Naomi traced the curving shape of the elaborate letter S. It was surprisingly heavy, solid-feeling, expensive. And then the little head, suspended from a wire fastened to the ring. The old plastic deformed beneath her fingers when she squeezed and the stubble of hair pricked at her skin.

'What is she, a Barbie head or something?'

'Something a bit like that, I guess. Her eyes are all faded, like the paint's been rubbed off. It's weird looking. Why would anyone want to thread a head?' He paused and was obviously considering how to phrase his next question. 'Is your friend all right, Naomi? He's not a bit odd, is he?'

Naomi laughed. 'Most of the time, no,' she told him. But just now, she wasn't sure she would swear to that.

Twelve

April

Simon was conscious, or rather, in that state between here and there that was neither sleep nor waking. He was aware of his mother sitting by the bedside, of the unfamiliar sounds of the hospital and his father's quiet conversation with a man he did not recognize. Lillian was talking to him. She'd done nothing but, Simon realized vaguely, not since she'd first seen him open his eyes a few hours before. At least, Simon assumed it had been hours before, the flow of thoughts and pictures travelling through his mind seemed to have taken a very long period of time. Now he'd come back to the world of the living, his mother seemed reluctant to stop the flow of communication, in case he should drift off back into that other world again and be gone for good.

Frankly, Simon wished she would shut up for a minute so he could catch the thread of his own inner words.

He tried to answer when she spoke to him. Sometimes, he thought he did, but couldn't recall the words of her question, never mind if he had answered it already. Mostly, he just drifted, and jolted back now and again into Lillian's reality when she bent close enough to whisper in his ear.

Simon was remembering. Drifting through one rain-washed night months before.

Simon sat outside Tally's apartment block for close on an hour before getting the courage to go inside. Despite what he had said to Naomi and Simon, he was not as ready to give up on Tally as he had declared.

Not that he'd lied. No, when he'd spoken to them, he'd really meant what he'd said; that he knew they, and his parents, were right and he should be moving on. But tonight, he had driven home past Tally's flat and seen her car parked outside for the first time in over a week. Tally was back home and, try as he might, he could not resist.

He glanced out of the side window at Tally's car. Her blue Maxda mx5 parked beside him in its usual spot had confirmed that she was home and encouraged him to get on with the task in hand, now, today before he could change his mind again. He had parked up but then continued to sit in his car, the heat gradually leeching out through the badly fitting windows, trying to convince himself that she might have taken a walk and that he ought to wait until she returned. Or he was half hoping that she might look out of the window and see him there. Come down and save him the emotional trauma of ringing her bell and perhaps being denied entry.

Neither of those things happened and the interior of the car was growing colder by the minute. Twice he had been forced to wipe the windscreen clear of condensation, and people walking by him to go into the apartment block looked askance at this stranger in the beat-up old Volvo with the steamed up windows who neither tried to go inside or prepared to drive away. Finally, as it began to rain, Simon decided that he should bite the bullet, grasp the nettle and whatever other handy clichés came to mind and present himself at Tally's door.

To his surprise and profound relief she buzzed him in without comment and her apartment door was ajar when he climbed the stairs.

He called her name as he pushed the door open cautiously. 'All right to come in?'

She was standing by the window dressed in old blue jeans and a crisp white shirt. Her feet were bare. Behind her, over the city, the rain clouds gathered, bursting down upon the streets.

'I wanted to see you,' he began. Then paused lost for words as she said nothing. 'I've missed you, Tally.'

She regarded him without expression and then she turned away, stood gazing out of the window at the falling rain. 'What did you come here for? Whatever it was you'd better say it and go. I've got better things to do with my time.'

'If you feel like that, why did you let me in?' He crossed the room to where she stood with her back to him, moving close enough to feel the heat from her body and smell the lilac and rose of her perfume. 'I want to help you, Tally.'

'I don't need your help.'

'Oh yes, you do. You think you can go on this way, pushing away everyone who might care about you. Making up some wild excuse whenever someone gets too close for comfort and you might have to feel something back.'

'You don't know what you're talking about.'

'Oh, I think I do.' He edged closer, warming to his task now. He had forgotten, made himself forget, just how intoxicating it could be standing this close to Tally Palmer. The clean scent of her hair, the subtle floral notes of her perfume, the warmth of her skin that made him think of sex and of their bodies moulded together in the half light of Tally's room. 'I want to help you, Tally,' he said again. 'I want to help you get rid of Jack forever, to break free of him and take control of your life again. You've got to be able to move on, Tally, whatever happened in the past that makes you think you need a scapegoat . . .'

'A scapegoat?' She sounded bitterly amused.

'Yes. I've got it figured out. That's what Jack is to you. There are things in your life that you can't deal with. That hurt too bad. I don't know all of them, Tally, and I don't need to know, but Jack's become your . . . your get-out clause, if you like, the thing you take it out on when you can't cope. If you blame Jack, you don't have to take responsibility or . . .'

He paused. Tally was laughing at him. Her shoulders shaking with mirth and when she finally turned towards him her face flushed was with it.

'Oh, Simon,' she said between bursts of breathless laughter. 'You don't have a clue, do you? You just don't have a clue.'

He was taken aback, the honest part of him admitting that she was right to laugh at his half-cocked ideas. That she'd have been well within her rights to do much more than laugh. But the sensitive part of him was resentful that his offer to help her should be so abused.

'I just want to help you, Tally,' he repeated and his voice sounded weak and plaintive even to his own ear. 'Look,' he said, desperate to begin again, 'I'll help find someone to . . . a counsellor, a psychiatrist. Whatever you need . . .'

She had stopped laughing and was staring at him incredulously. 'You think that I'm the one needing help? Simon, have you taken a look at yourself in the mirror lately? I'm not the one who has to come up with half-baked explanations that don't mean a thing.'

She shook her head and moved so close to him that he could almost feel the rise and fall of her breasts beneath the white shirt. 'Look at yourself, Simon. If anyone needs sorting out, it's you. What is it, can't you take rejection? Do you think you're so much God's gift that no one in their right minds would say no to you? Get back to that little slag I saw you with that night. Is she the same one you were seeing that other time? She looks just about what you deserve. And now, get out of my life again, and this time stay out.'

Simon said nothing though his body shook with anger and

his chest ached as he struggled to control his breathing. He turned on his heel and walked away.

When Simon left, Jack emerged from Tally's bedroom.

'Why did you let him in? You know I told you not to.' He paced restlessly for a while as though the very fact that Simon had been in that same room disturbed him. 'Once, I was the centre of your universe,' Jack reminded her. 'You didn't need the likes of him.'

'You still are, Jack.'

'So why have anything to do with him? Why have anything to do with any of them? You've got to admit, Tally, your track record when it comes to men isn't that bright.' He turned to face her, ticking names off on his fingers. 'First, there was Miles. Look what happened with that little shit. Then there was Adam. Tally Palmer's first big romance, I don't think.'

'Don't, Jack, please.'

'So perfect, wasn't he? Then he goes out and gets pissed because he thinks it's big, crashes his car and kills himself and his best friend. Is that perfect, Tally? Is that what you wanted?

'Oh and then, of course, Jon O'Dowd. Big man, big ideas. Nearly got you all killed. You could have ended up like that poor sod you found bleeding to death in the alley. Hacked up and left to die. And then this one. Another frigging journalist for God's sake.' He shook his head. 'Don't you ever learn?'

'I thought I should hear what he had to say. How can that possibly hurt *you*?'

'It *hurts* me. Anything that drives a wedge between us *hurts* me.'

'Jack, sometimes I just need some space.'

'Space! Tally, you and I are one soul, the one being, we don't need space and we can't give each other space. You belong to me, Tally, and I won't tolerate any stupid little upstart that wants to come along and take you away.'

He grabbed her by the arms and held tight, fingers sinking into the muscle. 'I will never let go of you, Tally, never, ever. You should have learnt that by now. Death do us part and then some.'

She pulled away sharply and turned her back on him. 'I've sent him away. Are you happy now?'

'Yes, I'm happy and so will you be. Forget him, Tally, he only wanted what you could give him. He didn't want you, the person, he wanted you, the icon, and sooner or later you'll realize that. He's a user just like all the rest. He'll dig and dig and dig until he gets to what he thinks is the heart of you and then he'll sell it to the highest bidder. I'm the only one that you can rely on, Tally, you know that. I've always been there and I always will be there.' He paused and reached out to her again and this time his hands were gentle and his voice softer. 'I've always looked after you. I want you, Tally. I came back to be with you. You can't have what we've had and then cast it aside when you've had enough.'

Tally shook her head. 'I love you, Jack, but sometimes I need something different. You demand a commitment I find hard to give. Sometimes there's nothing left for me.'

'I am you,' Jack said softly. 'What else is there?'

Thirteen

When Simon left Tally's flat it was half past six, the early evening rush hour not yet over and the streets crowded with commuters. He left his car where it was and walked swiftly, taking little notice of where he was going, intent only on finding somewhere he could get well and truly drunk.

About a half mile from Tally's home was a converted church, now a trendy bar, popular with students and the legal professionals that worked at the courthouse not far from the university. Simon knew it well. It was dimly lit and anonymous and, better yet, he had never been in there with Tally. He found a seat high up in the gallery bar, close against the wrought-iron railing that afforded a most dizzying view of the restaurant below, and he proceeded to drink himself stupid, as though that could purge Tally's words, Tally's scent, the very look of her from his mind.

Her accusations about another woman had cut him to the quick, the more so because, whatever excuses he could make – and he had designed for himself a fair few in the past months – he could not wholly rid himself of the knowledge that he had behaved abominably in that one regard.

He finished his first shot of bourbon and the second, was taking his third more slowly before he allowed his mind to roam back to the subject of Tally Palmer once more . . . and where there was Tally, in the background like a demonic shadow, there was always Jack.

When Simon had asked why he had never been introduced to Jack, Tally had just laughed. 'Have I met all of your friends yet?' she had asked him and at the time, only, to be fair, twelve weeks into their relationship, it had seemed a reasonable comment. But Simon could not be satisfied with it.

For one thing, Tally *had* met a great many of Simon's friends, and his family and, anyhow, it was more the *way* that she talked about Jack that bothered Simon. To be truthful, Tally mentioned Jack rarely – she mentioned *friends* rarely – but Simon was beginning to get the feeling that Jack had been around at practically every significant event in Tally's life and that had him wondering.

Who was Jack and why hadn't he got to meet such an important friend?

One night they had watched a documentary together. It was about a place called Mamolo in Somalia or Sudan or somewhere, if he remembered right, and was where Jon O'Dowd had been sent to report from. He knew Tally had been with him.

Simon recalled her mood on that night, the two of them lounging on Tally's bed watching on the little portable she kept tucked away in a discreet maple wood cupboard in the corner of her bedroom. She had watched in silence, drifting away into her own thoughts. Knowing that the memory of Jon O'Dowd and all that related to him must still be fresh and raw in Tally's mind, Simon had at first been reluctant to speak and break her silence.

'You were there, weren't you?' he had asked finally, half ashamed of how much he resented this distance that appeared between them whenever Tally reviewed her past.

At first, she had not replied. Had not in fact even seemed to hear.

'Are you listening to me?' Simon had demanded.

'What? Oh sorry, I was miles away.' Years away.

'I could see that. It doesn't matter. I just asked if you recognized this place.'

Tally had nodded. 'Oh yes.' She'd breathed the words quietly. 'We were there. One of the last times I worked with Jon. *Time* magazine ran a four-page feature. It barely scratched the surface. It was bad, Simon. The worst of times.'

Simon had waited. Sometimes Tally would be willing to talk, other times she'd give a tantalizing glimpse of her past and then shut down.

'We were running,' she had told him. 'It had been raining and the street was soaked from the downpour. The rains were coming. This storm had lasted just a bare fifteen minutes, but it had soaked us to the skin and the packed earth of the road was so hard-baked that the water sat there, like hot ice.'

Simon, drink in hand, watching the early evening meetings between friends and lovers in the bar, recalled that he had hardly dared to breath. He had wanted so badly to touch her, but had been too afraid that it might break the spell. Tally had been leaning back against the bedhead, knees drawn up to her chest and her shoulders hunched as though against sudden cold.

He had almost felt and seen the memories replayed behind her tight closed eyes.

'I skidded into Jon O'Dowd and he reached out to stop me falling. He never even broke his pace or looked my way. The gunfire was growing louder by the second and the rumours had been spreading all that day that foreign film crews were being targeted by both sides now. Two journalists had been killed in the past three days.'

One, Simon recalled, had been a soundman with a Scandinavian TV company, another was a photographer that Tally had trained with. Caught in crossfire, it was claimed, but no one believed that. O'Dowd's team had been ordered out hours before and even Jon himself was now ready to comply. If they could only reach the rendezvous point . . .

They had spent the past three weeks, she had told Simon, reporting on the worsening situation. Rival warlords making the UN troops look like children as they tried to keep what they hoped was order. 'Good intentions,' Jon had commented as the scenes of carnage replaced the optimistic images from only weeks before of UN troops being cheered by the locals, even greeted with some enthusiasm by the gang leaders, all of whom convinced themselves that fate had brought them a certain ally.

'Good intentions. What do they say about the road to hell?'

Tally was short of breath, her chest tight and the sweat running down into her eyes and pooling in her bra and at the base of her spine. She was scared. She'd been in tight corners before with Jon O'Dowd, but this was by far the worst. On foot in an unfamiliar town and separated from the main body of foreign nationals who were trying to make it to the airstrip, the three of them were alone, unarmed and too aware of their own mortality.

They veered into an alleyway between two ramshackle buildings as the gunfire sounded again, closer this time and off to their right, followed by the sound of running feet as they dived for cover.

Jon risked using his radio, praying that someone be still in range. The UHF sets were really little more than line of sight and there were rumours that one side or another were routinely monitoring transmissions and using them to track down those they now called enemies.

A low moan close by caused Tally to swing around.

'Oh my God, Jon.'

They pulled back the debris that covered him. A middle-aged man, badly wounded – the marks on his body easily recognizable by anyone who'd spent time in Mamolo – his body hacked with a machete, the man left to die.

Jon shook his head. 'Nothing we can do for him.' Then he turned his attention to the radio now crackling into life. He spoke urgently, giving their position as best he knew and asking for advice. Tally raised her camera; habit taking over shielding her feelings as she surveyed the man through the lens, the knowledge in his eyes cutting her to the bone. For a moment she hesitated and then O'Dowd was cursing at the radio and forcing them all to their feet once more and the running footsteps they had heard before they hid were coming back, purposeful this time and accompanied by further gunfire.

'They've got the base unit,' O'Dowd yelled as they ran. 'And I just told the bastards where we are.'

'There was this man,' Tally had told Simon. 'Old, I guess, but he was in so much pain it was hard to tell. I thought we were all going to die that day and when I looked into that man's face I swear he thought so too. It was a kind of recognition; I can't explain it any better than that. Simon, he'd been attacked with a machete. Someone had hacked off his arms and left him lying there in his own blood, and you know what? I lifted my camera to take his picture and all I could think for a moment was just what a fantastic image it would make. How much it would shock.'

'But you never used it,' Simon had commented.

She'd shaken her head. 'I didn't take the picture. I couldn't. The man was dying and I'd taken pictures of the dying more times than I want to count. But that time was different. I thought that would be our last day on earth, I really did, and I found myself wishing that Jack had been on that trip with us . . .' She hesitated and cast Simon an apologetic look. 'I needed him, I guess.'

'Jack?' Simon had not been able to keep the irritation out

of his voice. 'Why should *he* have been there? I mean, is he a journo or something? You never said.'

'Soundman. Jon used him occasionally.'

'Is Jack still in the same business?'

Tally had looked sharply at him as though surprised by the eagerness in his tone.

'Not any more,' she'd said. 'He quit the same time as I did.' She had leant back again and closed her eyes and Simon had known she was remembering the man whose picture she could not take, and he had wondered then if she regretted it, missing that decisive moment, deliberately setting it aside.

Her images illustrated the article in *Time* magazine written up from O'Dowd's sharp, compassionate television reports. She knew, had she seized the moment, she would have caught maybe the most powerful image of her whole career. She could still see the man's face in her mind's eye, as sharp and defined as ever, and still smell the stink of the dying as if she wore it like perfume.

At work the day after they had watched the documentary, Simon called an old friend he'd been with at university and who now worked for the BBC. Calum was known for his archival memory and his thorough knowledge of the industry and Simon asked him how he could find out more about Jon O'Dowd.

'O'Dowd? God, Simon, there's been reams written about the guy. He was practically a legend. Tell me what you need to know and I'll tell you where to start.'

'I want to know about his team. Who was his usual soundman? I know it's a bit odd but . . .'

'No, that one's dead easy. He almost always used the same crew. Mick Perl was his cameraman of choice, sometimes he'd take a photographer along too. Always reckoned dedicated stills pictures were better than anything you could grab from video. And his soundman was Nathan Sullivan.

Everyone calls him Nat. Little guy. Big shoulders. O'Dowd used to joke that the three of them could edit up a Pulitzer prize winner in the hotel broom cupboard. O'Dowd used the same team almost all the time. Especially late on when he had the clout to get what he liked.'

'Almost?' Simon questioned. 'And when he had to sub, who would that have been?'

'Sorry, wouldn't know,' Calum admitted. 'Look, got to go, but I'll see what I can dig up. Might take a few days though.'

Simon thanked him and hung up. Subbing for Sullivan. Jack what? Simon thought, realizing irritably that he didn't even know Jack's full name.

He took himself down to see the archivist and asked her to run a search on Jonathan O'Dowd for the six months prior to his death, but he was already wondering exactly what he thought he might be looking for and why. When she asked him if it was urgent he told her, 'No. It's background. Not urgent.'

'How's it going with the famous Tally Palmer?' she asked him with a mischievous grin.

Simon returned her smile.

'Pretty good,' he had told her. 'Really pretty good.' He had walked away, wondering even then if that were really true.

Simon knew he'd had too much to drink when he stood up and the gallery threatened to swoop down and tip him fifty feet on to the flagstone floor below. Somehow, he negotiated the spiral stairs that led down to the lower level, though twice his feet slipped on the iron stairs and the second time he landed unceremoniously on his backside. He was aware of people, of the crowd parting to let him through, of a large hand resting momentarily on his arm and guiding him the rest of the way outside. Just as well, Simon had lost all sense of how to find the exit doors.

'Just stand there a minute and get your breath,' a voice told him. The hand still rested on his arm. It was heavy and tattooed and, he noted, the nails kept short and scrubbed very clean. He followed the hand up an equally impressive arm, to a face that was not unfriendly exactly, but wary and just slightly amused. Simon took a deep breath of cold damp air and nearly threw up over the doorman's shoes.

He found himself being pointed back towards the main road. 'Take a walk that way,' the big man told him, sounding a lot less friendly now. 'Back towards town. By that time you might be sober enough to find a cab.'

'What time is it?' Simon asked him.

'Ten to eight, but if you ask me you've made enough of a night of it already. Get home.'

Released from the man's grip. Simon staggered forward, stumbling into a low wall and barking his shins before righting himself and shuffling off in the direction of the town centre. His mouth tasted foul; he knew that his breath stank. He could smell himself and it was not pleasant. Ten to eight, the man had said. It had taken him just over an hour to get this way.

Calum had phoned Simon at work with the answers to his questions about Jon O'Dowd. 'Sorry, no such luck with substitute soundmen,' he told Simon. 'But, look, if you want info on O'Dowd I could set up a meet. Nat's in town just now and he's a good guy, be glad to help out.'

Simon agreed, though he felt like a heel going behind Tally's back. 'Thanks, Calum. Oh, and ask him, will you, if they had anyone on the team by the name of Jack.'

'Jack what?'

'You've got me there. He'd be a friend of Tally Palmer's.'

'Oh?' Simon could almost hear the cogs turn in Calum's mind. 'And how is the lovely Ms Palmer? Good for you, bro.'

Simon thanked him again and put down the phone, very aware that the whole world seemed to be congratulating him on having won this beautiful, desirable woman and all the time Simon felt more and more doubt about holding on to her.

'Tally,' Simon muttered. He'd been talking to her, left his car there. He was dimly aware that he was headed in the wrong direction for Tally's flat but could not for the life of him work out the correct way to go. Maybe, he thought, he needed a map. He'd have to find a map shop. A map shop and something else to drink. Sickness and cold air were combining to take the edge off and he felt less inebriated than he had even ten minutes before. He walked on, touching the low wall that ran along the canal bank with the tips of his fingers as though keeping in touch physically with something strong and solid might infiltrate his own physical state. Not good, he told himself. This is not good.

He was almost as drunk as he had been that night with Nat Sullivan, that first time he had met the man. That had been a night to forget, Simon thought, wishing more than anything else that he could go back and wipe it all out, forget it for real. That had been the night his troubles had really begun.

Calum had called back to say that the meeting with Nat Sullivan would have to be the following day as Nat was off on another assignment.

'Sorry it's short notice. Maybe you could get together when he gets back,' Calum apologized.

'No, no, tomorrow will be fine.' Simon paused and drew

a deep breath, appalled at how desperate he sounded and unsure as to why. Calum had caught his tone.

'Anything wrong?' he asked. Never try to con another journo.

Simon laughed. 'No, it's fine. Honestly. Set it up for me, will you?'

Calum promised to ring him back with the details and Simon set about rescheduling his appointments for the following couple of days in case he should have to stay overnight in London.

He had called Tally and told her he had to go out of town, half relieved that they had no plans to meet that night. He knew he would never be able to fend off her questions.

'By the way,' he asked her, 'what's Jack's second name?'

'Why?'

'You never said.'

She sounded amused. 'Why should I? Actually, it's Chalmers. Jack Chalmers. What are you working on?'

Someone in the background called to Tally and saved Simon from the trouble of reply.

'Got to run,' she said. 'Tell me all about it when you get back?'

'Sure. Love you.'

He lowered the receiver slowly as though reluctant to break the contact. Should he have told her? What was there to tell? That he was jealous of a friend and wanted to know more about this possible enemy?

'Pathetic,' he told himself. 'Utterly pathetic.'

London was a nightmare for parking and Simon never bothered. He had friends at Edmonton with off-road parking in front of their house and he'd abandoned his car there and caught the tube into the city. He was a little late for his rendezvous with Nat Sullivan, a noisy bar just off the Charing Cross Road, crowded and stuffy after the cold outside.

Calum must have given his description because he had no sooner squeezed himself through the door than a voice was calling his name and Nat Sullivan appeared, fighting his way through the cram.

He was a small man, stocky and broad shouldered with an aura that preceded him by about three feet on all sides. Dark eyes gleamed in a tanned face and he exuded an energy that made Simon feel inadequate and slow.

'Nat Sullivan.' The man extended a large square hand. 'Come and have a drink.'

Somewhat overwhelmed, Simon followed him to the bar. Nat seemed to know everyone and to be capable of carrying on about a dozen conversations at once without missing a beat. Simon found himself surrounded by a crowd of eight or nine who seemed to be in Nat's immediate party. Nat was rowdy, noisy and very much alive and his companions seemed to have caught his mood. It occurred to Simon just how different Tally seemed by comparison. How fey and separate. What was Tally like when she was around the likes of Nat? Did she succumb to the man's energy in the way Simon felt himself doing?

They spent about an hour in the bar, Simon being interrogated by Nat's friends about his work, and inevitably – when Nat made the connection for them – about Tally. As the group slowly started to disperse, Nat took Simon to sit in a quieter corner with a couple of rounds of drinks to keep them going.

'Now,' he said, 'tell me. Calum spun me some yarn about a feature on Jon, but that's been done to death, so I don't go with it.'

Simon smiled at the man's directness. He guessed that the past hour had been so that Nat could sum him up properly, see if he was worth talking to or should be fobbed off. He figured he must have passed. He'd drunk far more than he was used to and hoped that his brain would hold out well enough to ask what he wanted to know.

'It's about his time in Somalia,' he said.

'That crap! God Almighty, was that one a farce.'

'But you were there both times Jon O'Dowd went out?'

'Damned right I was. Why?'

'Do you remember an incident, the second time? You'd got separated from the convoy. Tally was with you and Jon and you found yourself trapped between two rival gangs. A place called Mamolo, I think.'

'Christ, yes.' Nat leaned back in his seat and regarded Simon thoughtfully. 'Thought that was it for all of us,' he said. 'The rebels had attacked the control point, this little hotel on the edge of town. Jon radioed in for help and damned near got us all killed.'

'Tally told me about it. Nat, did you know someone called Jack? Another soundman?'

The man squinted, his brow furrowed with thought, though Simon didn't get the impression he was trying to remember, but rather trying to figure out why the question was necessary.

'Never heard of him,' he said finally.

'Tally told me he used to sub for you sometimes,' Simon explained.

Nat leaned toward him and placed his glass purposefully on the table. He'd seemed annoyed. 'Tally knows better than that. She's spinning you a line, my friend.'

'Why would she do that?'

Nat shrugged. 'Tally's odd sometimes,' he said. 'If you've taken notice of more than her knickers you'll know that by now.'

Simon shook his head to clear it but it didn't work. He excused himself and went to the toilets to wash his face but that didn't work either. He half expected Nat to be gone when he came back, but the man was still there, another drink in front of him and any irritation he might have felt gone from the broad, pleasant face.

'Maybe Jack's a nickname. Could be John or James or even Jonathan?'

'What was his last name?'

'Chalmers. Jack Chalmers.'

'Nope, no one with that name on our crew. What did he look like?'

Simon hesitated. Truthfully, he didn't know.

He started to speak but Nat held up a hand to silence him.

'Look,' he said. 'I don't know why this is so important to you but think on a minute. If Tally doesn't tell the truth about this then maybe there's a reason. Have you talked to her about it? No, I thought not. You're being too much Mr Junior Investigative Reporter and not enough Mr Tally Palmer. I worked with her. I liked her and when we were pushed into the corner she didn't let us down. If she doesn't want you to know something about her past, ask yourself this: are there things you don't like to talk about maybe, that you'd bend the truth over? What's it matter to you who was there that day?'

Simon didn't know what to say. He was aware that Nat waited for an answer but he had none to give.

And he had none to give, now, he reminded himself. Not if he were honest with himself. No reason beyond the feeling that remained, that Tally was somehow subject to Jack's will; that, and a simple, jealous need to know.

Fourteen

April

'What's he talking about?' Lillian wanted to know. 'Doctor, he keeps rambling.'

Simon heard the other male voice. The one Samuel had been talking to earlier. It was a comforting sort of voice, reassuring, pleasant. Simon struggled to open his eyes again and turned his head to look at Lillian. He struggled to smile at her.

Mum. Mum, it's all right. All right now.

She squeezed his hand, her eyes flooded with tears, but she smiled back at him. Simon closed his eyes and drifted again.

That night in London, Simon went out on the town with Nat Sullivan, club hopping like he hadn't done since his student days. Somewhere along the line they met up with a couple of Sullivan's friends, Claire and Antonia, and the four of them spent the rest of the evening getting increasingly pissed.

Simon had felt guilty when Claire had first attached herself, but as the night got later and then earlier, and the club they finished up in became more fragmented by the blur of alcohol, Simon stopped worrying and got down to having some serious fun, regretting only the increased lack in the co-ordination department.

The girls were relaxing company. Pretty, lively and – Claire especially – funny with it. The low intensity relationship was a relief, though he didn't go so far as to put that into words, even inside his own head. For all that he was crazy about Tally, life with her was so concentrated it could be hard to cope with.

Somewhere around three thirty in the morning the four of them wandered drunkenly back to Sullivan's flat and Nat and Antonia took themselves off to the bedroom leaving Simon and Claire alone.

'I could do with a coffee,' Claire confided, glancing into the kitchen. 'Do you want to make me one? Nat won't mind.' She wandered off muttering something about the bathroom and Simon went into the kitchen wondering if he could still remember how to handle an electric kettle.

Even through the heavy load of alcohol he could see how the night might develop. It didn't take any brains to know what Nat and Antonia had in mind, and it seemed kind of rude to say no to Claire. After all, she was an attractive lady with her long brown hair and big tits barely concealed beneath a bright red top.

But then there was Tally.

Can't do it to her, Simon told himself. Got a girlfriend and I can't do it to her.

He tried to get his head around telling Claire when she got back, but she seemed in no hurry to return. This was a disadvantage considering Simon's brain had become incapable of holding on to information for long, even if it could get it together in the first place.

Tally, he thought. Want to talk to Tally. Then it would be easy to say no to Claire, be nice about it but still say no.

He fumbled in his pocket for the mobile and squinted at the tiny numbers on the little black pads. It took him a couple of attempts to get it right but finally he remembered that her number was already programmed and he didn't have to press more than two.

Tally's phone rang several times and Simon glanced up

at the kitchen clock, realizing vaguely that it was after three. 'Must be asleep,' he told Claire who had wandered back into the room. 'Three in the morning . . . and a bit . . . must be sleeping.'

Then a man's voice said hello.

For a moment, Simon was stunned. Thoughts of a wrong number entered his head and then stalled.

'Who is this?' he managed to say, his words slurred and untidy.

'Oh,' the voice said. 'You must be Simon. Good night out, Simon?'

'Jack? Is that Jack? I want to talk to Tally.'

The man laughed and hung up. Stupidly, Simon stared at the mobile phone then he threw it angrily on to the kitchen counter. Drunk or sober, there was only one reason Simon could think of for Jack being there at 3 a.m.

Simon woke the following morning with a violent hangover and only a vague memory of the night before. He was lying on Nat's sofa with one leg dangling and a crick in his neck which only added to his pain. Nat was crashing around in the kitchen and the smell of frying bacon added nausea to Simon's list of misery.

Somehow he struggled to his feet and headed for the bathroom, not certain whether the need to pee was greater than the need to puke. His bladder won. Just. Nat was standing in the kitchen doorway when he staggered back.

'Good night?' Nat said, winking at him. 'Claire says to look her up next time you're down this way.'

'Claire?'

Nat tutted at him. 'My, but we did have a skinful last night.' He came over and handed Simon something disgusting-looking in a tall glass. 'Drink this then come and have breakfast. After that I'll have to chuck you out, my friend. I've got a plane to catch.'

A little later, over a breakfast that Simon was surprised

he was able to eat, he told Nat about his phone call to Tally.

'Sounds like you have a rival there, my man.'

'What did you think of her, when you worked together?'

Nat cocked an eyebrow at him. 'The hangover obviously makes you more direct,' he said. 'You spent all of last night not asking me that.'

Simon smiled wryly.

'Obsessive,' Nat told him. 'But then, you have to be. Talented, beautiful and totally impossible to get inside of . . . if you see what I mean.'

'She and O'Dowd. They were really close though.'

Nat whistled. 'And how. They had a real thing going for a while, then Tally started getting all distant on him. Said she needed space or something. I figured they'd just burned too hot, you know what it's like sometimes. You want something to last you have to go for the slow smoulder.

'Then Jon was killed.' He sobered suddenly as though touching too much reality.

'And Tally was there.'

'Yeah. We'd survived Mamolo, and then . . . a few weeks later, he was shot down right in front of her. In front of all of us.'

He got up and crossed to the shelves stacked high with videos. Selected one and handed it to Simon.

'I'll want it back,' he said. 'And, Simon, don't let Tally see it. OK?'

Shocked, Simon realized what Nat Sullivan had given to him.

Fifteen

April

'This is Patrick,' Naomi said. 'I've told you about him. He was with me when you called, so I brought him along.'

'Of course,' Lillian said. 'Patrick, I've heard a lot about you.'

'How is he?' Naomi wanted to know. 'You say he's been talking?'

Lillian nodded so violently Naomi could feel it through her clasped hands. 'Talking about all manner of stuff,' she said. 'But I don't understand it, Nomi. Samuel says he must have something on his mind, but he keeps talking about that woman and about the police.'

'Ah,' Naomi said. 'The police.'

'You know something, Nomi. Damn! Samuel said you would. He said the boy would be talking about something real and not his dreams like the doctor thought. What is it about, Nomi? What do you know that Simon's not been telling us?'

Naomi sighed. 'We made him promise, Lillian. He was meant to explain himself. Alec thought it would be in the papers, but Tally didn't press any charges and the officer . . .' She broke off, aware of Lillian's scrutiny even though she could not see the woman's face.

'Charges?' Lillian questioned. 'Officer? Naomi, my son said nothing about any of this. I would have thought that you might. You or Alec? What is it we had to be protected from? Has Simon done something so terrible? Or are you just not telling us the things you should, in the name of friendship, Naomi?'

She could hear the hurt in Lillian's voice and she sighed heavily. 'It's not so bad,' she said softly. 'Simon got very drunk one night and stood outside of Tally's flat shouting to be let in. The police were called and there was a bit of a scuffle. He managed to catch one of the arresting officers with his elbow, we think. Gave him a bloody nose, but Simon was lucky. The officer involved knew it had been an accident. He talked to Alec about it and didn't take it any further. Neither did Tally. Fortunately for Simon no one got wind of it. He was horribly embarrassed, Lillian. Knew he'd acted like a fool. We thought . . . Alec and I thought that if anyone told you about it then it should be Simon.'

'Sorry to drag you down here this time of night,' the custody sergeant told Alec, 'but he's in a right state. We've got the doc coming, but god knows how long that will take, and the only sense we can get out of him is that he wants to see you.'

'You say he was standing in the rain shouting for his girlfriend,' Alec confirmed.

'Ex, from what we can gather. We tried to persuade him to go quietly, as I told you on the phone, but he wasn't having any. We'd had three calls from the neighbours, so we couldn't just leave him there.'

'But the girlfriend, Miss Palmer, she didn't call in?'

'No. Not a peep out of her. We've sent uniform round to check things out. Make sure there's nothing else we should know about.'

Alec nodded. Domestic disturbances of one sort or another could get nasty, though he doubted this would apply in

Simon's case. Simon was just a fool – presently a drunken fool. 'He's not violent,' Alec said. 'But I know he's been upset by the split.'

'Upset! Screaming like a girl by the time we got him here. Then he threw up.'

Alec grimaced. Sick drunks were a pain in everyone's backside. Regulations said you had to check up on them at least every fifteen minutes in case they passed out and choked on their own vomit. Having to resuscitate when that happened was enough to turn you off police work altogether.

Alec had been at Naomi's when the call had come through and he was not best pleased at being forced to get up and dressed and back out into the cold.

'Anyone told his parents?'

The sergeant shook his head. 'He's asked for no one but you.'

Alec nodded. 'OK,' he said. 'Let's take a look at him.'

Simon didn't even raise his head when they opened the cell door. He was seated on the narrow bunk with his head resting in his hands. A blanket had been thrown around his shoulders but even so he was shaking as though chilled right through.

Alec sat down beside him, wrinkling his nose. Simon stank of vomit and booze and damp clothes and police cell. Naomi commented often these days on the particular odour of people and places and it had heightened Alec's own awareness. Police cells, however often they were hosed out and disinfected, still carried the same embedded stink within the very plaster of their walls. Alcohol and piss and despair and, Alec had noted, something like the faintest odour of wet dog. It got into your nose, your clothes, your pores, and Alec sometimes wondered if those who claimed they could 'smell a pig a mile off' might actually subconsciously be on to something.

'Simon?' he said.

The young man half turned his head, shifting his hands and letting them fall heavily down between his knees.

'Sorry,' he said. 'I didn't know what else to do. I was scared, Alec.'

He seemed to have calmed down at any rate, Alec thought.

'What were you playing at?'

Simon smiled wryly. 'Getting pissed. Making a nuisance of myself. Did *she* call the police?'

'I wouldn't know.'

'And wouldn't tell me anyway?' He sighed and straightened painfully, then leaned back against the wall. Alec winced. Touching the cell walls was something he would never willingly do. He'd seen what got smeared on them. The shit and vomit and blood. He could never convince himself that it really washed away.

'I really don't know,' he said. 'Simon, what the hell did you hope to achieve? I thought you agreed. It was time to let it go.'

'Thought I could do it, too,' he shrugged. '*He* was with her.'

'Who?'

'Jack. I told you about Jack. At the flat. I saw him looking out of the window. I *know* it was him.'

Alec was confused for a moment. 'You know . . . Simon, have you ever actually met this Jack?'

Reluctantly, Simon shook his head.

'Then it could have been just anyone.'

Impatiently Simon got up and began to pace back and forth across the narrow cell. He could barely manage three steps each way, being forced to curtail his final stride. It seemed to frustrate him even more. Angrily, he drew back his fist and drove it straight into the far wall.

'Everything all right in there?' The custody sergeant sounded concerned.

'It's fine,' Alec told him. 'Our young friend just letting off some steam.'

He waited until the man's footsteps trailed away and then called to Simon, 'Simon, sit down. Talk to me. What really happened between the two of you?'

'I blew it, Alec.' He turned around and Alec was shocked to see the tears coursing down Simon's face. 'I really blew it. Best thing that ever happened in my life and I fucked it up.'

'How? What did you do?'

'I went round there today and I confronted her about Jack. Told her what I thought, that she just used Jack as an excuse to run when anyone got too close. I told her how I felt, that I wanted her back, that I'd get her whatever help she needed. That we could see a counsellor and she just laughed in my face.'

'So you took the man's way out and went off to get drunk.'

'It wasn't like that,' Simon shouted.

'No, it never is. There's always some justification, isn't there. Some reason you can give yourself to make it seem like you're less the complete idiot and more the aggrieved party. What excuse did you use, Simon? It seems to me you're as guilty of using this Jack as a defence as you accuse Tally of being.'

For a moment or two Alec wondered if Simon would be stupid enough to throw the punch he had prepared. The arm swung back as it had when Simon had belted the wall, but then the moment passed and he let his arm fall limply at his side.

'I slept with someone else,' he said finally, his voice flat, almost toneless.

'And she found out?'

'I was down in London . . . with a friend. I mean, I'd only just met Nat Sullivan but . . .' He sighed and lifted his hands to scrub at his face as though that would make the whole thing go away. Then he sat down next to Alec, side on so that he would not have to see his face.

'I was down in London. I'd been seeing Tally for just over three months and things were getting serious. At least, I thought they were. But there were things about her that she wouldn't tell me. Stupid things, like Jack. Who he was. Why he was so goddamned important and this . . . Alec you've got to understand, I've never been in love before, not in love like this, and I was jealous, I suppose.

'Anyway, we'd met these girls, friends of Nat's and gone out with them, then back to his flat. Claire, she's nice. Easy to get along with and well, things got kind of intense. I called Tally. I thought, if I could talk to her then everything would be all right. I called her, it was something like half three, nearly four in the morning. Maybe later. And *he* answered the phone.'

'This Jack?'

'Yes. This Jack.'

'And so, to get your own back, you slept with Claire?'

'It wasn't that simple. I was drunk. I was being stupid.' He paused and lifted his head to look at Alec. 'Yes,' he admitted. 'I slept with Claire. And then later, just so I could rub in how mad I was about her seeing Jack, I told her about it.'

'Nice one, Simon,' Alec commented. 'God, but you do know how to screw up big time.' He thought about it for a minute and then asked, 'Did she say why Jack had been there?'

Simon laughed harshly. 'Why the hell do you think he was there? She *said* he was an old friend. She *said* he'd just come round to see her. I told her, what kind of a friend visits at that time of the morning, and she just said well, I'd phoned her at that time so what was the difference?'

He was on his feet again, anger building to its previous

level. Alec noted that the knuckles of his right hand were bleeding from where he'd struck the wall.

'Simon, I like you a whole lot, but frankly you've behaved like a right wanker. I hate to say this to you, old son, but it seems to me that you and Miss Tally Palmer are two of a kind and probably deserve one another.'

Alec got to his feet and, startled at the realization that he was going to leave, Simon grabbed him by the arm.

'You're not going?'

'Oh yes, I am. The police surgeon will be here later on to check you out. You'll sleep here tonight and if no one wants to press charges, probably be free to go sometime tomorrow. If you're very lucky, I'll get your mother to bring you some clean clothes.'

'You're going to tell them?'

'Oh yes, I'm going to tell them, Simon, they're good people. They've been worrying themselves stupid over you and this girl. I think they deserve for me to tell them rather than have them read about it in your own newspaper.'

'Newspaper?' He looked stricken. Clearly, the idea that this might have further repercussions had only just occurred.

'Next time, Simon. Try to think it through first,' Alec rapped on the cell door and called the sergeant to let him out. '"Journalist assaults arresting officer" would make a damned good headline, wouldn't it?'

'Oh God.' Simon sank back on to the bunk and the look of shock on his face almost made Alec pity him enough to offer reassurance. Almost, but not quite. Simon was quite sober now and had a big chunk of reality to chew over. Alec left him to it.

'Bit hard on him, weren't you?' the custody sergeant asked as they left the cell block. 'Timms knows it were as much his fault he got clobbered as it were the lad's. He'll not be pressing charges.'

'I know that,' Alec said. 'I'll let you tell him later, but

meantime I want him to think how close he's come to screwing up. If he's the Simon Emmet I know it'll do him the world of good to be pulled up short, and if you think I'm hard, you just wait till his mother has a go. Gentle as a lamb until she's roused, then she'd take on Tyson and come out winner. He's been a fool and he knows it and it's not like he's some daft teenager. He's old enough to know better. Anyone but Timms as arresting officer and like as not he would be facing an assault charge.'

'True enough,' the sergeant agreed. 'We'll leave it till morning then, to let him know he's off the hook.'

'Right,' Alec stretched wearily. 'I'm off to get some sleep. Take care of him for me.'

The custody sergeant laughed. 'Like he were my own,' he said.

Alec had left him, Simon returned to his brooding.

Alec was right; he did realize just how close he'd come to ballsing the whole thing up. In danger of losing the career he'd worked so hard for as well as the woman he knew he still loved.

He recalled the row they'd had when he came back from London. He'd gone straight to her flat, hung around, half expected, half hoping that Jack would be there. Been more than half afraid that he would . . .

Then, the argument that followed, and he could hear himself now, making those accusations, calling her all kinds of whore just because he believed she had slept with Jack and because it eased his conscience for having done the very thing that he accused her of.

'She didn't deserve that,' he whispered to himself. Alec was right, he'd behaved like . . . He couldn't find the words for it. Disgust sobered him like nothing else.

But he'd stayed angry with her. His sense of injustice building through the rest of that week as she'd failed to get in touch – Simon refusing to make the first move – until that following weekend when he'd taken himself back down to London and seen Claire. They'd gone out together and then wandered back to her flat. Tally had chosen then to try to reconcile their relationship. To make that first move that Simon with his stubborn pride had been unable or unwilling to do.

She called Simon on his mobile and told him that she had to talk to him, could he please come round.

He was at that moment in Claire's bed with other things on his mind. Claire, realizing who it was that demanded Simon's time, was far from impressed.

'Get rid of her,' she hissed. 'Christ's sake, Simon, can't she just leave you alone?'

'This isn't a good time, Tally, and I'm not home right now.'

'When will you be home? Simon, I've got to talk to you. I need to explain. To try and explain about Jack.'

'Jack,' Simon sighed. 'It's always about Jack. Tally, don't you see that was the problem? It was Jack, all the time. Not you and me but you and me and a third party.'

'I know what that's like,' Claire muttered in the background.

Simon grimaced. 'Look, Tally, this is not a good time. I'll call you, soon as I'm back and maybe we can meet for coffee or something.' He tried to ignore the daggers that Claire was shooting with her eyes. 'I really do have to go.'

'I want to tell you about Jack,' Tally said softly. 'I want to talk about Jack and about what happened. I really need to, Simon.'

Claire had had enough at that point and snatched the phone from him, breaking the connection and throwing it to the bottom of the bed.

'Decide, Simon. Her or me. I won't play second fiddle.'

'It isn't like that.'

'Isn't it?' She lay back against the pillows and glared at him. Her full breasts flattened slightly against her body, the nipples were hard, surrounded by large aureoles of darkest pink.

She moved slightly, parting heavy, muscular thighs and Simon groaned, pushing Tally from his mind as he reached for Claire.

She held him off, strong hands grasping his arms and keeping him at a distance. 'Decide,' she demanded. Then she let him go and he pulled her to him, sliding inside her as hard and as far as he could get, but it was Tally who filled his mind.

Sixteen

April

'Did you meet Jack again after that time at Tally Palmer's?' Patrick asked Naomi as they travelled home in the taxi.

Naomi nodded. 'Jack came to see me,' she told him. 'It was the day after Simon had made such an idiot of himself and I was working at the advice centre. Jack turned up out of the blue posing as a client. Sat for a couple of hours in the waiting room because he said no one else could help him. It was strange. A bit worrying too, I suppose. I wondered at the time how he knew I worked there. I didn't recall ever mentioning it to Tally.'

'Maybe Simon did?'

'Maybe, but why should he? I mean, he might have mentioned in passing that he had this blind friend who was an ex-copper and now made a nuisance of herself doling out advice to others . . . but somehow, I don't think so. And Tally didn't make any reference, any connection when I turned up on her doorstep. Had Simon mentioned me before, she'd have put two and two together.'

'Then Jack decided to track you down after you returned the photos,' Patrick guessed.

'Must have done, but I don't know how, or why. Anyway, he turned up cool and polite as you like. But there was no mistaking the threat.' She frowned, thinking back. 'You know, at the time, I kept telling myself I was being paranoid. Nothing he said was really unpleasant, just the way he said it.'

The morning after Simon's arrest Naomi was due to work at the local advice centre. She had done this twice a week for almost a year. It enabled her to go on using her knowledge of the law and the people skills she had acquired as a police officer. In addition, on what she saw as a rather selfish but invaluable level, it gave her back some notion of control. Naomi had grown used to being in a position of responsibility, to have to make decisions and act upon those decisions. Working at the advice centre and being able to point people with problems in the right direction was satisfying and boosted her self-esteem. It sometimes bothered people to be helped by a blind woman but for the most part it was a positive thing. It both distracted them and broke the ice, and often people seemed to find it easier to talk to someone who could not see their faces. It added to their feeling of anonymity or confidentiality, Naomi thought, odd though that might seem. Now, after eleven months of working at the centre she found that some people asked for her on the basis that if she had helped with one problem, she must surely have the solution to the next, an impression that Naomi wasn't always sure she wanted to cultivate.

It was just before twelve when a colleague, Shirley, came into Naomi's broom cupboard of an office and told her she had a 'repeat customer'. Shirley, an ex-practitioner of family law who now worked as a volunteer, had been at the centre only a little longer than Naomi and the two had become good friends, often enjoying evenings out together.

'The client says he's been to you before,' Shirley told her, 'though I can't say I remember him.' Shirley often ran the front desk, taking details as people came in and assigning them to advisors she thought could be most useful. She had a prodigious memory for faces and a pretty good one as regards names. 'He's quite insistent he wants to see you. Been waiting all morning'

Naomi's ears pricked up at Shirley's tone. A long career dealing with domestic problems had sharpened her instincts and Naomi had come to trust her colleague's intuition. 'Something wrong with him?'

'Um, don't know. Can't place it but he feels wrong. Won't give any details either, didn't even want to give his name until I pushed him.'

'That's not *so* unusual,' Naomi mused. 'What's he like?'

'Like someone you'd remember. Tall, dark hair, long on the collar and with curls most women would die for. Thirtyish, I guess. Says his name's Jack Chalmers.'

Naomi reacted to the name and Shirley spotted it. 'You know him?'

'No, but we've met. He's involved in something else. A friend with problems.'

'You want me to tell him you can't see him? Fred's on, we can hand him over, no trouble.'

'No.' Naomi shook her head, curiosity getting the better of caution. Her reaction was one of surprise, she told herself. Surprise and too much notice taken of Shirley's natural caution. 'I'll see him.'

'Well, if you're sure. I'll be just outside. Press the button if you're the slightest bit worried.'

Naomi nodded. 'Will do.' Panic buttons had been installed in every room since a rather nasty incident just before Naomi's time when a drunk with a knife had slightly injured one of the volunteers. Naomi could not recall one incident when they had been used. She smiled. 'Does he look like an axe murderer?'

'No,' Shirley admitted and Naomi could hear the smile in her voice. 'Quite the opposite, but they're always the worst kind, aren't they?'

She heard Jack enter. He closed the door and crossed the room towards her before he spoke.

'Won't you sit down?' Naomi asked indicating the chair on the opposite side of her table.

'Thank you,' he said.

She heard him pull out the chair, dragging it lightly across the uncarpeted floor. It scraped and then creaked as he settled his weight into it.

'How can I help you, Mr Chalmers?'

'Jack, please,' he said. 'After all, we have been introduced.'

'Jack then. How can I help you, Jack?'

He leaned forward and she felt the table shift slightly as he laid his arms on the edge of it. 'It's a delicate matter,' he told her. 'You can probably guess why I'm here. It's about your friend Simon and my friend Tally.'

Naomi leaned back in her seat and frowned. 'Jack, this is an advice centre. It's for people with problems: debts, difficult neighbours, court actions they don't know how to deal with. It isn't for things like this.'

'I see,' he said quietly. He seemed to consider her words and then he asked, 'If I came to you wanting a divorce, what would you do?'

'I'd make sure you understood the legal practicalities, talk to you about mediation and probably book you an appointment with a counsellor, if that was what you wanted.'

'And if it wasn't what I wanted?'

'Then I'd do my best to find out what you *did* want . . . or need, and address those issues.'

'Then that's what I want you to do now. Address my issues, if that's the way you'd like to put it. Simon and Tally are going through a messy divorce. I'm an interested friend. You're an interested friend. How can we help to make this better?'

'I'm not sure I understand the question,' she told him. 'Or, for that matter, what your part in this is.'

'I told you, I'm trying to help a friend.'

'Then why come to me?'

'Because *my* friend Tally is being hurt by *your* friend Simon. My job, my part in this, is to make things better for Tally. Your part in this, as I see it, is to make certain that your friend Simon stays the hell out of her life.'

Naomi's frown deepened.

'Don't screw up your forehead like that,' Jack said softly. 'You have a nice face, good skin. Bone structure that will last. It would be a shame to spoil it.'

'Are you threatening me, Jack?'

He laughed. A brief, harsh sound that startled both Naomi and Napoleon lying at her feet. 'Threat?' he said. 'I'm just giving good advice. No woman wants a wrinkled forehead.'

Naomi took a deep breath and exhaled slowly. The threat had been there, she was sure of it, but he was right, nothing he had said could be construed as anything other than an almost flirtatious observation . . . had it been made by anyone other than Jack and in a place other than here.

'Look, Jack,' she began again, surprised and annoyed by the ease with which he had knocked her off balance. 'Simon and Tally are both adults. Simon knows it's over, he's just having a hard time handling it and I'd guess so is Tally. What they both need is a little time and a lot of patience. What I don't think they need is friends with the best of intentions scurrying around behind their backs trying to do what the friends might think is best.'

Jack leaned back. She could feel him looking at her, his gaze harsh as though weighing her up and considering how best to proceed. 'Problem is,' he said at last, 'that people who are, let's say, emotionally damaged, don't always know what is good for them. What's best. Sometimes others have to show them. Give them a guiding hand.'

'I'm not sure that I agree,' she replied.

'No? You surprise me, Naomi. I'll just bet that after your

accident the last thing you wanted was to have to make decisions or even think things through. You were grateful to your family, friends, doctors, whoever it was that made those decisions for you. Told you what to do until you felt strong enough to take your life back.' He paused and waited for her response. Naomi did not reply. 'Am I right?' he asked her. 'Or am I right.'

'It's hardly the same thing,' she said at last, irritated at how lame that sounded.

'Isn't it? Maybe it's a matter of scale, I'll acknowledge that, but neither Simon nor Tally are thinking straight just now. You can't argue there.'

No, Naomi thought, she probably couldn't. Simon was certainly not behaving in a rational manner.

'Look,' he said, his tone placating, 'I know a little about Simon. I know he has a good family and I know now that he has good friends. People who'll see him through this little crisis, who'll be as ashamed of his behaviour last night as Simon himself should be and who, hopefully, will drag him back on to the straight and narrow. But you see, Tally doesn't have any of that. When it comes down to it, she only has me so I have to be the one to look after her interests.'

'Simon knows he behaved badly,' Naomi conceded. 'He won't be doing it again.'

'And I'm so glad to hear that. Tally is fragile, you see. She's had more than her share of tragedy in her life. Simon was a nice distraction for a little while, but it's over now and a broken love affair is bad enough without anything more traumatic happening.'

'Traumatic? Like what? Jack, you *are* threatening this time.'

'Am I?' He got up, scraping the chair legs again and then placing his hands on the table and leaning over her. 'I'm offering more advice, Naomi. You're Simon's friend. If you want to help him, keep him away from Tally.'

Seventeen

For the second time in as many weeks Naomi found herself climbing the stairs to Tally Palmer's flat.

Jack had rattled her but it took more than that to scare Naomi Blake and, as many people had found before, you annoy Naomi, you stir up the proverbial hornets' nest.

She had reported her conversation with Jack to Shirley and told her to call security should he come back again, but they had agreed it was probably not worth reporting the incident to the police. No actual threats had been made and Jack had left quietly without disturbance when Naomi had said she thought that he should go.

'Tell Alec about it,' Shirley had insisted and Naomi had promised that she would. It hadn't been until she was on the way home that she had thought about visiting Tally. Once the thought had occurred it had become nigglingly insistent and she had asked George, her regular taxi driver on advice centre days, to go home first so that she could collect something and then bring her here.

'You want me to wait for you?' he had asked as she paid him off.

'No, I can get the bus from the corner, I think. If I follow the line of the building right back towards the road, it takes me right to it, if I remember right. If I get stuck, I'll give you a call. I've got my mobile.'

'Right you are, love. I'll see you on Thursday. Just don't get too independent on me, will you? I'd miss you.'

Naomi laughed. George had become a good friend and though Naomi could now use buses on routes she knew with a degree of confidence, she was still a long way from dispensing with George.

Tally had buzzed her through the main door and was waiting as she reached the head of the stairs.

'Are you here on Simon's behalf?' she asked briskly. 'Because if you are, I've nothing more to say.'

'No.' Naomi had already thought of her excuse. It was a more or less truthful one. 'Actually, I'm not here for Simon's benefit. He behaved like a complete jerk last night and no one expects you to have any truck with him.'

'Oh,' Tally said. She sounded oddly deflated. 'For what then?'

'Two things,' Naomi told her. 'I've talked to Lillian and Samuel and they want you to know how bad they feel. They really liked you, said you'd been good to Darien, helping him with his photographs and everything. They don't know the details of what Simon did last night but Lillian is horribly embarrassed by Simon's inability to leave you alone.'

'Oh,' Tally said again. 'Oh, I see.'

'The other thing is, I wanted to return this. Simon left it at my place with the pictures, but I didn't realize.' She laughed self-deprecatingly. 'If people don't tell me where things are, it can take me a little while to find them.'

She reached into her coat pocket and withdrew the key ring then held it out to Tally.

'Simon's key,' Tally said. She sounded almost wistful as though his giving back the key was a finality she had not anticipated.

Cool slender fingers lifted the metal ring from Naomi's hand. She sensed Tally hesitate and then she said, 'Look, come in for a while. I feel bad about you having to come all the way here, the least I can do is make you coffee. Be careful though, there are bags just inside the door. Should I take your arm or something?'

Naomi smiled at her. 'Napoleon will sort me out,' she said. 'He's a bright dog.'

'He's beautiful.' She stood aside and allowed Naomi and her four-footed guide to enter the room. The space echoed in Naomi's ears. She had become very good as estimating the size of the room from the way it sounded, and this was big. Very big. She said so.

'It was a warehouse,' Tally told her. 'The offices were on this floor but the developers ripped out the dividing walls and now there's this big room, a kitchen at one end and a bedroom at the other.' She laughed suddenly and went on, 'Do you know what made me buy this place?'

Naomi shook her head.

'The most stupid reason imaginable. I bought it for the floor. Not the view or the space . . . well, kind of for the space and the view *is* fantastic, but mostly for the floor.'

Naomi tapped her foot. 'Wood,' she said. 'Not laminate. My flat has that phoney laminate stuff. It's nice, but not the same.'

'Polished beech,' Tally said. 'Here. Let me get you sat down.' She took Naomi's arm, a little nervously, Naomi thought, but she'd grown used to that reaction from people who wanted to be useful but were not sure how. Tally led Naomi to what felt like a small sofa and sat her down. Napoleon, at home just about anywhere, slumped down across her feet and deflated with an elaborate sigh.

'When I was a little kid,' Tally went on, 'my mum had a friend who owned this big house with a massive front hall. Polished wooden floors. We had to take our shoes off when we went in and . . .'

'You used to slide.' Naomi laughed. 'Oh Lord, do you remember the big hall at school? It had that, what's it called, parquet flooring. We used to sneak in after the caretaker had finished buffing. I got caught once, sent to the head. She kept me waiting outside her office for a full half hour before I got my dressing down. Then she went on about respect for school property or something.'

'Can't imagine you getting sent down for anything,' Tally said. 'I remember you, the prefect, deputy head girl, wasn't it?' She giggled like a child. It was a contagious sound and Naomi laughed too, shedding the tension that had brought her here.

'I think it's a perfect reason for buying this place,' she said.

Tally made coffee and they talked, exchanging reminiscences about their school days, the teachers they had hated, and those few that they had actually liked. Ordinary things such as people talk about when they have a common past, and from that talk they turned to the lives they led now, the careers they had chosen and eventually, inevitably, back to Simon.

'You know the ironic thing? It was Simon's idea I go on this trip. He suggested it. Thought it would be a brilliant idea for me to go back and re-photograph the places I had visited, put the then and now images together in the retrospective. The gallery loved it and want to call it my "Homecoming" exhibition. So now, I've got to actually go and get on with it and it doesn't give me much time.'

'Does it worry you? Going back. I mean some of the places you photographed were in war zones.'

'Most still are, but they've quietened down now for the most part. The fighting has . . . relocated. I'm not going to high risk areas. I've no story to tell except for the way things have changed. If they haven't changed, there seems little point in reprising something I did the best job I knew how to do the first time round.'

Naomi nodded. 'I went to your last big exhibition,' she

said. 'I'd love to come to your new one, see what's changed in Tally Palmer's world.'

'Would you?' She could not keep the surprise and doubt from her voice. 'I mean . . .'

'Because I can't see?' Naomi shook her head. 'I guess if I'd been born blind, I'd have a different attitude. It may sound strange, but I still don't know how blind people think, how they perceive the world. Those who've never been sighted, I mean. I know that most of the time I still think like a sighted person. I still get pictures in my head that I use when I'm trying to work out where I am or what it might look like. I still love films, either video or on at the pictures and my friends know that if they take me anywhere it has to be described in the minutest detail.' She laughed. 'My sister says I'm a right pain in the backside, but I've got my nephews well trained.'

'I never thought about it that way,' Tally mused. 'I couldn't cope with it. I really couldn't. It would be like dying . . . sorry, that must sound really, I don't know, selfish. Stupid.'

Naomi shook her head. 'No, I know what you mean. All my life it was the thing I was most afraid of. I'd always been very short-sighted and it was a family joke that the first thing I put on in the morning was my glasses. Then when I woke up in hospital after the accident and they eventually told me I would probably never see again, there was a moment when I wished I hadn't survived.' She smiled awkwardly at the memory. 'You know, I think the thing that got me through was that I was too ill to care much about anything at first, and by the time I'd actually started to get better there'd been a month, six weeks maybe, of living in this new world. I found I'd – well a part of me at least – kind of got used to the idea.'

'It can't have been that easy,' Tally objected.

'Oh, no, I never meant to say it was.' She paused and

frowned. 'I had this friend who was a recovering alcoholic. He always said you had to take things one step at a time, one day at a time, and I guess that's what I did. And you know the odd thing, it was the small details, like figuring out how to put on lipstick without looking like a clown, that made me feel most myself again. I guess it's different for everyone.'

'How *do* you do it?' Tally asked. 'I have to use a mirror.'

'Oh, I cheat, use my finger and stick to glosses or light colours. Anything really red and I get my sister to do it.'

Tally laughed. 'You know,' she said, and there was a sadness, a loneliness in her voice that caught Naomi completely off her guard, 'if things had been different, I think the two of us could have been really good friends.'

'Are you really OK?' Naomi asked her as she left. She sensed Tally hesitate for the merest instant before she said brightly that she was fine, looking forward to getting back to work and trying her best to get over Simon. But as Naomi heard the door close behind her, she could not shake the feeling that the younger woman had wanted to say so much more. That Simon, wrong headed as he may be and going about things in totally the most stupid of ways, actually might have a case when it came to his suspicions over this Jack character.

'You know she's coming to our school?' Patrick told Naomi the next day.

'No, I didn't. What's she going to be doing?'

'It's one of these careers talks we keep having,' he said. 'You know: "Do you want to be a doctor or a lawyer or a merchant banker. Well hard luck 'cause most of you'll end up stacking shelves."'

Naomi chuckled. 'I'm sure they don't say that.'

'No? I told the careers advisor what I wanted to do and he

was all, "Well –" he deepened his voice in fair imitation of Mr Baxter – "It's good to have ambitions, Patrick, but don't you think you'd better have a realistic fallback position as well?".'

Naomi laughed at him. 'You could always become an accountant like your dad,' she said wickedly.

'Oh wow, thanks. I'll be lucky if I pass maths GCSE. I don't think I inherited a single thing from my dad, especially not the maths gene.'

'You'll do OK,' she told him affectionately. 'Harry's dead proud of you, you know that. So am I for that matter. You know, I don't think careers advisors have changed much from the sound of it. I had one who tried for two terms to talk me into becoming a nurse. I mean, can you see me as a nurse?'

'Oh, I don't know,' Patrick told her slyly. 'Bet you'd look good in the uniform!'

Naomi aimed a playful thump in his direction. 'Cheeky little blighter,' she said. 'Anyway, when's Tally Palmer coming to talk to you?'

'Friday,' Patrick told her. 'She's coming on Friday. You know,' he added, 'they showed us a picture of her on her publicity stuff. Simon must have been out of his head.'

'How do you mean?' Naomi asked him.

'She's gorgeous,' Patrick told her. 'If I found someone like that, I'd never play around the way Simon did,' he added with all the confidence of his fifteen years.

Eighteen

Saturday afternoon a few days after Naomi's visit to Tally's flat, Alec, Harry and Patrick gathered at Naomi's flat and began to collate the material Simon had brought over.

'How did you get on with Tally Palmer at school?' Naomi asked.

'Oh, good,' Patrick said.

'School?' Harry asked. 'What's all that about?'

'Oh, one of these careers things. You know, people come and talk about their jobs and we decide if we want any more information. *She* was good though.'

Naomi laughed. 'I take it some of your visitors weren't?'

'No, dead boring. I mean, who wants to be a banker or a manager or – no offence, Dad – an accountant.'

Harry humphed in that way he had when he didn't know whether to laugh at his son or disapprove.

'What about photographer?' Alec asked

Patrick shook his head. 'Don't think so. I'll stick to my original ideas, I think.'

This was new to Alec. Patrick was generally rather shy of saying what he wanted out of life. 'What's that then?' he asked.

'Patrick wants to design computer games,' Naomi told him.

'He could change his mind a thousand times yet,' Harry added, as though this were not his idea of a proper job.

'Oh,' Alec said. 'I think that's a good choice, Patrick. Should suit you down to the ground. And what was Miss Palmer like then?'

Patrick thought about it for a moment. 'Cool,' he said. 'Very . . . attractive and she . . . she really thought about things. You know, why she was doing what she was doing and why she stopped.' He paused and Naomi could feel the cogs turning. 'I don't think I could do that sort of thing,' he said. 'I mean, when you play computer games about war and you go round blasting the hell out of things, you know they're not real. You get kind of involved, you know. It's like being in a different place where . . . where you're powerful and can do anything. But the pictures Tally Palmer took weren't like that. They were real, you know. Real people dying and when real people die, it's not just them it's . . . well, you know.'

Harry cleared his throat again and Naomi smiled in Patrick's direction. Patrick knew all to well how events cast shadows across the lives of those who came after. When Harry's sister, Naomi's best friend, had been abducted, Naomi had been only twelve years old. But not a day had passed, not a major decision been made in her life, where Helen's disappearance had not been an influence and a constant pain. It was an influence that had continued to cross the generations, affecting Patrick himself in the most direct of ways. It didn't surprise her that in some ways Patrick preferred his fantasies.

'That's very perceptive,' Harry said at last. 'And you know . . . whatever you want to do, I'll back you all the way,' he added awkwardly.

'I know, Dad,' Patrick mumbled, embarrassed but, Naomi thought, pleased as well. 'It's a pity you took the key back,' Patrick mused. 'If she's gone away we could have had a look around.'

'We?' Alec queried.

'Well. Maybe just you.'

'You trying to get me the sack?' Alec enquired.

'It wouldn't be illegal,' Patrick argued. 'Not really. You told me once, if you had the key, it isn't breaking and entering.'

'I tell you far too much,' Alec said. 'And you've got far too good a memory. It wouldn't be right,' he added sternly, though he sounded a tad wistful all the same. 'I found two Jack Chalmers on the voters' register,' Alec went on. 'Neither of them could be our man. One's in his seventies and the other's a teenager, registered for the first time this year.'

Naomi knew from experience that the register of electors, though invaluable, was never complete or completely accurate. People moved house and missed out on registration, or for other reasons chose to slip through the net.

'I've cross-referenced with similar names: John, Jonathan, Jason and so on, but nothing seems to fit the bill. Chalmers is not a particularly common name and I've got only three households of Chalmers that have a male member of around the right age.'

'That's probably not his real name,' Patrick commented.

'Maybe not, but it's all we've got to go on right now.'

'And that's the whole crux,' Naomi added mournfully. 'If we could figure out who Jack really is, what his relationship is to Tally Palmer, what hold he has over her, we can get to the bottom of this.'

'I'm not so sure it's as simple as that,' Alec countered. 'It seems to me that this is a reciprocal thing. That Tally is as reluctant to part with Jack as he is with her.'

'What have you found, Patrick?' Naomi asked. She had been listening to him shuffling around among the newspaper clippings that Simon had collected. Now his riffling had ceased and she could sense his interest.

'Something about a car accident,' Patrick said. 'It's fastened together with a bit about a murder.'

Alec reached over and took it from him. 'Miles Bradshaw and Adam Hunter. Let me see. "Teenage driver killed in fatal accident",' he read out. Then: '"Quiet Close Shocked by Brutal Murder".'

'What's the connection?' Naomi asked.

'Simon's scribbled a note on here that Adam was Tally's boyfriend,' Alec told them. 'Apparently, he'd just passed his test, went out to celebrate with three of his friends and crashes the car.'

'It says he was drunk,' Patrick put in.

'Blood alcohol levels twice the legal limit. By all accounts, Tally must have been devastated.'

'And Miles Bradshaw?' Harry asked.

'Oh, you must remember,' Naomi insisted. 'Miles was in my year. Nasty piece of work, thought he was God's gift. I remember the murder because of all the fuss it caused. The school was buzzing for weeks and his girlfriend was in my class, we did history together. She was off school for about a month.'

'And how was Tally involved in these cases?'

'I don't know,' Alec admitted. 'One kid that survived the crash. He was in a coma for a long time so no one took any notice, but he swore that someone ran across the road and caused Adam to swerve.'

'Twice the legal limit would take care of that without the pedestrian,' Harry observed.

'Sure, but there's a brief mention in one of the articles on Miles. A paper quoted a neighbour who saw a blonde girl knocking at Miles' door earlier that evening. She went inside. It says that she was small with long blonde hair, wearing a blue coat. Tally, I believe, was small with long blonde hair.'

'Hmm,' Harry commented. 'I bet that tea's ready for pouring. I'll go and get it.'

'You're suggesting that Tally somehow caused the death

of her boyfriend and that she was somehow implicated in Miles Bradshaw's murder?' Naomi asked. 'Sounds at bit weak to me . . .'

'Yes, it does, doesn't it,' Alec agreed. 'Interesting though, don't you think?'

'You want to move things over?' Harry asked, coming in with the tea tray.

Papers were shuffled out of the way and pots chinked as he set things down.

'Tally's had a lot of tragedy in her life, according to Simon's notes.' Alec added. 'Family deaths, then her boyfriend, then Jon O'Dowd.'

'Deaths in the family?' Naomi queried.

'Hmm, yes. Her father when she was about thirteen, but before that, her brother Zechariah. He was a year older than Tally and Simon notes here, on the report of his death, that they were really close.' He paused. 'He's attached notes to most of the clippings and there's reams of scribbled pages to wade through when we get the time. Well, anyway, Zechariah fell on to a railway line from the embankment. Slipped and bashed his head. He hung on in a coma for a while but they finally pulled the plug.'

'Was this before or after the father died?'

'Hmm, let me check. Oh, before. He left the following summer, just after Tally's younger brother, Carl, was born. It turned out he'd been having an affair. He had a kid with another woman and then died a couple of years later. Simon's made another of his helpful notes. Patrick, is that clipping under your arm about Tally's father too? Thanks.'

'It must have hurt so much though,' Naomi commented. 'First the death of a sibling and then your father taking off like that.'

'Divorce isn't good for kids,' Patrick said. Then he added, 'But I'm glad my mum left my dad – no offence, Dad. But at least with the Atlantic ocean between the two of you, you can't argue any more.'

Her father had so little impact on her life that he had been gone three days before she even noticed that he'd left.

It was the summer that she was ten and two months after her baby brother had been born. Her father had not been keen on the new arrival, who had appeared without permission and proceeded to invade the house and her mother's affections in a way that no one else had ever dared. She had grown used to her father coming home from work, staying long enough to eat and then absenting himself until long after she had gone to bed. Days would pass with barely a word spoken and, although Tally had been vaguely aware of something being extra wrong in those three days, it was only the arrival of her aunt and uncle that told her what it was.

She had, of course, been sent to play while the grown-ups talked, but instead had watched and listened, hidden behind the half open door, as her mother wept and railed against her father and called him words she had to write down quickly and look up later. After three days of silence, of her mother being moody and withdrawn, this noisy shift in tone was an entertaining thing.

Tally watched through the crack in the door as her mother flung her arms around the aunt and wept noisily into her shoulder. Then she pulled away, first waving her hands in distraction, then pounding with fists at her armoured chest, crying out against the injustice of it all. Tally had heard the preacher at Sunday school talk about folk in ancient times beating their breasts in grief but she had never seen it done before now.

She wondered if it hurt. If it did, then her mother seemed not to notice.

It was only after several minutes of this carry on that Tally was discovered.

'Hush,' her aunt counselled. 'The child.'

She hustled towards the door, smiling at Tally and gave her the briefest of hugs. Tally could feel the wetness on her shoulder from her mother's tears.

'Go and play now, Tally,' Aunt Bee said. Then as though inspired: 'Find that nice dolly I gave you. You find that baby and some clothes and later on we'll have a tea party together.'

She was pushed gently but firmly from the room and this time the door was closed.

Tea party! Tally was disgusted. Only little kids played that sort of game. Didn't her aunt remember how old she was? And as for finding that doll . . .

Tally went outside into the garden trying to recall exactly where she had buried it this time. She figured she'd better dig it up again, just in case Aunt Bee remembered and wanted to play. Today didn't seem such a good one to court adult disapproval.

She found the body of the doll under her mother's orange rose. The legs were in the mint patch and the arms shoved into the big pot of geraniums just outside the back door together with the brunette head. She had long since lost track of the blonde one.

Tally washed Tallulah Two Heads under the kitchen tap, scrubbing the doll clean with her father's toothbrush. Then she sat it to dry, splay-legged on the steel draining board in a patch of sunlight that heated the bright metal almost hot enough to burn flesh.

'My father's gone to live with a bitch of a painted whore,' Tally told the doll. 'Mum says he's a fucking wanking bastard.' She looked around quickly, scared of being overheard but the adults were still closed up in the other room. And the words sounded pretty good so Tally said them again and again, a little louder each time until a slight sound from the living room had her certain that the

grown-ups must have heard. Panic-struck, she dodged out of the back door and ran down the garden, plonked herself on the swing and pretended she had been there all the time. But it was a false alarm. Several minutes passed and no one appeared. Tally began to breath again.

Slowly, she crept back up the garden path and peered around the kitchen door. There was no one there except Tallulah Two Heads, still sitting on the hot patch of steel. Hopefully, Tally looked for some expression of discomfort or even pain on the painted face, but Tallulah Two Heads, calm as ever, merely stared back at her, unblinking.

Her father had taken everything, emptied the bank account and was refusing to pay a penny to Tally's mother. She was taking him to court, but in the meantime they were existing on what little her mother could squeeze out of the DSS. Bills went unpaid and her complaints that her feet were cold, still wearing summer shoes in November, were met with tears.

She saw her father only twice that winter. Once when he came by to pick up the remainder of his things and the second time when she waited for her mother outside the court.

The first time, she saw him only through the window. She stared out through the rain-streaked glass as he scrabbled on the ground gathering the clothes and books her mother had thrown there. He saw Tally as he stood up, his arms full of his sodden possessions and rivulets of water streaming down his face from his wet hair. For the briefest of times their eyes met and she tried to read in them if he was sorry to be going or if life was better with his bitch-whore woman. But she couldn't tell. The rain fell too fast, thumps of wet grey sound against the window. The sound of the sky too loud for her to hear the lesser message in her father's eyes.

She tried to catch a glimpse of the woman in the car as her father struggled to open the door and dumped his bundle of belongings on the back seat, but rain and glass got in the way and all she saw was a blurred red shadow in the driving seat of the car.

The second time, in February, he didn't even look her way. He walked swiftly through the panelled corridor, the squeak-flap of new shoes against the wooden floor almost drowned by the sharply painful tap of her mother's heels as she pursued him down the hall. Her solicitor ran after her calling for her to 'calm down Mrs Palmer, please calm down'. His robes flying out behind him like a vampire's cloak.

Things began to improve then and Tally had new shoes the week after. She chose red trainers with white stripes that her mother hated but let her have because, as she said, they needed cheering up. Tally wore them that year right into the autumn until they had all but fallen apart and her feet had grown another size. She wore them even with her best pink dress or her yellow jeans though her mother winced at the clashing colours and sometimes the loudness of the visual noise they made hurt Tally's eyes and burned her ears.

But she couldn't not have chosen them, not from the moment she saw them in the shop window. It had been raining and the grey water streaked the glass so heavily that the shoes were like red shadows at the back of the display, the exact same shade as the clothes the bitch-whore woman wore the day Tally had glimpsed her through the windscreen of the car.

The feeling that stayed with her from that winter, and one that she had been reminded of many times as she had travelled, is that there is a stink to poverty that has nothing to do with the price of soap. It's the smell of damp rooms in houses that are truly warm only in the best of summers, and of clothes that dry too slowly inside when the cold rains fall. It is largely a winter smell. Even the poor can have their share of summer. They can let the sunlight into their houses and sit outside in their yards or on the front step, storing up the heat against the winter. But it's the cold time that truly shows the difference, that breeds the odour of too many bodies crowded into the one heated room. The stale air kept in by windows closed tight and sealed with stretched polythene to keep the precious warmth inside.

After her father left, the house was cold. The kitchen only really warm at the end of the day when her mother cooked. They ate their meal at the kitchen table, leaving the oven door open wide so the last vestiges of heat leached out into the room. They would sit in the moist, food-fragranced room until the chill crept in under the back door.

Her mother cooked bread and pies and fruit cake that they spread with butter. Even at the worst of times she refused to buy margarine, they just spread what they had more thinly and made it last.

Tally grew afraid of the cold. For a long time afterwards, even when things were better and the heat came back into the house, she kept her fear of chill and draughts; she would scorch her cheeks sitting too close to the fire and always wore her socks to bed.

'I'd guess it was losing Zechariah that really got to her,' Naomi commented softly, thinking of her own childhood scars. Having had to deal with Helen's murder, Harry's sister and her own best friend, was not something that could be painlessly or easily put aside, especially when it seemed so random and so pointless and had taken close on twenty years to solve. 'It never stops affecting you,' she added. Sometimes I even used to see Helen.'

'Nan and Dad still do,' Patrick put in. 'They pretend to each other that they don't, or that's it's no big deal, but I know they do. You know,' he went on, 'I'll bet Jack's someone she knew a long time ago.'

'What makes you think that?' Harry asked his son.

'I don't know. I guess . . . I mean . . . Well, you know

when Helen . . . when Helen went. I remember, Naomi, you said that everything seemed so empty and when Joe Jackson got involved and was nice to you, you kind of became attached to him?'

Naomi frowned. 'You think, after Zechariah died and Tally's father left and all that, Jack was someone new to depend upon? It's a thought,' she added. 'Maybe you're right.'

They were silent for a moment, a silence interrupted by Patrick scrabbling in the piles of paperwork once again.

'Did you wear uniforms like this?' he asked suddenly.

'What's that then?' Naomi asked

'It's a school photo,' Harry explained for Naomi's benefit. 'You know, one of those panoramic things they used to do. No one ever wanted them really. I mean, you couldn't put them on the wall or anything, not without a frame a yard long.'

Naomi giggled. 'Lord, yes. Still got one or two stashed away somewhere. What year's this?'

'Tally's first year, according to the helpful Simon,' Harry said, finding a note clipped to the back. 'It says she's on the second row, third from the end and on the right. This must be her I think.'

'So Naomi must be on it too?' Patrick asked.

'Oh, Lord, I suppose I must.'

'Show me,' Patrick demanded.

'OK, I'll bet I can find her . . . yes. Just here. My Lord, all that hair. I'd quite forgotten,' Harry teased.

Naomi laughed. All so long ago.

Nineteen

'I knew what I wanted to do from being fifteen years old,' Tally said. 'I guess I was lucky, not having to hunt around for a direction.'

It was, Simon remembered, the final time, the final chance to make things up before they broke up for good. They had met one evening, both feeling the need to at least try to bring things to some proper conclusion. The evening had been melancholy, the two of them going through the motions of civilised conversation. Both showing restraint. Both committed to allowing the new wounds they had inflicted upon each other to heal over, however thinly. So their conversation had been about general things, external, safe. Such care, such cowardice, could never last, Simon thought. It could never last.

They had left the flat and walked beside the canal towards the marina. Night had fallen and a soft moonlight filtered through a mist of rain reflected brokenly in the water. Night, Simon thought, was never truly dark in the city. It was neon blue and smoky yellow and tonight the colour of a rain-drenched moon.

'I guess I must have known early too,' he said. 'For me it was always words. I was hopeless at sports and couldn't draw a carrot without instructions, but I had power over words and that made me feel strong.' He smiled wryly. 'Most of the time anyway.'

'When I was due to leave for Sheffield,' Tally confided,

'my mum moved house. She said now I was going off to university they didn't need so much space. I spent my last night in her new house and it was like suddenly everything I had known was changing and ending.'

'And you cut off your hair,' he added for her; he had heard the story before. Tally's small act of final defiance as she left childhood behind and went out to conquer the world.

He breathed in the damp night air. The canal was clean enough these days for fishing competitions to be held along its banks, but he could recall a time when it had been a mere resting place for supermarket trolleys and old prams and had stunk of rot and decay. The city fathers had decided it was time to redevelop, convert the old factory units into high-priced loft apartments and the canal into an artery for the tourist trade. It was a good change in the main, Simon thought, though he could never foresee a time when he might afford to live beside it.

'Who is Jack?' he asked softly. 'Who answered the phone to me that night? Tally, what was he doing there?'

She sighed. 'He's just a friend, Simon. His name is Jack Chalmers and he's a soundman.'

'I don't buy that.'

'Don't buy what?' She became angry again, turning away from him as though that meant she could avoid his questions. 'I don't care what you do or don't "buy", Simon. Jack's a friend and it's bugger all to do with you anyway.'

'Fine. So it's nothing to do with me. Tally, I love you. That makes it something to do with me.'

'Loving someone doesn't mean you own them.'

'I never said it did.'

'Simon, you spy on me, you go behind my back and ask questions and you stand there looking all aggrieved and self righteous ready to believe anyone rather than me. Fuck it, Simon. Just get out of my life.'

Raucous laughter from a nearby bridge reminded them

of how public a place they had chosen for their argument. A group of half drunk youths were standing on the bridge enjoying the show.

In the yellow of the sodium lights Simon could see the colour rise to Tally's cheeks. She turned from him and began to walk back down the towpath, the set of her shoulders making Simon realize that she really did not want him to follow. At that moment he felt too confused and angry to want to anyway.

'Fine,' he muttered. 'Well that's just fine by me.'

He walked swiftly away in the opposite direction feeling that his world had just fallen apart.

Simon walked without thinking of a direction and realized suddenly that he was close to the newspaper office. The night man signed him in and he wandered upstairs to his desk in the shared, partitioned office.

The archive material he had requested lay in his tray together with a list of messages that had been left for him. He sat at his desk and flicked through the papers, reading about Jon, the man who had shared such an important episode in Tally's life, but on the face of it there was nothing there that he had not heard or seen before. Several papers covered the Somalia incident, emphasizing how lucky Jon and his crew had been to get out alive. The reports said that they had run with rebel forces in hot pursuit until they had reached the main road and miraculously caught up with the back markers from the US army convoy. To Simon's mind, the reports of their escape were vague and sketchy, but, he figured, so much had been going on that O'Dowd would have seen as more important in his coverage and Jon O'Dowd was a man who was well known for his acceptance of the risks that went with the job.

All of this was reprised on the reports that covered his death and some of these were complete features that ran to several pages. Jon O'Dowd had been a respected man who had finally stretched his luck that step too far.

One cutting showed a picture of Jon O'Dowd taken not long before his death and Simon stared at it long and hard. A man of great presence with his mane of jet black hair and his piercing blue eyes that seemed to look into the soul of the viewer. These things were trademark O'Dowd.

Looking at the clippings reminded him that he had not watched the video given to him by Nat Sullivan. He'd been unable to face it, knowing that it recorded those last moments of O'Dowd's life and would expose Tally's grief as nothing else could do.

He took himself home and, before he could change his mind, loaded the tape straight into the machine and sat down to watch before even removing his damp coat. The event had taken place only scant weeks after the return from Mamolo. The actual recording was only minutes long. The crew stopped at a checkpoint close to a railway siding and the camera showed Jon getting out of the truck to show their identity papers to the guards. Prisoners were being brought out from another truck for transfer at the siding where a cattle wagon waited.

In the film he could see Jon gesturing at the line of men who were shackled hand and foot and being prodded by the guards. As they watched from the truck, one man turned on his guard, knocking the rifle from his hand, and began to run. Shackled as he was there was no hope of escape. Maybe he thought that with a foreign film crew present he would be safer, but there was no truth in that. As the man ran, a guard raised his rifle and shot him down. Jon O'Dowd turned furiously on the guard and the next moment he too lay on the ground while the guard simply moved away and continued to help load the prisoners into the cattle truck. In the background, Simon heard Tally's voice screaming Jon O'Dowd's name.

Twenty

April

The morning had been a busy one and Naomi had stayed on to have lunch with a couple of her colleagues. George, therefore, did not collect her from the advice centre until after two and it was approaching the half hour when he pulled up outside her door.

'Are you OK to see yourself in, love, only I'm running a bit late today. I'm due at the school for three.'

'I'm fine, George, thanks.' She'd been fine for months, but more often than not George waited outside until she'd closed her door. George was part of a small family-run company and most of their work came from repeat custom. George knew the virtue of taking care of his clientele. His three o'clock job was a daily one, collecting a child and her carer from the local comprehensive.

'I'll spin round at the end of the road,' he told her. 'You take care of yourself now.'

Naomi kept her door key in her pocket. She had just slipped it into the lock when a voice behind her said, 'Hello.' It was Jack.

'How did you find me?' Naomi demanded.

'Easy. I followed you from the advice centre. Good restaurant you chose for lunch. Reasonably priced too.'

'You watched me? Followed me? What the hell—'

'It's cold out here,' he interrupted her. 'Let's go inside.'

He pushed past and swung the door open. Naomi shouted

at him, reached out to catch his arm, but Jack had already gone beyond her reach.

Naomi's phone lived in her other pocket: easier than fiddling about with her bag when it rang. She dug it out now and began to dial the nines.

'No, I don't think so,' Jack said. He took the phone from her hand and threw it to the ground. Naomi heard it crash, break into pieces against the concrete. Napoleon whined, knowing things were wrong, waiting for Naomi to tell him what to do but Jack had her arm and pulled her sharply away from the dog and through the door.

Napoleon, scratching and whittering in his anxiety, was left outside.

'What the hell do you think you're doing?'

He had taken her keys from her and they now stood in her living room, Jack pacing restlessly. She could hear him as he moved about the room, shifting things, inspecting her books and ornaments. Flicking through the photo albums that sat on one of the shelves beside the window. She was glad that Alec had moved Simon's boxes into the spare room.

'I needed to talk to you,' he said. 'I was told at that place you work in that I'm persona non grata. Not nice, Naomi, not nice at all.'

She heard his footsteps coming closer, felt the heat and size of the man as he pressed so close that his breath warmed her cheek. And the memory of what he had done to Simon weighed like a stone in the pit of her stomach.

'You went to see her, didn't you? When I specifically asked that you keep your business out of Tally's life.'

'I had something to return to her, that's all. You don't own her, Jack, and you don't control whom she chooses to let through her front door.' She hoped she sounded more confident than she felt. She clenched her fists hard to stop her hands from trembling.

He reached out and took her arm, his fingers digging

painfully into the muscle. 'I won't stand for it, Naomi. I won't put up with any of it at all. Tally's had enough to cope with in her life without little people like you screwing with her feelings.'

'If any one's "screwing with Tally's feelings", Jack, then it strikes me it's you. Not me, not even Simon. She's not a child that you should rule her life like this. She's a grown woman, an intelligent, passionate, confident woman, except when it comes to dealing with you. If anyone should butt out of Tally's life, it should be you and if you cared anything for her – really cared, I mean – you'd clear off somewhere and let her be.'

Jack hit her then, still holding her fast with one hand, he brought the other one slapping hard across her face. Naomi's head snapped back and she would have fallen had Jack's fingers not pinched deeper into her arm and his strength kept her upright.

Her head was spinning, but Jack had made a major mistake in thinking he could intimidate her this way. The stone in the pit of her belly melted away into anger. Clawed fingers aimed at Jack's eyes, she missed, but raked down the side of his face. Then she dropped her full weight downward, against the grip of his fingers, twisting at the same time, then kicking back, hoping to hit Jack somewhere on the shins or knees. She made contact with something and Jack, shocked that she had turned on him, loosened his grip long enough for Naomi to break away. She made for the door but Jack, cursing and swearing, was only inches behind.

Outside, George had swung the cab around in the entrance of a local factory and was heading back past Naomi's house towards the promenade. The sight of the black dog scratching at the closed front door was not one he had expected to see. He pulled up at the kerb and got out of the taxi. 'Poly? What's wrong, mate? Where's the missus gone?'

The dog turned and whined at him then bent his head and snuffled at the ground. Naomi's phone lay broken at George's feet. Moments later, George was on his radio and calling for the police.

'Who the hell is that?'

Jack had her pinned against the door, both hands gripping at her arms this time and his body pressed too tight against her for Naomi to kick. Relief flooded through her at the sound of George Mallard's voice accompanied by the barking of an excited dog.

'George!' she shouted at the top of her lungs. 'George, call the police.'

She heard Jack swear and then he flung her aside. She fell heavily to the floor. She heard the door slam and his footsteps on the stairs and the kick as he broke down the rear door. Naomi in her turn stumbled and tripped her way down the stairs. She dragged the front door open and almost fell into the arms of a startled George Mallard.

Twenty-One

'Do you know what he might have touched?'

She shook her head, then forced herself to think carefully. 'George said he saw him leaning on the windowsill,' she said. 'It's glossed, should have taken a good print. And he touched the photo albums, I'm pretty sure of that, and he was fiddling around with the stuff on that shelf, but I don't know exactly what he touched.'

'When do we expect SOCO?' Alec asked.

'With luck, this afternoon,' Peterson told him. 'Maybe tomorrow.' He paused and Naomi could imagine him shrugging his shoulders. 'You know how it is.'

'Yeah, I know how it is.' Alec sounded bitter. Bitter and angry. 'You say he followed you from work to the restaurant,' he asked her for the third time.

'Yes, like I said. I can't believe I didn't know. Can't believe Shirley didn't notice him, she turned him away earlier when he came to the centre. She's usually so sharp when it comes to faces.'

'Lunchtime crowd,' Alec said. 'And she was talking, concentrating on you, not on some face in the background. She saw him at the advice bureau though. I've arranged for some time with the police artist. We'll put the picture out as Simon's attacker,' he reassured her. 'No need to mention this to the press, Nomi, not unless you want to.'

'No. I don't want that. Not at all.'

He stroked her arm and she flinched, realizing suddenly how much the bruises hurt.

'Nomi?'

She hadn't even taken off her coat, chilled and unable to get warm again. 'Bruised arm,' she told him briefly. 'I've had worse.'

'Let me see.'

She felt the tiredness of the after-effects of adrenaline setting in and reluctantly she allowed him to remove her coat and slip her arm out of the sleeve of her sweater. He was silent as he studied the bruises on her arm, then moved his fingers back to smooth those on her face.

Impatiently, Naomi shoved her arm back into the sleeve and dragged her coat back around her shoulders. 'Just bruises, Alec,' she told him impatiently. 'It's nothing.'

'It could have been.' His voice shook slightly and she reached out instinctively as much to comfort herself as him. Alec pulled her to him and held her tight.

Twenty-Two

Tally Palmer was not at her flat, though a small knot of media types had gathered at the entrance to the car park. Alec ignored them, recognizing a couple of the locals from Simon's paper. They, of course, would have known about Tally, he thought. He should be grateful the knowledge had not spread faster, no doubt the editor wanting his story before the nationals got hold of it. Probably the reason for Miss Palmer not being home, Alec guessed.

Alec tried the gallery and got the name of her agents, but they could shed little light on her whereabouts. When asked about Jack Chalmers their response was a simple 'who?'

Rose Palmer was the next logical step. A phone call to Lillian at the hospital provided him with the street on which Rose now lived, and a glance at the voters' register the number. After calling to check that Naomi was still safe at her sister's house, Alec went in search of Rose.

She had made him welcome and almost immediately asked if there was any news of Simon's attacker.

'It's a terrible thing,' she said. 'He's such a nice young man and Tally was happy with him. I called the hospital a couple of times, but of course they won't tell me anything.'

Her shock deepened as Alec told her about Jack Chalmers, that he was the chief suspect in their investigation and about his assault on Naomi – a friend of Simon's, Alec was careful to say, giving no details that Rose could inadvertently give to the press.

'I'm sorry,' she told Alec, 'but I know nothing about Jack Chalmers.'

'You know that he's Tally's friend. Her close friend?'

Rose Palmer raised an eyebrow and her lips quirked in a half smile. 'Inspector Friedman,' she said quietly, 'my daughter is an adult, at least in chronological age. It's a very long time since she consulted me about her friends. There was a family called Chandlers or Chalmers lived on our street for about a year, I seem to remember. But that was years ago, I've no idea where they went after. I'm sorry, Inspector, but my daughter and I . . . It's a long time since we were close.' She sighed and frowned as though puzzling something out. 'To be truthful, Inspector, I don't remember that we were ever close. Tally was an insular child, and after her brother died became even more so.'

He rather liked her, he decided. Small and delicately made, it was clear to see where Tally had got her looks, though Rose looked very different in other ways. She wore her hair long, grey and undyed, tied back in a neat braid. Her clothes were slightly hippyish. A long black skirt, embroidered at the hem, and an Indian cotton blouse; it looked as though Rose Palmer had settled on a style years before and saw no reason on earth to change it. It suited her though, he had to admit. She looked comfortable with herself.

'Mrs Palmer,' Alec went on, 'we believe Jack seems to be very concerned about Tally's mental health. His previous threats against Simon seemed to centre on this concern. I know it's a delicate question but has Tally . . . has there ever been any reason to be concerned about . . . ?'

'Tally's mental state?' Rose nodded slowly, her lips pursed as though holding something back or deciding how much to say.

'I know she's been through some rough times,' Alec said gently. 'Maybe . . .'

'It was after her brother died,' Rose told him. 'She couldn't seem to come to terms with the fact that he was gone.' She shrugged. 'Understandable, I suppose. No one finds it easy to let go of a loved one, but Tally seemed to find it especially hard. Impossible in fact. In the end, we had her see a counsellor and for a time things seemed to settle down. She no longer talked to us about her brother as if he were still around.' She smiled a little sadly. 'Afterwards, I realized that the only thing Tally got out of the experience was that she learnt to say what we wanted her to say. I don't believe she ever let go of her Jack.'

'Jack?' Alec questioned. 'I understood—'

'That his name was Zechariah, yes. Well it was, but it was such a mouthful for a little one to say and Tally couldn't manage it. She tried to call him Zech. We all called him Zech, but it came out as Jack and somehow it stuck. Her pet name for him.'

Alec frowned. Simon's theories about Tally using a scapegoat to get out of difficult situations was nagging at him. But that still didn't explain Jack Chalmers. The man who had bruised Naomi's arm had been utterly here and now. So who the hell was he?

'Zech was brain-dead right from those first hours,' Rose continued. She spoke softly and her gaze moved from Alec's face to some distant point in that painful past.

'It was about three weeks before the school holidays were due to start,' Rose said. 'A Monday evening. They had been playing in the fields behind the house. Playing hide-and-seek with a group of other kids from our street. Zech had run off to hide. He'd said he knew a new place down by the embankment where he was certain they wouldn't find him. I saw him heading off down the hill and then he disappeared behind the thistles and the long grass in the bottom field. He must have fallen from the bank on to the railway line. By the time they found him almost an hour later, he was deeply unconscious. His brain had swelled, and he slipped into a coma and never woke up.'

He wanted to press her for more details. This simple retelling of Zechariah's death was so stark and cold, and he wanted the rest of it: the emotion, and not just the bare words. But he couldn't ask.

'Someone saw him running. Someone standing in the bedroom of one of the new houses they were building on the other side of the track. He was running along the embankment, they said, and he kept glancing behind him as though he was being followed. The witness said he looked scared, but when everyone heard they were playing hide-and-seek no one asked any more questions. The witness said he saw a man following him. That the man stood on the rise where the embankment breaks for the black pad to cut through and the bank is higher. The man shouted and started to follow Zech and then he turned away. He was too far off for a description.'

'You think someone scared him and he fell?' Alec asked.

'I don't know. Tally used to go to see him at the hospital and watch him for hours. She said she was trying to feel what he might be thinking, or dreaming, but they kept telling her that there was nothing going on in Zech's head. I know she used to fantasize that he would be like that forever. That he would grow up, still attached to that machine, become a grown man on the outside but still a little boy in his head. She went back to school after about a week, I suppose, because it was better than sitting around at home watching her father and I grieve and fight. She used to go and see Zech straight from school and tell him what they'd done that day and read her books out loud just so he wouldn't fall behind. They said he was brain-dead a few hours after the fall but it was another four weeks before we agreed to switch off the life support.'

'That must have been terrible for you,' Simon whispered.

'Tally never forgave us for it. She said we'd killed him and as far as I know, she's never changed her opinion on that.'

At the end of term that summer Tally went to her brother's teacher. Zechariah had been due to change schools that September and the new school always set a project for the summer to be done by the new students.

The teacher was taking down the last of the drawings and displays from the walls. Chairs were stacked upon tables and the classroom had a deserted, relieved air about it as though it too looked forward to the weeks of play and peace.

The teacher was a young woman. Pretty with dark hair and calm grey eyes. She wore short skirts and a sweet perfume that smelt like spring, exploding blue and fresh in Tally's head. She turned in surprise as Tally pushed the door and came inside.

'Hello,' she said, 'I thought everyone had rushed away. Have you forgotten something?'

'Can I have Jack's project for the summer, please?'

'Jack? Oh you mean Zechariah?'

Tally nodded. The teacher looked confused. 'But Tally, I thought, your brother . . .' She hesitated, not wanting to upset this child with her wild blonde curls and sad blue eyes. Desperately, she looked for clues as to what to say in the young girl's face but found none. 'Is he getting better then?' she asked finally. She had heard different, but maybe there was more cause for hope than they had been led to believe. Children could recover from some amazing things.

'Tally –' she came over to where the child stood expectantly – 'the project doesn't matter. I doubt he'll be well enough for project work.'

Tally shuffled her feet and looked away, gazing out at the school playing field and the bright sunlight and the children playing as they started for home anticipating the weeks of freedom that lay ahead. Then she looked back at the woman.

'Please,' she said. 'Jack doesn't want to get behind.'

The teacher nodded. Nothing in her training had anticipated this but she felt it would distress Tally far more to argue with her. She found the photocopied sheet with the notes she needed and made certain Tally had paper and card to make the folder. She watched from the classroom window as the solitary child crossed the field heading for home.

That evening Tally took the project work with her when she visited Jack.

'It's got to be something about history,' she told him. 'We've got to find something that happened near here and write about it and do drawings. There's a list of suggestions or we could do something of our own.'

She looked at him, waiting for a response. 'Did you hear me, Jack? It can be something of our own if you want. I'll help you, we can make it really good together.'

Jack lay unmoving and unmoved.

'You've got to listen,' Tally yelled at him. 'How can I help you unless you listen? Talk to me, Jack, talk to me.'

She had begun to cry, the project sheet and the paper and the green card she had selected to make the folder crushed against her chest. And Jack wasn't listening. Jack was never going to listen again.

For her brother's funeral, she had a new blue dress – her aunt had chosen it, she did not like children to be dressed in black. In the morning they took her to see Jack for one last time before the coffin lid was sealed and the small white box packed and decked with flowers was lifted into the hearse.

Tally had a plastic shopping bag gripped between her hands and from it she took Jack's favourite toys: the rabbit he'd had since babyhood, the marbles in the green velvet bag, the books and games they had made together, and wild flowers she had gathered from the fields behind their house, a little wilted now from the summer heat and the tight grip of Tally's sweaty hands.

The grown-ups stepped away, ushered by Aunt Bee, who, for all her halitosis breath and smudged pink lips, had a heart that knew grief and understood that sometimes grief must be left alone. Tally could hear their quiet voices as they talked to the black-coated funeral director and his staff. The condolences voiced once more. The nervous suggestion that in a way it must be a relief at least to bring things to a close. Tally's mother softly agreeing that it was.

'I don't believe you're gone,' Tally whispered, knowing she mustn't cry or be upset in front of her family. She had fought long and hard to be able to see Jack this final time and she mustn't spoil it now.

She lay Jack's things beside him wishing they were grander, more important, like the swords and fine jewels that accompanied the Vikings on their death boats or the precious objects buried with the pharaohs. But these little toys and shared memories were all she had to give and she knew intuitively that they would be enough.

She couldn't reach to kiss him, the table on which the coffin rested was too high and there was nothing on which to stand, so Tally kissed her fingers and touched them to Jack's lips. The skin felt cold and dry and an odd smell of antiseptic and something chemical seeped from the pores as she leaned close.

'You're not gone, Jack. I can feel you here, inside of me, and I'm going to live forever just so you can see it all.'

Twenty-Three

April

Alec was back at work studying the minutiae of a rash of local burglaries when Rose Palmer called him only a few hours after his visit.

'It's probably nothing,' she apologized. 'I thought about it after you'd gone.'

'Tell me anyway,' Alec encouraged. 'If it's not relevant, no harm done.'

Rose Palmer paused and then she said, 'It was when Tally went away to Sheffield, she did a photo journalist course there, though you probably know that. Anyway, she had this friend when she was there. A young man she used to introduce as her brother. She called him Jack.'

'Her brother?' Alec confirmed. 'Why would she do that?'

'Heaven knows. She passed it off in the end as some sort of practical joke. Covered for herself by saying that he was a friend from home who was like a brother, only I know he wasn't, Inspector Friedman. He wasn't from here, she met him there.'

'Did you talk to her about him?'

Rose Palmer laughed. 'If you knew my daughter then you'd know that you don't talk to Tally as in have a conversation, you receive from her what she wants you to know and you give back that which she requires.' It sounded harsh, bitterly put, and she must have realized that because she continued more gently: 'I love my daughter, Inspector Friedman, but I don't begin to know her, not even after all this time.'

Alec let the silence grow between them, then he prompted her: 'How do you know about all this if Tally didn't tell you?'

'Because it caused sufficient anxiety for her tutor to get in touch and ask me about this Jack. Her tutor, a Mr Bentley if I remember right, he told me there were rumours about this man and Tally, that if they were indeed brother and sister that their relationship was, how did he put it, inappropriate.'

'They were lovers?'

'They slept together. Not always the same thing, but yes, that's what he meant. Tally was challenged, and that's when she tried to backtrack. I imagine it took a while for the fuss to die down, but she was only in her first year and as far as I'm aware behaved herself the rest of the time.'

'And this Sheffield Jack,' Alec asked, 'you have a last name for him?'

Rose laughed uneasily. 'His first name wasn't Jack,' she said. 'That came out later, when Tally tried to cover herself. It was Robert. Robert Principle. He worked in construction or something. Not part of the university crowd at all, which, I suppose, was how Tally got away with her story for so long.'

She could tell him little more, but it shed new light on Tally Palmer and on her Jack obsession. Though what light, Alec wasn't too sure. Had she kept in touch with this Robert Principle? Had he followed her here to Ingham? Did he have a record? And was he the man who'd threatened Naomi? Rose had never met him and had no description to give but a few phone calls had him put through to Professor Bentley, Tally's tutor from her student days, and he confirmed Rose's story.

'I hope she's in no trouble.'

'No, it's the man she was involved with that we're trying to trace.'

'I see,' Professor Bentley sounded doubtful. 'Detective, if we all spent our lives being answerable for the stupid things we do at eighteen then it's going to be a poor lookout for all of us.'

'I couldn't agree more,' Alec told him. 'There are a fair few things I'd like to keep quiet from back then. No, this involves the here and now. We have reason to believe that Robert Principle was involved in an assault.'

'Oh, I see. Well, I'm sorry, Inspector, but I've had nothing to do with the young man since then. As far as I know Talitha broke all contact with him.'

'Can you give me a description, Professor? Did you meet this man?'

'Once, briefly. He waited for Tally after a tutorial. He was perhaps a little older. Dark hair, curly or wavy, I think. Quite well built, though I imagine his job kept him fit. He was a builder or scaffolder. Something like that.'

'Didn't that strike you as odd?'

'What, that a student should date someone outside of the university? Detective, my father was a builder and my mother worked as an accountant. Attraction happens.'

Alec got the feeling he had stepped on a proverbial corn. He persisted anyway. 'Any idea how they met?'

'No . . . Oh wait a minute, we were having work done, I believe. The library block . . . I don't recall clearly, it was some years ago. But I think that's probably how they met. I'm sorry, I really don't know anything more.'

Alec thanked him and hung up. At least he had an age and confirmation of description to give the Sheffield force should he need it, though he'd start with local checks, just in case Robert Principle had moved south. His profession might cause problems too. Workers in the building trade were often self-employed and frequently mobile.

He picked up the phone and called Naomi for the second time that day. He had, with difficulty, persuaded her to move for a few days at least and stay with her sister. Naomi, predictably, had protested against all of this but Alec could tell that she'd been shaken by the experience with Jack. Jack had invaded her space, a place she had held sacred and safe, and that hurt.

'I'm still fine,' she told him. 'Just as fine as I was two hours ago.'

Alec smiled. 'And I'm glad to hear it. I may have a lead on Jack.'

'Oh?'

'Yes. Something from Rose Palmer. She called me, recalled an incident from Tally's university days. It might be the break we need.'

Swiftly, he filled her in on Robert Principle and Tally's involvement with him.

'Sounds bizarre,' Naomi commented. 'Anything else? Did she recognize Jack Chalmers' name? Did she meet him, or does Tally keep her mother at a distance too?'

Alec laughed. 'Which order do you want me to take those in? Yes, she keeps her mother at a distance. Her mother didn't recognize the name, said they'd had a family of Chandlers or Chalmers living close by years ago, but she'd never really heard Tally talk about Jack and had never met him. I got the feeling she didn't see her daughter very often anyway.'

'Hmm,' Naomi mused. 'You going to check out these old neighbours? You know, I've been thinking about what Patrick said about them being childhood friends. I think he might have a point.'

'Maybe, but I can't make it a priority, Nomi. Just don't have manpower to track down distant neighbours who may or may not have had the right name. This Sheffield thing, it strikes me as a more positive lead. What are you doing with yourself this afternoon anyway?'

'We're going shopping.'

'Shopping? Are you sure . . . ?'

'Alec, I won't be put under house arrest! I'll be fine, we'll keep to busy places and check the street when we get back. Anyway, I need a new phone. I fancy one of those tiny little clam shell things with the fancy trim Patrick was going on about.'

Alec laughed. 'OK, love,' he said, 'but just take care. We know nothing about this man and he's already shown he's not above using violence.'

'I will,' she promised. 'Now get on and find him or I'll be forced to write to our local MP and complain about the inefficiency of the local police.'

The afternoon was a fruitless one. Alec had other projects on the go alongside the assaults on Naomi Blake and Simon Emmet.

By five he knew that no one answering Robert Principle's name, age and description had ever been arrested in the Ingham area. SOCO had been to Naomi's flat and fingerprinted the areas she had indicated. They called Alec to say they had lifted a partial palm print from the windowsill and a clear thumb from the surface of one of the photo albums. It was something at least, though Alec knew it could take a long time for comparisons to be made and results to come back. And Naomi's case, though serious, could not be given top priority just because Alec Friedman wished it so.

He ended the day faxing a request to Sheffield for information on Robert Principle, possible alias of Jack Chalmers, with what description he could put together. Looking at the brief typewritten details on the request he knew that he'd be unimaginably lucky to turn up anything from them. Too sketchy, too vague. Too long ago.

Shirley and Fred from the advice centre had been scheduled some time with a police artist for the following afternoon which would hopefully at least give Alec something to put out in the local paper. Until then . . . He stretched wearily, slow finicky days always more wearing than busy ones, he may as well go home. Or at any rate, go to see Naomi's new ultra tiny clam shell phone.

Twenty-Four

Lunchtime on the Wednesday found Patrick in the school library examining the archive of past photographs kept in map drawers in the stock room. He had shown the librarian the photo he had taken from Naomi's flat – a fact he'd not confided to her, and about which he felt guilty, recalling his protestations the day he'd found Simon's key.

'It's a kind of project,' he told the librarian, a harassed middle-aged woman who was trying to fit in his questions between stamping books and directing students to the right shelves. 'No, British history is over there. You'll find what you're looking for second shelf down. This book's a week overdue, *and* it's on restricted loan. Didn't you get a letter?'

She turned back to Patrick. 'A project, did you say? Do you have a slip from your teacher?'

'A slip?' Patrick was thrown by this.

'Yes, if you need to look in the archive, you'll need . . .' She paused, looked at Patrick with proper attention for the first time, then glanced back at the picture he held between his outstretched hands. 'Good Lord,' she said, noticing the date, 'that was my first year here.' She laughed and pointed to the line of staff on the back row. 'Look a bit younger there, don't I . . . No! Don't answer that. Oh, come on then,' she added glancing back at those queuing for her attention. 'I'll let you into the stock room, then you're on your own, the drawers are marked by years. Photocopies of the school play posters, that sort of thing. But I'll need that slip from your teacher. OK?'

She pushed him gently through the door and, pausing only to switch on the light, left Patrick in the large, musty smelling storeroom behind the reference shelves.

'Wow,' Patrick said as he looked around at the long shelves stacked with text books and topped with stuffed birds and animals, the cardboard boxes filled with props for school plays and musical instruments. Two, marked with the legend 'Christmas Decorations' in blue marker pen balanced precariously on the top together with the little tree the head teacher had up on the stage for the final assembly of the year. Boxes full of hymn books and scruffy school Bibles stood alongside, heavy with a generation's worth of dust.

The chests the librarian had indicated stood at the back of the storeroom. They were heavy wooden benches with wide but shallow drawers beneath, similar to those kept in the art room used to store students' work. Patrick began to pull open the drawers. They were marked up in date order, sometimes covering a couple of years, some close to a decade. Curiously, he pulled several open to look inside. School photos, bits and pieces of art work, fliers advertising the school play that year or the carol concert, programmes for the same. All the flotsam and jetsom of college life, left here to gather dust because no one could either quite bear to throw it away or spare the time to archive it properly. Patrick wondered how long it had been since a person had last opened the drawers and looked inside – probably closing them again swiftly when they realized the enormity of the task of sorting through this stuff.

Patrick almost shut the drawers and walked away. Already he was a quarter of an hour into his lunch break, knew he probably wouldn't have time to eat and, if he were honest with himself, didn't even know what he was looking for. He just had the solid conviction that somewhere in this picture was Jack Chalmers and he was possessed, especially after what Jack had done to Naomi, of a burning need to find him.

Sighing, he found the drawer dated closest to the photo and began to sift, looking only for the photographs and resolutely ignoring everything else, choking on the dust and aware of the gritty dryness against his hands as he riffled through.

More photos were produced. The whole school lined up on a succession of June days to have their images captured for posterity. These unnamed faces, black and white images of massed ranks of kids and teachers. Naomi's position moving year by year as she got older. Tally Palmer too shifting across Patrick's frame of reference. Patrick stared hard at the boys in Tally's class, wondering if Jack were there. Trying to discern some secret sign that would give him away. What had a man like Jack Chalmers looked like when he was twelve years old? Thirteen? Fourteen? What would set him apart?

But there was nothing, just row upon row of anonymous faces gazing out into the middle distance.

Patrick gave up and shoved the long strips of panoramic photographs back into the drawer. But then he noticed something. He'd been so fixated on looking for these massive pictures that he'd failed to note the blue folders packed into the bottom of the drawer. Blue folders with a photo studio's logo printed in gold upon the corner. Eagerly, Patrick pulled them out and realized what he had. The last year Naomi attended Ingham Comprehensive, the school had adopted class pictures and done away with the panorama. Form teachers posed with their thirty odd students. Tally Palmer easy to pick out in Mr Frederick's class, but better than that, row by row they were named on the inside cover of the paper folder. Tally Palmer, and behind her a boy with dark wavy hair and intense blue eyes that challenged the viewer. Jacob Chalmers, Patrick read and his moment of doubt at the different name was quickly put aside. This was Jack, Patrick was certain of it.

He glanced at his watch. Ten minutes to go before registration. Biting his lip nervously, Patrick crammed the picture into his bag, then slammed the drawer closed and made his way out of the storeroom. The librarian had left the keys in the door, a trust that made Patrick feel immediate guilt for the purloined picture in his bag. He wondered briefly if he should take the photo to her and ask permission. And wondered also how the hell he was going to get it back into the storeroom. Maybe he'd have to try and get a permission slip from one teacher or another. Deciding he would have to cross that bridge later, Patrick dropped the keys back on the librarian's desk, and with a shout of 'Thanks, gotta go now', he took off down the corridor as if Jack himself was behind him.

Naomi had never been good at taking a back seat. Not when she'd been a serving officer, not as a child and certainly not now. She'd always needed to be at the heart of events, often watching them unfold rather than taking an active role, but nonetheless, there. The idea that she should sit back now and wait for Alec and her ex-colleagues to solve the Jack Chalmers problem, was something she could not countenance and she had found a surprising but willing assistant in the form of Harry Jones.

Harry had done something today that he'd never done in his working life: he'd called in sick when he was patently anything but. He felt like a kid playing truant. Excited and scared of being found out at the same time.

'So, where do we start?' he asked as he parked the car in Tally Palmer's old street.

'Begin with her closest neighbours and work outward,'

Naomi told him. 'You take one side of the street and I'll take the other.'

'Oh.' Harry was taken aback. 'I'd rather stick with you, if it's all the same . . .'

Naomi laughed. 'OK, we'll stay together. Might take longer though.' She frowned. 'It's a while since Rose moved, I just hope there's someone round here remembers the Palmers.'

Harry got out of the car and she heard him open the rear door for Napoleon, pausing to fix his harness in place before coming to the passenger door and helping Naomi out.

'So,' he said, 'our story is, we're looking for old friends who moved from here a while ago. The Palmers and the Chalmers.' He laughed sharply. 'Rhymes, almost,' he said. 'No one's going to believe us, you know. They'll think we're trying to sell something. Religion or encyclopaedias. Do people sell encyclopaedias door to door any more?'

'I don't know,' Naomi told him, recognizing the display of nervousness for what it was. She squeezed his hand before taking Napoleon's harness from him, reflecting that it wouldn't really have been a good idea to set Harry off on his own knocking on doors. Slipping back into her own investigative mode, she'd almost forgotten that far from having another experienced officer sharing the house-to-house with her, she had a well meaning but understandably uncomfortable friend. Touched by his loyalty, she smiled. 'Thanks for coming, Harry. I appreciate it no end.'

'Couldn't let you come on your own, could I? But God knows what Alec's going to say to the pair of us. And if I catch even the glimpse of someone I don't like the look of, you're back in that car and we're gone. All right?'

'OK, Harry. I'll agree to that. Let's make a start, shall we?'

The first few houses they tried were empty. People out at work or just not answering the door. The next told them rudely that he didn't care what they were selling they could piss off and when Naomi persisted with their lost friends story, was equally curt in informing them he'd only lived there three months so how was he to know.

Naomi could feel Harry quail under the verbal attack. She took it in her stride having done this too many times to be really fazed by impatience, rudeness or both.

The next replies were politely suspicious but unhelpful, one neighbour bemoaning the fact that no one stayed for long round here any more. Not like the old days.

'Old days?' Naomi questioned.

'You know, ten years ago everybody knew everybody else. Friends like. Now it's all young families moved in. They stay a while, then go and buy if they can. And the council's moved so many problem families in. It's not like it used to be.'

But despite being there for more than a decade and her claims of universal friendship, the woman remembered neither the Palmers nor the Chalmers and certainly not Jack.

'I'd forgotten this was council owned,' Naomi mused.

'Looks as if a lot of the properties are private now,' Harry told her. 'New front doors and double glazing. Down the bottom of the road looks a bit scruffier,' he added, 'but the houses are a different style too.'

Naomi nodded. 'If I remember right, the road that runs across was mainly private letting. Short-term stuff. Used to be students but the uni's built so much accommodation I don't suppose it's like that now. I suggest we stick to this end,' she added, feeling Harry's relief at that. 'Anyone living on Coulter Road, at the bottom, is unlikely to have been there more than a short time, I'd think.'

They moved on to the next house and then the next. A progression of negatives met them at the door and followed them along the road. Harry noted that they were being watched. Curtains twitching and other occupants looking more openly from their windows. At the next house, Napoleon guided Naomi carefully though the garden gate and paused to let her know that there were steps.

'Two,' Harry told her, taking his cue from the dog. 'Sorry, should have said. Elderly lady looking at us like we're thieves from behind her curtains,' he advised as Naomi negotiated the steps and followed Napoleon's lead to the front door. It opened before she knocked, but only to the length allowed by a short brass chain.

'Good morning,' Naomi began.

'I'm not buying. Whatever it is. I don't buy and I don't let anyone in unless they've got identification.'

'Very sensible,' Harry approved.

'We're not selling anything,' Naomi assured. 'Actually, we're looking for old friends who used to live here. Wonder if you might know them. Mr and Mrs Palmer from number seventeen and the Chalmers family who—'

'Never had any truck with them,' the old lady interrupted her. 'The Palmers were all right. He went off with some other woman, you know. Nearly broke poor Rose's heart. Don't know where he went to. Someone told me he'd died, but he wasn't that old, so I don't know. Rose moved across town somewhere. I wouldn't know where. But those Chalmers. Never had anything to do with them, especially the boy.'

'Jack?' Harry asked hopefully.

'Jack? No, his name wasn't Jack. Joseph or Jason or something. Flaming nuisance whatever he was called.' She paused suspiciously. 'Thought you said they were old friends. How come you think he was Jack? I'd bet money on it his name wasn't Jack.'

'It was a nickname,' Naomi said smoothly. 'His parents called him Jack.'

The woman snorted. 'His mam might have done, though I

never heard her. Come to the end of the road and screech for him she did and she didn't call him Jack. No, it was Jacob or Joseph or some such. No sign of a father as I could see,' she added, archly, then paused suspiciously again. 'What do you pair want with them anyway? Where did you live then? Not round here, I know.'

'No, not round here,' Naomi confirmed. 'We knew them before. Before they moved here.' But she knew she'd lost all credibility. She could feel the woman scrutinising her carefully and almost hear the cogs turning as she decided whether or not to call the police. But they had more than Naomi had hoped for. A name possibly and a reputation and confirmation that Tally Palmer could have known Jack Chalmers when both were children.

'Patrick was right,' she observed as they made their way back to the car, deciding to leave now while they were still ahead and unarrested.

'Certainly looks that way,' Harry agreed, a touch of pride in his voice. He laughed. 'He'll wonder what's got into me when he finds out how I've spent my day,' he added.

'Oh, I think he'll approve,' Naomi told him, smiling.

Twenty-Five

Simon had been moved out of ITU and was now conscious and stable. Alec was allowed five minutes with him, Samuel hovering anxiously in the background.

'Any idea where she might have gone?' Alec asked him. He'd not told Simon about Naomi's run-in with Jack, merely that there'd been a sighting of Jack and they needed to speak to Tally, ask her some more questions about the night Simon was stabbed.

Simon shook his head. 'You've talked to Rose?'

Alec told him that he had.

'Not that Rose is likely to have much of an idea, anyway,' Simon considered. 'Don't think they talk much.'

'Anyone else that Tally might be close to?'

Simon thought about it and then shook his head. 'Not that she'd confide in,' he said. 'You know, the more I think about it, the more it strikes me. Tally knew loads of people. Dozens of them. You go anywhere with her and it could take half an hour just to cross the room, but they were all acquaintances. Just people she knew. Tally is a very lonely person, Alec.'

'She let you through her reserve.'

'Yeah and look what happened. You know, it's like Jack's been holding her hostage all this time and like she's got so used to it she can't function any other way.'

Alec sighed. 'I know it's not what you want to hear, old man, but Tally Palmer must have known that Jack could get violent. She knows he stabbed you, but she still won't give us anything that might help. Swears she doesn't know where to find Jack, not even where to contact him.'

Simon absorbed that, then shook his head against the white hospital pillows. 'You know, Alec, you've got to consider something. Where Jack's concerned, she may just be telling you the truth. Far as I could make out, Jack used to just turn up, out of the blue. He'd go away for periods of time and I think Tally would hope he'd gone forever. Than back he'd come and when he did he'd make it his business to destroy anything he didn't like. Anything Tally was involved in that he didn't approve. Tally's as much the victim here as I am. I'm sure of that, Alec.'

The nurse had returned and was telling Alec that his time was up. Alec rose to go. 'You take care of yourself,' he said.

Simon smiled weakly. 'Don't need to,' he said. 'Got a whole army of willing bodies doing that for me.'

On the way out, Alec paused to have a word with Samuel.

'How are you bearing up?'

'Oh, better. Now he's here on the ward, it's not so bad. We go home at night and get some sleep at any rate and I've persuaded Lillian to take the car and do some shopping. We've nothing in the house and it'll do her good to concentrate on something ordinary for an hour.'

'What about work?' Lillian worked part-time as a legal secretary and Samuel was office manager for a large company down by the marina.

'Thankfully, they've all been very good. I've got leave on compassionate grounds until Monday and the doctor says he'll sign me off with stress if I need more time.' He smiled awkwardly. 'Frankly, Alec, I think I'll go back in for a few hours next week, or I will be off with stress. He's out of danger now, and I'm climbing the walls.'

Alec laughed. 'I can imagine,' he said. 'I'm only sorry not to have more news for you.'

'You'll get him,' Samuel said with quiet conviction. 'We know you will.'

Simon closed his eyes and allowed his mind to drift again, wondering about Tally and where she was and knowing that if she wasn't with Jack, she'd be somewhere alone. He thought about the first time he had met Rose Palmer and the curious relationship these two women had. He found it hard to reconcile with the relationship he had with his own mother.

They were both free one Saturday and Tally announced that she was taking Simon to see her mother, Rose. He was surprised, she rarely talked about her parents and, he knew, phoned her family only once or twice a month. By contrast, Simon rarely let a day pass without speaking to his.

'Will your brother be there?'

'Carl? I don't know. He's out a lot, plays Sunday league football, got a girlfriend and he's just joined yet another band.'

Simon was surprised. It was perhaps the most information about her younger brother that she had volunteered in one go. 'What instrument does he play?'

'Keyboards and guitar. He's good too, last band he was in I went to hear him, but these things never seem to last long. They're all just kids.'

'You don't talk about him much. Him or your mother.'

'We're not close.' She grinned at him. 'Look I'm very fond of my little brother, but I suppose the age gap made it difficult. Mum and Carl always have been, close I mean. I think after Dad left she felt she had to make it up to him.'

'And you? Did she feel she had to make it up to you?'

Tally looked surprised. 'I hardly noticed the difference,'

she said. 'Dad left when I was ten and didn't even apply for access. Next time I saw him was at the funeral.'

It would be Rose Palmer's birthday the following week. Tally had bought her a Celtic knotwork brooch, heavy silver, set at the centre with a cabochon of lapis lazuli. She had shown it to Simon before wrapping it carefully in a piece of handmade Japanese paper, folding it in a way he couldn't quite fathom so that the package held together without need for tape or string.

Her mother lived at the end of a terrace of four red-brick houses in a quiet street on the outskirts of town. Tubs of winter pansies stood outside the blue front door, beside a welcome mat that spelled out the greeting in a dozen different languages.

Inside was as cluttered as Tally's place was sparse. Sports equipment – Carl's presumably – dumped just inside the door. Brightly coloured rugs scattered at all angles across a dark grey carpet. Busy wallpaper and paint effects upon the walls and every available surface crammed with books and knick-knacks and family photographs. There were pictures of Tally and of a teenager that must, thought Simon, be her brother Carl. Others too, group snapshots of Tally with other children, one with a sandy-haired boy who looked a lot like her.

Tally's mother was dressed in a long blue skirt and a neat white blouse. She was past fifty, Simon knew, but still wore her hair long, tied off with a blue band and decorated with a copper slide at the crown. She wore no makeup, beyond a trace of lipstick and her skin was pale but as clear as Tally's own.

Looking at them both, Tally in tailored trousers and a blue silk shirt, a fitted jacket thrown casually around her shoulders and her hair tightly cropped, Simon could not have imagined two more radically different women.

Only the pale skin and the eyes showed the family

resemblance, he thought. Tally's ice blue eyes were like her mothers, though the older woman's seemed to have faded a little with time and the laughter lines at their corners gave them a softness that Tally's never had.

The two women hugged and Simon was introduced and scrutinised, but it was clear that their visit would not be a long one. For all her effusive greeting and the announcement that she 'must make them some tea', Tally's mother kept them hovering in the small living room, standing awkwardly as though ready to make a bolt for the door while she fussed over Tally's gift – and then shoved it into a drawer – and answered Simon's polite questions about her health and the talents of her son.

'We have to be going now, Mum,' Tally said. 'I've got to work later on and Simon has a story to call in.'

Simon blinked at the blatant lie, but left it unchallenged, as glad to make his escape as Tally.

'Oh, must you?' her mother asked and Simon felt that he had slipped unnoticed into a well rehearsed play. 'Oh well, if you must, my darlings.' She waved a hand vaguely towards the door, then hurried over and held it open for them. 'Do phone me sometime, Tally dear, and it's been so nice meeting you er . . .'

'Simon,' he reminded her.

'Yes, of course.' She beamed at him as though congratulating him for remembering and leaned forward to kiss Tally on the cheek. Just for a moment, Simon saw something pass between the two women as Tally's mother lifted a hand and rested it upon her daughter's cheek, saw Tally smile and her eyes grow warm. It was as though there were genuine feelings to be had between these two, but feelings that had been put on hold sometime and left there for so long that the line of communication had died for lack of use. It saddened him.

The door had closed before they had even reached the car

and Tally collapsed into her seat with a sigh of relief. She looked drained and Simon felt bewildered. He glanced at his watch. It felt as though they had spent hours at the little red house, so tired and confused did he feel, but glancing at the time he was amazed to see that less than fifteen minutes had gone by since they first knocked on Rose Palmer's blue front door.

But, Simon now reflected, that wasn't really Rose Palmer. That was Rose Palmer with Tally around and Simon's next meeting with her had revealed a totally different woman, one he felt drawn to. Shortly after that first meeting with Nat Sullivan, impulse had taken Simon away from his route home and he went to see Tally's mother. He had thought that she might not be there, maybe at work, maybe shopping, realizing that a major part of him did not want to ask the questions in his mind.

She was surprised to see him, surprised and a little confused. Simon reminded her of their meeting and suggested that Tally might have left her scarf there when they had called.

'I've not seen it,' Rose told him, 'but come along in and have a look around.'

To his surprise she made him welcome, had him sit down in the tiny living room and made tea. Set it on a tray with ginger biscuits and the little chocolate rolls Simon hadn't eaten since childhood. It seemed that when her daughter was absent, Rose could relax and allow herself to enjoy company. It was, Simon thought guiltily, not a difficult attitude to understand if you knew Tally.

They did not even make pretence of looking for the scarf.

'What do you see yourself doing in the future?' Rose wanted to know. 'Do you think you'll keep with the provincial papers or try for the nationals?'

Simon was astonished. Last time he had met Rose she

seemed barely to have noticed him, yet clearly she remembered more than he thought.

'National paper, definitely,' he said. 'And maybe sideline into television if I can find the opening.'

'Ah, television,' Rose laughed. 'Carl has one in his room but frankly I don't have time to watch. I'm out almost every evening and I work four days a week. When I have the time I'd rather read a good book.'

Simon grinned at her, suddenly intrigued. Tally had given him the impression of a rather defeated woman with little interest in life. Rose was telling him a different tale. 'What do you do?' he asked. 'In the evenings, I mean?'

She smiled back and then crossed over to the sideboard where Tally's brooch had been stowed away. She came back with a bundle of papers. Play bills from the local YMCA theatre and the church hall.

'I'm an Am. Dram. queen,' she announced laughing at herself. 'I act, I make costumes and I help out with the tea.' She waved a careless hand in Simon's direction. 'Oh dear, I've no illusions about my lack of talent but we have a damn good time. I've been a kitchen maid and an undertaker's assistant and even a corpse. Then there's my painting classes and I'm learning to speak Spanish. When Carl goes off to university next year I'm giving myself a Spanish holiday.'

'Good luck to you!' Simon applauded. 'Where in Spain?'

'Oh, Seville, Toledo. A grand tour, I think. I might even take up flamenco.'

She struck a pose still sitting in her armchair and Simon felt himself warming to this woman who was so unlike her daughter. As if Rose could feel his thoughts she asked, 'How's Tally? Is everything going well between you two?'

He hesitated, a little taken aback that she'd brought the subject up first. 'I'm not sure,' he admitted finally. 'Sometimes I feel we're really close and others . . .'

Rose nodded thoughtfully. 'It's always been like that with Tally. Blows hot and cold. You want her enough, Simon, you've just got to learn to hang in there.'

'Yeah. It's just knowing if she wants me enough to let me.'

'Oh?'

Simon shrugged. 'Rose, do you know of anyone called Jack? A close friend of hers, only . . .' He broke off. Rose had stiffened and the openness of her expression became guarded and enclosed.

'Jack,' she said. 'You don't know about Jack?'

'I know about Jack, I mean I know he's a friend, but, Rose, if he's more than that then why doesn't she tell me?'

Rose shook her head sadly. 'I thought that was all over,' she said and Simon felt his heart sink.

'She's always found it so hard to let him go. But Simon, how can you have problems with memories? You've no rival in a dead boy.'

'Dead? But . . .'

'Jack was a nickname,' Rose went on. She spoke swiftly as if to get things over with. 'She couldn't say Zech, short for Zechariah, when she was a little thing, so she took to saying Jack. And it stuck.'

She got up and fetched a photograph from the sideboard. The sandy-haired child that Simon had guessed was Jack.

'This is him,' she said. 'Tally's brother Zechariah.'

'Tally's brother! But I thought . . . Carl . . .'

'No,' Rose insisted. 'You're not hearing me. Zech was Tally's older brother. There was only just over a year between them.' She looked away as though suddenly upset. 'He died the year before Carl was born.'

Twenty-Six

Much against Alec's wishes, Naomi had returned to the flat and, with help from Harry, had spent an hour or so scrubbing fingerprint powder – and the residue of Jack's presence – from her home. Harry went to collect Patrick from school. He did this so rarely that his son immediately thought something must be wrong.

'No, no, nothing wrong,' Harry said. 'I just took the day off work.'

'You did? Why?'

'Ah, Nomi and I will fill you in when we get back to her flat.' He gestured towards a plastic bag on the back seat. 'And you can help me fit some extra locks,' he added.

'*I* can? Dad, I don't know anything about locks.'

'Well, that makes two of us,' Harry said comfortably. 'We can help each other.' He glanced sideways at his son, noting for the first time his air of suppressed excitement. 'What are you so excited about?' he asked.

'Ah,' Patrick said mysteriously. 'I'll tell you later. After we've fitted the locks.'

By the time Alec arrived, champing at the bit with annoyance that Naomi had come home, Harry's attempts at DIY had finally met with success. Naomi, listening to the pair of them discussing just how and what order to do things in, wondered if she'd have been faster doing it herself. Discreetly, she returned to her kitchen to listen to the radio news and make tea. It was good that Harry and Patrick were working together on this anyway, she thought, and if it took then twice as long as it would anyone else, well, what did it matter. They loved one another deeply, but as people they were so different that it was often difficult to find common ground. Though neither had any regrets, Naomi was certain, about Patrick coming back to England to live with his father – his mother being with her new husband and stepsons in Miami – it hadn't been an easy ride, particularly as Patrick had arrived back in the middle of a murder inquiry.

Alec's arrival brought them all into the living room, gathered with fresh coffee around the dining-room table.

'I thought you agreed to stay away for a few days,' Alec said.

'No. You agreed. Anyway, this place is like Fort Knox now.'

'Last time, he didn't break in, he used your key.'

'I won't be frightened off, Alec. This is my home.'

'I just think you're unwise, to say the least. Nomi, this man is dangerous. If I had my way, you'd go right away until we catch him.'

'Fortunately, you won't be having your own way.'

'Dad took the day off,' Patrick said, sliding his statement into a brief pause in the conversation.

'Oh?'

'We had a little something to attend to,' Harry said. He cleared his throat nervously as though suddenly concerned about what they had done.

'We went looking for Jack,' Naomi told them.

'You what!'

'Now, Alec, don't throw a fit. We got to thinking about what Patrick had said about Jack possibly being Tally's childhood friend, so we went back to where Tally lived as a child and lo and behold—'

'I've got a picture of him,' Patrick said quickly, interrupting them.

'What?' Harry asked.

Patrick left the table and rummaged in his bag.

'Naomi, don't you realize how dangerous that was? I don't care where you went looking. If he got wind of it—'

'You want me to sit back and do nothing?'

'Well, preferably. Yes,' Alec said bluntly. 'And dragging Harry into this . . .'

'I didn't need dragging,' Harry said indignantly. 'And for what it's worth, if you expect Naomi to keep out of this, then you don't know her nearly as well as you should.'

Naomi could feel Alec bristle with anger.

'I would *prefer* to see her safe,' he told Harry pointedly. '*I* would not have gone along with any such hare-brained . . . What did you do, go knocking on doors in the hope that someone remembered him?'

'Well, yes,' Harry began.

'A couple of years ago we'd have called it making house-to-house enquiries,' Naomi reminded him pointedly. 'Alec, I'm blind, not stupid.'

'Sometimes, I wonder about that,' Alec told her angrily.

'Well if that's what you think . . .'

'Look, I've got a photo of him,' Patrick said loudly. 'That's if anybody's interested.' He sounded aggrieved.

'All right, let's see it then,' Harry said. 'A class photo. Well, well. How did you get this, Patrick?'

'In the school library,' Patrick told them, skimming the details. 'They keep them in the storeroom. I borrowed it.'

'Borrowed it.' Harry noted the slight hesitation in his voice.

'Well, yes. I'm going to put it back. I just thought maybe you could copy it.'

'How old is Jack in the picture?' Naomi cut in before Harry could question his son more thoroughly. She felt there was enough tension in the room without that and Patrick was clearly hiding something.

'Hmm, judging by the year, I'd say about Patrick's age,' Harry mused. 'He'll have changed quite a bit by now.'

'Well, yes,' Patrick agreed, 'but maybe you could get an expert to age it on a computer. I've seen it done on television.'

'I doubt we've got the resources,' Alec said heavily. 'Patrick, get that picture back before you get in trouble. This whole thing's getting way out of hand. What do you all think you are? Some kind of vigilante group? This isn't some kind of computer game. When people get killed in the real world, they stay dead. I mean . . .'

'You're telling *me* that?' Naomi was outraged. 'Alec, up until two years or so ago I was your colleague. I've been—'

'And now you're not!' Alec almost shouted the words. He took a deep breath trying to regain control. 'Naomi, I nearly lost you in that car crash. I nearly lost you again bare months ago. When I saw that building on fire and knew you were inside, what the hell do you think I went through? And now this. You put yourself in the line of fire because of what? Pride, stupidity? What?'

'Alec, I didn't stop being *me* after that accident. I didn't stop being *me* when you were tracking Helen Jones' killer. I've not stopped being me now and I won't be told to butt out of what *is* my business by you or anyone else.'

'Fine,' Alec told her. 'That's just great. That's just . . .'

Whatever it was, he was interrupted by his mobile phone. He listened intently for a minute then announced he had to go. 'Tally Palmer's been arrested at the hospital,' he said.

'Arrested? On what charge?'

'Obstruction,' Alec said shortly. 'I'll speak to you later, Naomi.'

Ignoring the others, he headed for the door and moments later, he was gone.

*   *   *

Tally listened in shocked silence as Alec recounted Jack's attack on Naomi. As he finished she was shaking her head as though to deny his words.

'No,' Tally said. 'I can't believe Jack would do a thing like that.'

'What he did is not in doubt, Miss Palmer. Neither, it seems is why.'

'I'm sorry, I don't understand.'

'Oh, I think you do. This Jack Chalmers, this friend of yours, seems to have taken your welfare very much to heart. While I might understand his motives, there's no way anyone could condone his actions.'

She stared at him, then rapidly she shook her head again. 'You're assuming I . . . No, no, Inspector Friedman, I had no idea Jack would do this. I *like* Naomi, she came to see me with the best of intentions, I know that. Jack gets carried away sometimes.'

'Did he get "carried away" the night he tried to kill Simon? Miss Palmer, if Jack hadn't been scared off at Naomi's, might we be investigating another attempted murder? Simon got lucky. I might be a little old fashioned here, but I judge "intent" to be almost the same thing as "action". Jack wanted Simon dead. Does he always take such violent means to get people out of your life, Miss Palmer?'

Something in her expression made Alec wonder. Had he hit the mark in some way? He remembered the news clippings concerning the many men in Tally's life who had met violent ends, then pushed the fanciful thoughts to the back of his mind.

'I never thought he'd threaten Naomi. Why should I think that?'

'He gave you no indication that he had any grievance against her?'

She hesitated for a fraction too long and Alec pushed her

hard. 'Miss Palmer, if there's anything he might have said to you, I want to know about it. Now.'

She looked away. 'It wasn't anything,' she told Alec. 'Nothing really, but that first time Naomi came to return some photographs, Jack was there. He said he didn't like her. Didn't trust her or something. I think he felt she was taking Simon's side, pleading his case.'

It crossed Alec's mind that he was not the one who should be sitting here, questioning Tally Palmer, his personal involvement was far too deep. His role was in some way parallel to Jack's, a friend coming to the defence of a friend, a lover trying to protect a lover. He knew that should the worst happen and the situation flare again, he would have to hand it on, but for now . . .

'Did you feel that his words constituted a threat, Miss Palmer?'

'No. No threat. I swear I didn't think anything like that. Jack would say things, would be suspicious of strangers. He's always been like that, overprotective. Worried about me being hurt.' She shrugged awkwardly. 'I've not seen him since that night Naomi came.'

'Not at all?'

She hesitated and he got the impression that she was genuinely searching in her memories. Finally she told him, 'One time more. I'd done a talk at the school. Ingham Comprehensive. I was on my way home and stopped off at a local shop, the newsagent's on the corner of Turnbull Street. When I got back to the car Jack was there, waiting for me. I told him I was going away for a while.'

'And what did he say?'

She shrugged awkwardly, uncomfortable beneath Alec's insistent gaze. 'He said – it was just a joke, I was sure of it – that he'd just have to pay more attention to Naomi while I was away, then, wouldn't he.'

Alec questioned her further, but she was strangely reticent when it came to disclosing anything useful about Jack.

How long had she known him? Since childhood.

How did she get to know him? He lived close by.

Where did Jack live now? She really wasn't sure. They never discussed things like that.

That final statement had Alec choking in disbelief. 'Miss Palmer, excuse me, but you've known this man all your life, he regularly interferes in your most private affairs. He's obviously a close friend, perhaps more than a close friend . . .'

'What are you saying?'

'I'm suggesting that you and Jack Chalmers may well have been intimate. Still may be for all I know.'

'I was *seeing* Simon Emmet,' Tally protested.

'And that means?' She said nothing so he continued. 'Forgive me, but Jack's actions are more like those of a jealous lover intent on protecting his interests than they are of a simple friend.'

And Alec's own interests, he realized, were not so very different.

'If you're suggesting I played around while I was dating Simon, you're dead wrong. I loved Simon.' She sighed heavily and slumped back in her chair. 'Maybe . . . maybe I still do,' she admitted sullenly. 'But whether I do or not has nothing to do with you. With you or with Jack.'

'Jack thinks it does. He thought it did enough to make threats to a woman who could not defend herself. Who—'

To his surprise, Tally laughed harshly. 'I don't see Naomi as that incapable,' she said.

'I think you're failing to see the seriousness—'

'Oh, I see the seriousness, I just . . .' She gave up trying to explain, gesturing her frustration with outstretched slender hands. 'I'm tired, Inspector Friedman. I want to sleep. I've told you all I know and as far as I can make out I've done nothing wrong, nothing you can accuse me of, so if you don't mind, I'll go home now.'

'I want Jack's address,' Alec told her. 'Where can I find him? Where does he go when he's not sleeping in your bed?' He in turn leaned back in his seat and waited. Tally stood exasperated.

'I want to go,' she told him, pronouncing the words slowly and carefully as though talking to a deliberately wilful child.

'Jack's address,' Alec repeated. 'Look, Miss Palmer, you're here on an obstruction charge. That's just for starters. I'm sure we can think of something else later. This is an enquiry into two serious incidents, Miss Palmer. The attempted murder of Simon Emmet was the first, then Jack forced his way into Naomi Blake's flat, assaulted her, made threats. So far we've kept most of that out of the press, but you've a famous name, Miss Palmer. I'm sure there'd be considerable interest in the actions of one of your so-called friends.'

'Jack's not the only one to be making threats then,' Tally said angrily.

'No,' Alec agreed. 'Maybe not, though let's think of them as observations, for the time being, shall we? Now, where am I likely to find Jack?'

Furiously, as though forcing out the words, she gave him an address and the names of a couple of clubs that Jack frequented. Alec didn't believe her. She was stalling, he thought, but he knew instinctively that he'd pushed far enough tonight. Best to leave her with a little thinking time.

'You'll be hearing from my solicitor,' she told him coldly as he took his leave.

'As you like, Miss Palmer,' Alec told her. 'I shall look forward to it.' He knew, even exhausted as she evidently was, that she'd get very little sleep that night.

* * *

Tally went back to her apartment, getting the taxi to pull right up to the door, avoiding the odd stray reporter still hanging around. She tried to go back to bed but could not settle. Impatiently, she pulled on her robe and went into the kitchen to make tea, drinking where she stood by the kitchen counter, staring out through the slats in the half open blind.

'Where are you, Jack?' she whispered. 'Where did you go to? Where did either of us go to?'

Beside the kitchen door hung the one telephone she had in her apartment. It was smooth and white and minimal against the bare white walls. Her hand hovered over the receiver for a moment then dropped back to her side, though the desire to call the hospital, beg to be allowed to speak to Simon, tell him that everything would be all right, was almost too much to bear. Shocked, she realized that for the first time in her life she was missing someone more than she was missing Jack . . . and neither she nor Jack could accept that. Whenever she had tried to replace Jack in her life or even bring another soul to stand beside him in importance, Jack, or Tally herself – and the truth was she could not always tell the two apart – had scuppered the attempt, destroyed the relationship. On occasion, destroyed far more.

And she had lied to Alec Friedman. She knew exactly what Jack was capable of.

At fourteen Tally had her first boyfriend. He was three years older than her and going out with a girl from his own year. Two-timing with Tally.

Tally was infatuated. Miles was her first big crush and she threw herself heart and soul into the relationship, unsatisfactory though it was to have to keep it secret. He kept promising her that he would finish with the other girl, kept coming up with new excuses why he hadn't yet done so, and Tally, in love, she thought, for the very first time, let him get away with it. Her life was coloured by the joy of stolen moments with Miles. Quick kisses on the way home from school. The odd evening in the back of his dad's car when she had told Rose she was studying with a friend. Inexperienced groping in dark shop doorways on nights his other girlfriend thought he was out with the lads.

It was exciting and it was frustrating and it was the first time that Jack had taken second place in Tally's life.

Keeping things from Rose was one thing, but keeping Jack out of the picture was quite another. It was only a matter of time before he began to question her more frequent absences from home; notice that she wore make-up when normally she rarely bothered and that she seemed excited by something other than himself.

'Who is it?' Jack questioned her one night. 'Tally. I know you're seeing someone, you stink of him.'

She glared at him. 'I've got homework to do, Jack. Let me get on with it.'

'Not until you tell me who it is.'

Tally knew that she could only hold out for so long but she was determined that she would keep Jack guessing for as great a time as she could. Miles had told her that his parents would be away that weekend and suggested she come round. Asked, gloated Tally, that she go round to see him, not that other girl that he still hadn't got rid of. Tally was under no illusions as to what Miles wanted her for. Virginity had to be abandoned at some point in her life and if that time was now and the place Miles's bed, then so be it. The thought excited and frightened and the last thing she wanted was for Jack to interfere. So far she and Miles had confined themselves to half-clothed groping as occasion and circumstance allowed. He had seen Tally's breasts, fondled them, sucked and chewed on her nipples in a way that both excited and appalled her, and once, on the back seat of his dad's car, he had persuaded her to suck him off, though she had chickened out at the last minute and he had come all over her hair and his dad's upholstery. The rest of that evening had been spent cleaning up.

Even to Tally's inexperienced mind, sex play with Miles was a little iffy, but, she decided, given the right circumstances and a less risky scenario, she was willing to bet that it could be worthwhile.

She had her doubts of course. Friends in school said that he was only ever after one thing and that he collected girls like an old time hunter collected trophies. Tally had to allow that much of that was probably true. She had heard his official girlfriend complaining that he slept around and threaten to get rid of him many times, but he always seemed to smooth things over. For Tally, this seventeen-year-old with green eyes and dark, swept-back hair and a muscular definition that was universally envied, was just perfect and the fact that he had noticed her, selected her from among the waiting crowd made Tally feel like she was walking in the clouds.

Saturday took an age to come and Jack hassled every hour that she was with him. She spent the daytime in town with Rose – anything to get away – and came home for long enough to change and have tea before setting off for Miles' house. If Rose thought she might be overdressed to be doing homework with a girlfriend, she didn't say, and if Jack thought her to be distinctly underdressed for decency, she didn't care. This was a night, Tally swore, that she would remember for the rest of her days.

'I'll just follow you,' Jack told her.

'Don't even think about it. I'm entitled to have friends and you have to learn when to butt out.'

'He's not a friend. He's just using you.'

'Oh, and what would you know about it? You don't even know who he is.'

'Anyone that wants you to dress like that can't be any good.' He frowned at her short blue skirt and the little silver top that barely covered her bra. 'You look like a slag and a cheap one at that. Do you think your mum would let you out of the house if she knew you were dressed that way?'

'She didn't see.' Tally reached for her coat and fastened it over her clothes. 'Satisfied?'

'No. I know what's underneath.'

'What do you think you are, Jack? My dad? Some know-it-all vicar? Everyone wears stuff like this.'

Jack said nothing. He turned away from her and gazed out of the window across the fields where they had played as children.

'I've got to go,' she said, but Jack ignored her and Tally found herself swallowing down the tears. Jack's indifference, real or feigned, was far worse than anything he might have said.

When Miles opened the door he was already naked from the waist up and Tally was momentarily taken aback. She had wanted to be coaxed and romanced now that they had the time for it, not met by a man half-stripped for action. But she smiled at him and he led her through to the living room, pulling her down beside him on the couch.

'Thought you might change your mind,' he said.

Tally shook her head.

'Glad you didn't.' He kissed her, his hands moving to unfasten the buttons on her coat. She shrugged out of it, wondering if she could get it out from underneath her before it creased, but he was already pushing her back against the arm of the sofa, grunting with approval as he saw what she was wearing.

'Nice,' he said. 'Easy to get into.' He pushed up her skirt and pulled at her knickers, dragging them down to her knees before thrusting one hand hard between her legs.

Startled, Tally drew back. 'Hey,' she said. 'Slow it down a bit.'

Miles just grinned at her. 'Why?' he asked. 'We both know what you came here for.'

'No, I mean, yes, but not like this.'

'No, I mean yes,' he mocked. 'That's what they all say, Tally.'

He leaned over her again, his mouth harder on hers this time and the hand still rummaging between her legs, trying to push his fingers inside. With his other hand he pulled up the silver vest top and grunted again in further satisfaction to find that her bra fastened at the front with a little blue clasp. He freed her breasts and fondled them roughly, the fingers of his other hand still pushing between Tally's tightly clasped thighs.

'Please. I don't want to any more.' She was aware of how weak that sounded, how naïve, but he was hurting her, frightening her. This was not the scene she had dreamed about all week. Not the way it was meant to be. She felt humiliated with her knickers round her knees and her skirt pushed up to her waist, as well as totally scared.

She tried to wriggle away from him but there was nowhere to go. He had her pinned tightly against the arm of the sofa and one hand pressed down on her shoulder, while the other tried to prise her legs apart. He withdrew that hand for a moment, reaching for Tally's knickers and pulling them towards her ankles. She reacted instinctively to stop him, leaning forward, but he took that opportunity to grab both of her legs and pull her further down on to the sofa, pinning her right leg beneath his knee and pushing his other leg between her thighs. Tally screamed and tried to hit out at him, her hands clawed to scratch his face. He grabbed both her hands in one of his and held them fast, then moved the other down to unzip his flies. Tally screamed again, knowing what he was about to do. She fought him hard, bucking her hips and jerking her arms back, but it was no good. He was totally aroused and absolutely determined he would get what he wanted from her. He positioned himself over her and pushed hard.

'Jack,' Tally screamed out loud as the pain between her legs grew and the tearing sensation spread through her abdomen. 'Help me, Jack!'

And then Miles cried out in shock and agony and suddenly he was no longer on top of her but lying sprawled across the hearthrug, his head bent at a strange angle against the papered wall.

'Jack!' He stood over the inert Miles. He was breathing heavily and his pale face was flushed. 'Is he dead?'

Jack shook his head. 'Get dressed,' he said, 'and get yourself out of here. Make sure no one sees you.'

'What are you going to do to him?'

'Does it matter?' His look made her all too aware of her messed up clothes and dishevelled hair, of the blood that she could feel seeping, slick and sticky between her thighs. 'Jack . . .'

'Just go, Tally. Now.'

She hesitated for a moment more and then leapt to her feet, pulling her clothes back in place the best she could and scooping her underwear from the floor. She wrapped the coat tightly around her, grateful that she had taken Rose's advice and bought something long. She needed the warmth of it now, her whole body shaking as though she had a fever. She stumbled to the front door, remembering only at the last minute Jack's admonishment to make sure she wasn't seen. Then she ran for home, tears pouring down her face.

Twenty-Seven

Alec drove to the address Tally had given him. He was unsurprised to find, when he reached his destination, that it did not exist. Carson Street ended at number fifty-two. Tally had told him that Jack was living, or staying at sixty-eight.

He considered giving her the benefit of the doubt. Maybe she had the number wrong. Then he abandoned such sympathy and called in to base, giving instructions that Miss Palmer should be brought in for questioning first thing next morning. He knew he'd have to talk to his boss as well, tell him just how involved he personally was in this whole thing and ask advice. The last thing he wanted was for Tally to get Jack some clever-assed lawyer when they finally caught up with him. Someone who'd play the personal vendetta card when it came to court, and Alec was determined that this would come to court. His anger at Jack, even though Naomi had come to no real physical harm, went far beyond anything he had felt in a long, long time.

Tally was brought in first thing the next morning but refused to say a word until her solicitor was summoned. Now Matthew Jaques had arrived and insisted on time with his client before the official interview took place.

Alec sat in his boss's office, nursing a cup of strong coffee and discussing their next moves while Mr Jaques and client made themselves ready for Alec's next assault.

'I spoke to her agent this morning,' Alec said. 'Not best

pleased at me using her mobile number or interrupting her breakfast.'

'And . . .' DCI Dick Travers asked, pressing Alec for more.

'I asked about stalkers. About anyone Tally Palmer might have mentioned who was giving her grief.'

'You're going for a blackmail angle?'

'Yes . . . sort of, yes. I don't think it's as simple as that. I get the feeling there's a kind of dependency grown up between Tally and this Jack Chalmers. He's using her, yes, I've no doubt about that. I've no doubt either that access to her financial records would show payments she wouldn't want to account for.'

'Unfortunately, we just don't have enough to apply for a court order,' Dick reminded him.

'No, I realize that. My guess is that our friend Simon was right about one thing. This goes back a long way and probably to the deaths of either Miles Bradshaw or Adam Hunter.' He took a sip of his scalding coffee. 'My money's on Bradshaw.'

'You think she might have killed him?'

Alec nodded. 'I pulled the old case files. A young girl, small and blonde, was seen both arriving and running away from the house. She was never traced and the neighbours that reported her couldn't give any more of a description. There was evidence that Miles had recently had sex. Sperm samples. Also blood that wasn't his, and was the wrong group for his official girlfriend: group B when the girl he was dating was group O. We know she wasn't there anyway. She was at a family celebration twenty miles away with a pub full of witnesses.'

'Was Miss Palmer interviewed at the time?'

'Only in the general run of interviews that went on at the school. They had the kids in three at a time, asked them if they knew Miles socially, that sort of thing. There was no reason to think Tally had an involvement. She was fourteen, Miles was several years older.'

'And now, apart from your gut instincts, what is there to link her?'

Alec grinned wryly. 'Bugger all unless I can get a blood sample,' he acknowledged. 'If she's a B, then maybe DNA analysis would . . .'

'And how are you going to manage that? There's no evidence. No reason to suspect a link. Alec, for what it's worth I go with your reasoning about the blackmail angle. I even accept the possibility that this Miles jumped her, raped her and got killed for his trouble. If she was the victim, if she killed him, then I can understand her need to hide what happened, how she could have laid herself open to blackmail. But you've got to ask yourself, how did this Jack know? Was he a boyfriend she confessed to or what?'

Alec nodded. 'That's why I talked to her agent again. I figured she might have mentioned something, however small, if she felt threatened.'

'And?'

'Nothing conclusive. Tally's like all celebrities, she gets her share of fan mail and her share of obsessives. She's young, beautiful and rich and that can be a difficult combination. All her fan mail is vetted by her agent. Some they send on, the majority they simply send a set acknowledgement and Tally never even gets to see them.'

'Any of it threatening?'

'Very little, though apparently there was a nasty incident about three years ago they saw as serious enough to report to the police.'

'Oh? Action taken?'

'No, the police were involved but the sender wasn't traced although Tally was complaining about a stalker at the time. Someone who came to every public appearance and hung around outside her flat – not here, she was living down in London then. Her agent said it was really that which decided her to move back. She gets more privacy here.'

'And the letters?'

'I've contacted the Met, see if they can track the case file. But as far as the agent can remember they said something like: "I know what you did. He died because of you and one day you'll pay for it". They thought at the time it referred to Jon O'Dowd.'

'Nasty. Did they go for the newsprint option or the computer printer?'

Alec laughed. 'Bits cut from the newspaper apparently and they never made a direct link between the letters and the stalker. The letters stopped coming, there's been nothing since.'

DCI Travers nodded. 'The price of fame,' he grinned. 'OK, Alec, we'll go with your theories for the time being and see what comes out, but I don't need to tell you, it's flimsy at best and certainly not enough for us to recommend the expense of DNA analysis at this stage, even if the samples have been kept and it's recoverable.'

'No,' Alec agreed. 'I know that. But the Miles Bradshaw case was a murder enquiry. It's cold, but it's still open.'

His boss nodded. 'And if you were right, she was a juvenile at the time and probably scared as hell. Don't lose sight of that, Alec. And right now your focus is on getting even because of Naomi and your friend Simon, not looking for justice for a boy you didn't even know. Don't kid yourself about your motives, you start doing that and I'll have to pull you off. We're short enough personnel-wise at the moment, I don't want to have to do that.'

Alec swallowed the last of his coffee before replying, then he nodded. 'You're right,' he said. 'I'll keep it in mind. But I'm finding Jack Chalmers, with or without Miss Palmer's help.' Or yours, he implied, knowing Dick Travers could read him well enough to know.

'Miss Palmer, I'd like to know why you chose to send me on a wild goose chase last night.'

'My client doesn't know what you mean.'

Alec glanced briefly at the lawyer. 'The address you gave me,' he continued, 'it doesn't exist. Can you explain why you would send me somewhere that does not exist?'

'My client probably made a mistake. She was tired and stressed.'

Alec held the ground that he had won. Instead of answering, he asked, 'Miss Palmer, how long has Jack Chalmers been blackmailing you?'

'Blackmail?' It was the solicitor's turn to be surprised. 'Detective Inspector Friedman, just what are you suggesting my client might have done that would open her to blackmail?'

Alec said nothing in reply. Instead, he turned to Tally once more and reminded her, 'There's still the little matter of a false address.'

'Not false; mistaken,' Jaques insisted. 'Miss Palmer supplied you with what she thought was Mr Chalmers' address. If he gave her a false address, she can hardly be blamed, can she, for simply passing that erroneous information on to you?'

Alec stifled an irritated sigh. He was tired and hungry and very pissed off and in no mood for smart, expensive lawyers to play games with him. He was wise enough to know, however, that he needed more if he was going to break through Tally Palmer's costly defences.

When the solicitor rose and gestured for Tally to follow his example, Alec had to let her go. He had nothing to charge her with, not even wasting police time. Any lawyer worth his salt would argue, as Jaques had done, that she was merely passing information on. If false information had been given to her, there was nothing she could do about it.

'Well, thank you for your cooperation, Miss Palmer,' Alec said with as much dignity as he could muster. 'I'll be in touch again.'

'I advise you not to harass my client,' Jacques told him frostily.

Twenty-Eight

There'd been a new boy in school, started midway through the term. It was a couple of days before Tally really noticed him and it was the gossip that first drew her attention.

'Did you hear what he called Miss Frazer?'

'Well, she is!'

'I know, but to say it . . .'

'Must be some kind of a record. Detention on your first day.'

'Did you hear, Tally? They're moving the new boy into our class. Mr Fredericks is supposed to be a steadying influence.'

'Who told you that?'

'I overheard the head telling the secretary when I took the registers down. Miss Frazer says she won't have him.'

'Shh!' someone warned. 'They're coming.'

Tally, along with everyone else in the class, looked towards the door. Their form tutor, Mr Fredericks, an unassuming man in an old tweed jacket and trousers that never quite coordinated with it, could be heard chatting amiably to someone in the corridor. He didn't seem to be getting much of a response, the replies were vague mumbles and words that could not be made out no matter how they strained. Mr Fredericks sounded unconcerned by this lack of enthusiasm, but then, Tally thought, Mr Fredericks was unfazed by just about everything. He was a man possessed of a consuming optimism and a willingness to think the best of everyone, even when they proved him wrong time and time again. Everyone liked Mr Fredericks, but all acknowledged that he really wasn't of this world.

The boy he had in tow was dark haired, skinny and tall. He slouched into the classroom behind the teacher, his backpack slung carelessly over one shoulder. He glanced about him with the kind of surly unconcern that Tally immediately marked down as an attitude hiding something else. He's scared, she thought. Scared and pissed off with the world making him that way.

Mr Fredericks was introducing him. 'Jacob Chalmers,' he told the class. 'Though I understand you like to be called Jack. I'm sure you'll make him very welcome.'

Jack, Tally thought. They called him Jack. She looked again at this newcomer, about as different from Zechariah as anyone could be, with his dark hair and slouching posture and his I don't care attitude . . . and then this new Jack happened to glance her way, his blue eyed gaze meeting hers with an intensity that was both frightening and stimulating. The connection between them was made and solidified all within an instant.

There was a spare desk behind Tally, next to Mark Jones, a quiet, studious kid whom the class considered to be also from another planet, so vague it'd likely be a day or two before he even realized the empty space beside him had been filled.

Tally watched as Jack Chalmers crossed the room, dumping his bag with a heavy thump on the wooden desk and dropping heavily into the chair. She turned right around to look at him, meeting the suspicion of those blue eyes head on. 'Hi Jack,' Tally Palmer said.

News of this newcomer had reached Rose by the time Tally came home from school that day. The Chalmers had moved into the rented house down the hill, the house that no one stayed in very long. Rose – as always suspicious of the occupants of this tall, scruffy-looking establishment, with its untended garden and short stay tenants, and the Chalmers, with four kids and a mother that had done nothing but shout – so it was reported – since the minute they'd arrived, was not likely to add to the community.

'Mrs Frith at the post office says he was expelled, the oldest one. A troublemaker, Tally. You keep away from him even if they have put him in your class.'

Tally shrugged. 'He seems OK,' she said, more to judge the depth of her mother's opposition than because she really believed it.

'OK! He was in trouble the first day at school. Any more and I hear he'll be suspended and whose stupid idea it was to put him in Fredericks' class I can't think. That man couldn't control a butterfly farm.'

Tally wondered at the analogue, which was typically Rose. 'I guess they thought if Ja . . . Jacob had someone being nice to him for a change it might rub off,' Tally replied with a shrug. 'How long till dinner time?' she went on before her mother had time for further expressions of concern. 'I've got English tonight, should I do it before or after?'

'Oh,' Rose said, distracted as she always was when Tally showed a willingness to do her homework. 'I should leave it 'til after, love. It won't be long.'

Jack, Tally thought as her mother bustled away back into the kitchen. She felt a sudden and almost overwhelming need to cry but couldn't place a name on the emotion that prompted her tears. Anger and grief and all of those things she had been feeling since her beloved Zechariah had been taken away. But beyond that, beyond reason or comprehension, tears also of quite profound relief and utter joy.

Naomi was alone in her flat, still smarting from her quarrel with Alec. Harry and Patrick had stayed for a while the night before, discussing the events of the day, but somehow, the mood had been broken and they felt deflated after their initial excitement.

This morning, Napoleon, sensing her mood, had kept close beside her, leaning against her as she prepared breakfast and laying down beneath the table while she ate.

'It's not right,' Naomi told him. 'I've a right to do what I want. I don't have to ask Alec's permission to live my life.'

Napoleon lifted his head and woofed amiably, his tail sweeping across the floor.

'You know, maybe he'd be happier if I went into a convent or something. Took the veil. Opted out.' She frowned wondering if that was an appropriate thought. She'd only ever known one nun and she was a fully qualified nurse who could certainly never be accused of retreating from the world. 'OK, bad idea. Don't think I could be celibate anyway. But I still won't be bossed around by some man. Not any man.'

She remembered guiltily Harry's actual enjoyment of the situation the night before. Harry was subtle about it, but he enjoyed the rare occasions when he won out against Alec. He made no secret of his admiration for Naomi and she knew that should the occasion arise when her relationship with Alec slid in even the smallest degree, Harry would be there to fill the gap with Patrick urging him on.

At home in her flat Tally had a restless day. Not wanting to be still but not able to endure the thought of going out into the world. She felt exposed, flayed and anxious. What did he know, this Inspector Friedman who probed and poked into her life, prising his way beneath her defences in a way that reminded her so strongly of both Simon and of Jack.

Why could none of them just leave her be? Did he know about Miles?

Tally shook her head. How could he? How could he know anything?

That night, just after the experience with Miles, Tally had been in bed by the time Jack came to see her. It was close to midnight and Tally was finally drifting off to sleep. He appeared in the shadows, climbing in through the window she had left open for him. He moved to the side of her bed, his weight as he sat beside her waking her from her doze.

She turned over and reached for his hand.

'Did your mum see you come in?' he asked.

She shook her head. 'She was watching TV. I just shouted that I was home and that I had to dash to the loo. Then I had a shower and everything and got into bed. She bought me a cup of tea later on but I pretended to be asleep.'

Jack nodded, an indistinct movement in the darkness. She peered at him, then lifted herself on one elbow to see more closely.

'Jack, Jack? What?'

He silenced her and then took both her hands in his, stroking the fingers gently. 'Listen to me, Tally, and listen hard. You were never there tonight. You knew Miles only as someone at school that everybody fancied. You had nothing to do with him and you never spent time with him outside of school. Have you got that?'

Tally gaped at him, then she nodded.

'And if anyone wants to know where you were tonight, you were home with your mum. You came up here early to get your homework done and before that you watched the television with her. It's that soap opera thing she likes so you can catch the reruns tomorrow.'

'But Mum knows I wasn't here. And who's going to ask,

Jack?' She stared at him, her eyes wide with fear. 'Is he dead? Is that what you're telling me? Is he . . . ?'

Jack leaned forward and kissed her.

'Just remember,' he said, 'you were here all night.'

The death of Miles Bradshaw occupied the collective mind for weeks until the summer break finally separated Tally from her classmates and she could breath more easily. She had been questioned, of course, as had all of the school. One of Miles's friends had mentioned that he fancied Tally but no one suggested that anything had been done by either side. The girlfriend had been absent for a fortnight, apparently distraught, and the sight of her, red-eyed and clearly distressed when she returned to school, was enough to have Tally on the verge of confessing many times.

But then, she thought, what was there to confess? She had no real idea of what had taken place that night. What should she say?

That Miles had raped her.

It had taken Tally almost a week to say that even to herself. She felt betrayed and not just by Miles, feeling as she did that she had given him the motive and opportunity. But Jack kept telling her that it hadn't been like that. Yes, that she'd been foolish, yes, that she'd played a game she had not been ready for, but no, it had not been her fault.

'No one should do that to you, Tally,' Jack told her. 'But now he won't do it to anyone again.'

Back in the here and now, her reverie was broken by the harsh shrilling of the telephone. It was Alec Friedman.

'I just wondered, Miss Palmer,' Alec said, 'what your blood group might be?'

'Blood group? What the hell . . . ?

'Just researching some old cases, Miss Palmer. I've just

one more question. Do you recall a boy called Miles Bradshaw?'

Silently, Tally lowered the receiver back on to its cradle, and as the phone went dead Alec smiled. He knew that he had guessed right and that he'd hit home.

Twenty-Nine

Late morning had brought a breakthrough, of sorts. Alec was notified that Sheffield had an address for Robert Principle. He was still working in the building trade as a scaffolder, had a wife and a couple of kids. A few points for speeding picked up over the years and an arrest for possession, but otherwise no police record.

Three in the afternoon found Alec loitering with intent outside Principle's place of work trying to pick the man out from the rest of the work crew. He felt a certain wariness coming to meet the man who might be Jack Chalmers, though now he was here some instinct told him that he was barking up entirely the wrong tree. To think that a man earning his living the way Robert Principle earned his keep could drop everything as often as he wanted and make the four-hour drive to Sheffield just didn't ring true and that was not even taking account of the fact that the man now had a wife and kids.

Somewhat reluctantly now, he made his way to the site hut and made himself known to the manager.

'I can't believe Rob's done owt wrong,' Alec was told. 'What do the police want with him?'

'I'm not here because of something he's done wrong,' Alec said. 'It's part of a missing person's inquiry. Robert Principle's name came up as having known the missing party.' He awarded the manager a wry, apologetic smile, hoping to get him on side before admitting in the most confidential of manners that: 'Frankly, we're clutching at straws here, but if you could spare Rob for a few minutes, it would help me out.'

'Missing persons, is it?' The man frowned and Alec didn't know if he was believed or not, but whatever the site supervisor might have felt, he got on the radio and called Robert Principle down.

'Something up, guv?' Robert asked.

Alec knew he didn't have his man. Robert was a thickset man with a weathered face and bare brown arms even in this foul weather.

'I'll leave you to it,' the manager said. 'But try not to keep him too long. We've a schedule, you know.'

Robert frowned, clearly puzzled as the man left the Portakabin. 'What's up?' he asked again. 'You police or summat?' A worried look flitted across his face. 'Nothing's happened?' he asked. 'To Jan or the kids, I mean?'

'No,' Alec hurried to reassure. 'Nothing's happened, but because you're married now, settled down, I didn't want to talk to you at home. I've told your boss this is part of a missing person's investigation, someone you used to know. It's not so far from the truth.'

Robert Principle still regarded him with some suspicion, but he sat down in his boss's chair and waited for Alec to go on.

'Talitha Palmer,' Alec said. 'You knew her when she studied here.'

At first he looked as though he might deny it. A look very close to fear passed across his eyes and got Alec wondering. This was not a man who frightened easily, he'd bet on that.

'I knew her. Even went out for a bit. Why?'

'She told people you were her brother,' Alec said. 'I find it hard to believe that anyone took her word on this, but apparently it was believed.'

Robert looked away. 'Oh,' he said. 'That. Her idea of a joke. I went along with it for a bit because I fancied her. But it got too stupid. So I told her it had to stop.'

His gaze lifted and as he once more met Alec's face, he said simply, 'I liked her. We met in the union bar. I had friends studying engineering but in the end the lass was a bit too weird. And her so-called friends . . .' He shook his head. 'There was this one guy, nothing to look at him. Tall but skinny, you know. He came up to me one night when I was walking home. Told me I'd best leave her alone or he'd know why. I near laughed in his face. I could take on two like him, one hand behind my back, or so I thought. This night, before I knew what was going down, he'd got me pinned against the wall and was beating seven shades out of my hide.' He half smiled, clearly embarrassed even after all this time. 'The cops found me an' I ended up in hospital for the next three days. Told them I'd been mugged. I mean look at me, you think I could admit a shrimp like that one took me out? I'd have been a laughing stock.'

'How many did you say there were?' Alec asked. 'Been me I'd have claimed at least three.'

'I said three maybe four,' he said. 'But I couldn't get a proper look at their faces. They were never caught any road.' He grinned then and Alec felt the man's relief that after all these years he had finally come clean and not met ridicule. 'You know this man, don't you?' Robert said. 'That's who you're after. I always knew he were some kind of psycho.' He sat back in the chair, content now that he'd not been beaten by just an ordinary man. Then he sat forward again and asked anxiously. 'You won't have to tell the wife about this?'

Alec shook his head. 'Like I told your boss,' he said. 'Missing persons. Did Tally finish with you after that?'

He shook his head. 'I dumped her,' he said. 'She knew

who'd done it, never even came to see me in the hospital. So, I thought, that's it. Over.'

Naomi went to visit Simon. For the first time in days his parents were not present. They'd gone to have lunch together, he told Naomi. He'd threatened to have them both thrown out if they refused.

'It's been harder for them than it has for me,' he confided. 'All I had to do was lie here and be looked after. The first days I was out of it anyway. *They've* had to watch.' He sighed heavily. 'Nomi, I don't know how I'll make it up to them, you know.'

'They won't want you to,' she told him. 'Just get yourself out of here and let Lillian mother you for a week or two.'

'Oh, Lord, don't.' He laughed and then winced. 'Mother playing mother is a pain in the backside. Anyway, what can I do for you? Don't expect they'll give you long. The ward sister's a right gorgon.'

'I've been finding out about Jack,' she told him. She dug in her bag for the purloined photo Patrick had brought home. 'Take a look at this while I fill you in.'

Briefly, knowing she'd have little time, she told Simon of the enquiries she had made with Harry's help. What little they had found out about Jack. 'Ring any bells?' she asked. 'Anything Tally might have said?' She hesitated. 'You know she came to see you?'

He grimaced. 'One of the nurses told me. Mum and Dad sent her away, apparently.'

Naomi nodded. 'How do you feel about that?'

'I don't know, not really. Truthfully, I don't think I'm ready yet.' He paused thoughtfully. 'She once told me she . . . I don't recall exactly . . . confused the two of them. Jack and Zechariah, I mean. Claimed that sometimes she couldn't make out where one began and the other ended. When she remembered one it was like remembering the other. We were in the middle of a row at the time, so I wasn't paying much mind, but if Jack Chalmers came into her life at the right moment, maybe he did sort of take over from her brother. Fill the same space somehow.'

Naomi nodded. 'I thought something very similar,' she said. 'I was remembering what it was like when I lost Helen. After Helen disappeared, there was a hole in my life that no one could fill. Not my other friends, not Mum and Dad or my sister. Nothing. Then Joe Jackson came into my world and he plugged the hole. He understood me, so I thought. Didn't tell me I had to let Helen go. Didn't say anything I didn't want to hear. I clung to him. He became my mentor and my confidant and my support. I became a police officer because of Joe. I decided life was worth living because of Joe, but realizing that Joe cared about other people, maybe cared about them more than he cared about me . . . God, you can't believe how painful it was to know that.'

'Joe Jackson was a guilty man,' Simon said heavily. 'And in giving his attention to you, he hurt others.'

'Neither of which I knew at the time. Neither of which I'd have cared about, to be honest. I *needed*. Nothing else mattered. I'm guessing that's how Tally must have felt. Then, finally, I grew up. Joe had backed off by then. Made me stand on my own two feet, and you know, Simon, I hated him for it. I really did. I felt abandoned. I felt like I'd lost Helen all over again, you know that? But if he hadn't, if he'd kept that dependence going, would I have ended up hating him for that? Trying to break away? And what if, like Jack, Joe had let me start to build a new relationship and then snatched it away just when I'd begun to get really involved. How would I have coped?'

Simon shrugged stiffly.

'But you know,' she said, 'I think Joe was as obsessed

by his relationship with me, at the time, as I was with him, and, Simon, we know just how destructive that was.'

In school, Jack remained aloof. He became the class 'man of mystery', moody and awkward but clever and alert enough to know the answers when challenged. Girls vied for his attention, boys copied his effortless swagger. Teachers rolled their eyes in despair before recounting some other tale of Jack's exploits, their recounting accompanied by comments of: 'I know I shouldn't laugh but . . .' All except Miss Frazer, who had not forgiven Jack for that first encounter.

The Chalmers were living in the rented house while their own was undergoing repair. The early rumours that Jack had burned it to the ground proved to be nothing more than romantic fiction. The house was being underpinned due to subsidence and there was talk, it turned out, of whether even this would prevent its eventual collapse. Legal matters were being entered into, talk of compensation – the house being on a newly built estate – but however things turned out, the Chalmers – with the mother that shouted and the kids that ran wild – would be living at the end of Tally's road for some time to come.

In school, Tally – herself known for aloofness – kept her distance from Jack Chalmers, watching as he conquered and created his own kingdom. Once out of school, the friendship between them was swift and vigorous . . . and secret, a concession to Rose's continued concern about their unwanted neighbours.

In the early days of their friendship, it was still warm enough to meet outside, but as autumn galloped towards winter and the days grew shorter, it became easier for Jack to come to Tally, creeping through the back garden, up the apple tree and across the kitchen extension into Tally's room; Rose usually ensconced in the front living room by early evening.

These clandestine meetings were in fact absurdly innocent. They talked, listened to music and, as they both grew older, experimented with first kisses and awkward, fumbled groping. But, perhaps surprisingly, this had not progressed further until much, much later when both had experience of others.

For Tally, her relationship with Jack simply followed on from her relationship with Zechariah and, given time, she would have moved on from this, expanded her horizons, lost her dependency both on Jack and on those other memories.

But this was not to be. Jack Chalmers did not want to let her go.

Thirty

Alec and Naomi spent another night apart, neither quite ready to give in and admit to being wrong. Alec's arrival, therefore, the next afternoon at Naomi's flat, was meant to be a conciliatory gesture. He asked her to go with him to see Rose. He wasn't sure she'd accept the gesture for what it was – and anyway, he still believed himself to be utterly in the right – but he figured that curiosity would be a compelling factor.

Naomi wasn't fooled either, he knew that. His taking her along on this visit to Rose made it an informal, unofficial affair and he hoped he might elicit more information by arranging it that way.

Rose was surprised to see them and not in the least fooled by the vague excuses Alec had prepared.

'If this is about my daughter,' she told Alec, 'if you think she may be in trouble, then I want to know.'

Alec nodded, appreciating her forthright attitude. 'I think she's being blackmailed,' he told her. 'I think Jack knows something, has known something for years, and is taking advantage of her.'

'Tally? What could Tally have done?'

Alec was not yet ready to reveal his fears about Miles. He said quietly, 'Rose, I'm not sure, but I'm sure she's the victim here. The long-term victim. It's not so unusual, you know, people often put up with it for years when coming clean about whatever happened would have been much easier for everyone. The blackmailer often goes to great lengths to keep their fears alive and once this has started, once you're on the treadmill, it can be very hard to jump off.'

'And Jack,' Naomi continued, 'whoever Jack is, he's past master at keeping the pressure on. Tally's reluctance to talk about him; the fact that she knows or claims to know so little, even though she says that he's a long-term friend; the control she allows Jack to have over her private life: it all adds up to something being very wrong.'

Rose was silent for a moment, she shook her head slowly, taking in what they had said. 'You know, it's almost as if she's always needed someone else to be in control. The world sees her as this dynamic, wonderful go-getter, and in her professional life that's all true. Tally would dare anything, endure anything, but otherwise –' she looked hard at Alec – 'she lets people in only so far and when they try to get further in, Tally backs away. She's been like it ever since Zechariah died.'

She paused then for such a time that they thought she might not continue. 'Rose?' Naomi prompted gently. She could feel the other woman's distress so intently.

'I think, you know, that she must have been spying on her father,' Rose said finally. 'Seen him with that other woman. She spent so long after Zech's death trying to convince us that he'd told her about them and she knew a great deal. Where they'd met, what they'd done together . . . She must have been hurting as much as I was and not known what to do about it. She tried to cover herself, protect her feelings, I suppose, and maybe to protect me, I don't know, by saying that Zech had told her all these things. I suppose, as she knew we couldn't question Zech, it was easier to let him have the credit or the blame.'

She drew a deep uneven breath as though her lungs were

reluctant to accept the air. 'She said . . . she said that he, their father, had been with that woman on the day Zech died. That he saw them on the embankment and then his father spotted him, chased him away. Tally swore that was why Zech fell. Why our son died.'

She shifted in her seat and leaned over impulsively to take Naomi's arm.

'But how could she have known that? I ask you, how could she have known? Zech died. He fell and struck his head. He never woke up again. She couldn't have known unless she had been there too, spying on the two of them.' She sat back abruptly. 'Can you imagine how it must have felt for me, to think it was his father who chased Zech, who scared him so much that he fell to his death? Who killed him over a cheap fuck in the grass.'

Naomi said nothing. She was shocked by Rose's outburst. More shocked, she realized irrelevantly, by the woman's use of the obscenity. It seemed so unlike Rose. So not in keeping.

No one spoke, then into the growing silence, Alec asked, 'Rose, do you remember an incident when Tally was about fourteen? A boy called Miles Bradshaw?'

She turned sharply, Naomi conscious of the new alertness in the woman's body.

'Miles?' Rose asked. 'The murdered boy? In his own home, they said. We all thought he might have disturbed a burglar.'

'That was the theory at the time,' Alec agreed. 'One of them anyway, spoiled by the fact that nothing had been taken. No door or window had been forced.'

'I remember Miles,' Rose agreed. 'Or at least, I remember it happening. But Tally didn't really know the boy. You can't possibly see a connection there.'

Something in the sharpness of her tone alerted Naomi. She asked, 'Rose, are you certain Tally didn't know him?

By all accounts, he was a bit of a lad, always chasing after the girls.'

'She didn't know him,' Rose said flatly. 'No, she didn't know him.'

They left soon after that, their welcome wearing a little thin and Naomi knew that she had touched upon an unhealed wound. More than one, but the second not so public. Naomi knew from her own teenage experiences, boys she wasn't supposed to see, friends her parents didn't entirely approve, that although she had been confident at the time that she had kept these liaisons hidden, her parents had known. Her sister certainly had. They had chosen not to confront her being wise enough in the ways of Naomi Blake to realize that the more they pushed the further she would shove back, and that such relationships, ignored on the surface and monitored quietly, would soon burn themselves out. Rose, Naomi guessed, had taken a similar tack with her own child.

'She knows, doesn't she?' Alec commented as though reading her thoughts.

'Oh yes. Or suspected and we've just confirmed it. Alec, I don't like what we're doing here. Are we losing sight of things? We're supposed to be helping Tally, not putting her future on the line.'

Alec didn't reply straight away. He weighed her words and then his own reply. 'What I don't understand,' he said eventually, 'is if Rose suspected the truth about Miles, had an inkling that Tally was seeing him, then how come she didn't suspect anything about her seeing Jack Chalmers?'

'Because,' Naomi surmised, 'she was used to hearing about Jack. It never occurred to her that this was a different Jack, someone new. If it concerned Jack, Rose probably stopped listening. She didn't want to hear about him any more. It hurt too much, and besides, she wanted desperately to believe that Tally had recovered.'

'Maybe,' Alec agreed reluctantly. He returned to the question of Miles. 'If she killed him in self-defence,' he said, 'if Miles raped her and she fought back, the courts would be understanding, Naomi.'

'Would they? You believe that, Alec?' She sighed. 'You know, if I'd been in Tally's place, I guess I'd have paid off Jack as well. I couldn't have faced that.'

Alec looked sharply in her direction. 'You'd have faced it,' he said. 'And she's got to now, or spend the rest of her life running. What's worse, Naomi? Knowing the worst that can happen or just speculating about it? What was worse with Helen, knowing she had gone or knowing for certain she was dead?'

Naomi said nothing. She had her own parcel of guilt to carry with her from childhood. At twelve years old she had quarrelled with her closest friend, and on that one morning when Helen had walked to school alone, she had been abducted. It had been years – only a few months ago in fact – before Naomi had known for certain that her friend had died. She had been murdered only a short time after she had disappeared. It had been . . . yes, almost a relief. Death bringing a proper chance to say goodbye and move a little out of Helen's shadow cast so long ago.

'I'm not sure it's the same thing,' she said stubbornly.

'Not the same, no. But I'm talking about grief and guilt here, Nomi, and you know what it's like to live your life overwhelmed by both of those. Tally, if she did kill Miles, has served worse than a prison sentence. I'm not talking about ruining her life. I think it's time she took it back.'

'Not by forcing her into the open,' Naomi said. 'She'd never cope with it. I know what it was like for me. Everyone knew. They all wondered, what if I'd been with Helen that morning. Even Mari, and I know Helen's family never blamed me. They're the best friends I could ever have had, but they knew and they wondered. How could they not? And

I was a kid, just an ordinary kid with nothing much to lose in terms of reputation, or life, or even friends. Think of Tally's life in comparison. If she'd come clean at the time, run to fetch help even, she'd have been seen as a child who'd acted out of fear. For a woman with her influence, her money, her power, to be implicated in such a sordid, nasty death . . . Alec, I don't think she could cope with it, let alone walk away purged by it, or whatever it is you're thinking.'

'So what do you reckon I should do?' Alec demanded. 'Miles died, however you look at it. Should I ignore that just because by all accounts he was a little prick?'

Naomi said nothing. She shrugged her shoulders uncomfortably and left Alec to interpret the gesture as best he could.

Thirty-One

When they returned home from the funeral, Tally went straight to her room and lay down upon the bed.

The box containing Tallulah Two Heads was on the windowsill, its presence scarring Tally and heightening her distress and heartache.

Tally's room was painted a light pink, with a white ceiling and cream woodwork. The curtains were gingham, white with two shades of pink. She had opened the window and they blew gently into the room. Pale flags signalling defeat. She had learnt long ago that these shades were most restful to her mind. They were colours that had melodic tones to accompany them, insipid and unobtrusive, they spoke to her thoughts in muted whispers and allowed her fevered imagination and overstimulated brain to rest. Later in life, even the palest pink became too obtrusive when she was tired or stressed, and then only white would do, though at times the purity of that colour burned with a fire that even the darkness could not quench.

She lay back, fully dressed, upon the soft cream quilt that her mother had embroidered with chain stitch and tiny flowers. She allowed the tears to pour unchecked from her eyes and run down her face on to the bed.

'She brought you a doll!' he laughed. 'She must know by now that you can't stand them.'

Tally sat bolt upright. 'Jack? Is that you Jack?'

'Who else d'you think it was?'

He was standing beside the window, the light streaming through him on to the floor.

'Are you a ghost?' Tally wasn't scared. How could she be scared of Jack? But she was puzzled as hell.

Jack came over and perched on the side of the bed. He seemed quite solid enough to do that, though she could see the pattern of the quilt through his jeans-clad leg. The daisies did nothing for the blue denim.

'How can you do this?' She reached out and touched him. She gasped. Touching Jack was like drenching her hand in the coldest water. He was there, he was solid enough to touch and he was clear as glass, just tinged with colour.

'I don't know, Tally, but I didn't want to leave you.' He reached and took her hands. 'Maybe wishing was so strong it just brought me back here.'

Tally pulled from his grasp and leapt off the bed. 'I've got to tell Mum and Dad. Tell them you're not dead. Oh, Jack, I can't believe this. Mum's cried so much and so have I and Dad's gone round like he didn't know where he was.' She paused, puzzled as Jack shook his head. He was frowning and looking as though something caused him pain.

'I've got to tell them, Jack. I've just got to.'

'Not yet, Tally. I don't think . . .' He lay down on the bed, the slight colour in his clothes and hair fading so that Tally could hardly see that he was there.

'Jack!' She leaped back towards the bed, trying to grasp him before he faded out completely. 'Don't leave me, Jack!'

'You've got to help me, Tally.' His voice became fainter now. 'I don't want to go away.'

She lay down beside him, plunging her hands into his body, unable to feel him well enough to know where his outline lay, relying instead upon the chill against her hands and then against her body as she moved close, occupying almost the same space and time as her beloved Jack. The chill almost too much to bear, she shivered uncontrollably even in the summer heat.

'I won't let you go, Jack. I'll never let you go. I'll live for both of us, Jack, just like I promised. I'm you and you're mine and we'll never be taken apart.'

Her mother found her later when Tally failed to answer her call to come and have supper. Tally lay on the bed shivering, her lips blue with cold, though her skin burned to the touch.

Tally was ill for almost two weeks, feverish and delirious and calling out for Jack. Shock, said the doctor, and probably the summer flu that was going around. Her mother read to her when she felt well enough to listen and her father moved the portable television into Tally's room so she could watch her favourite programmes. Even after she got better, Tally remained quiet and upset. She seemed lost without Jack. More lost with the passing time, not less as her parents had hoped.

In September Tally went back to school. It would in any case have been her first year without Jack who would have gone across the playing fields to the secondary school. By now, Tally had worked out a strategy for helping Jack and on the first day back she set about carrying it forward. Jack had to go on learning. To continue to grow up as he would have done had he still been alive.

'What teacher would Zech have had at the new school?' she wanted to know.

Tally's head teacher looked surprised. 'I don't know, Tally dear, but most of Zechariah's class were going to be with Miss Jones. Is it important?'

'I don't know. I mean, I'm sure Miss Jones would pass things on if she wasn't Zech's teacher?'

'What things, Tally?'

Hesitantly, Tally held out the folder she had been holding. It was made of bright green card and the front had been decorated with coloured pictures cut from magazines and hand drawn sketches.

'What is it, dear?'

'Zech's project. He wanted me to hand it in. I just don't know who to give it to.'

Mrs Dean was silent. She looked anxiously at the girl. 'Did Zech get his project question early?' she asked. 'I mean, did he get it before his accident?'

Tally shook her head. 'No, Miss, I got it for him on the last day of term. His teacher gave me the question sheet and the green card for the folder.'

'So . . . who did the project, Tally? Did you do it for him?'

Tally sighed, knowing that her answer wasn't going to be believed. 'He wouldn't want to get behind,' she said unwillingly, knowing that would mean nothing to Mrs Dean.

The bell was ringing for the end of break and Tally lay the folder on the teacher's desk. 'Please,' she said. 'I kind of promised.'

'All right, Tally, I'll see what I can do.'

She watched the child go and then picked up the phone and called Tally's home. 'Mrs Palmer? Oh, this is Mrs Dean at Oakfield School. I've just had a little chat with Tally and I wonder if you'd mind popping in to see me. I think we have a bit of a problem.'

Thirty-Two

The day after Tally handed in Jack's project, Mrs Dean talked to Tally's mother and showed the project to her.

'Tally's been deeply upset by all this,' Rose said. 'But she'll come right. All she needs is a bit of time.'

'I really think she could do with some professional help, Mrs Palmer. She doesn't seem to be coming to terms with her brother's death at all.'

Rose shook her head. 'It's only been a short while,' she said. 'Tally and Zech were so close . . . of course it's going to take her time.'

The head teacher sighed. She had known that this would not be easy. 'Take a look at this, Mrs Palmer.' She pushed the history project over the desk and Rose obediently opened the folder.

'I saw Tally working on this,' she said. 'I thought it was just homework.'

She flicked through the pages, drawings, written work, maps. Tally had chosen to write about Lady Jane Grey, the nine-day queen who had been born close by. 'I suggested the subject to her,' Rose said. 'We went out to Bradgate to take pictures. Look –' she pointed at the photographs that Tally had used to illustrate the project – 'I think it looks very good, but I don't see what this has to do with Zech.'

'It was to have been Zech's assignment,' Mrs Dean explained, 'ready for secondary school. They always set

a project for the summer. When Zech couldn't do it, Tally felt compelled to complete it for him.'

'Really? Oh, Mrs Dean, don't you think that's rather sweet?'

'No. No, I don't. I think it's rather worrying. And even more worrying . . . Mrs Palmer, look at this.' She selected two pages of text and lay them before Tally's mother. 'Look. I've compared the work to both Tally's and Zechariah's. Not only has she done his project for him, but much of it is in what looks like her brother's writing.' She shook her head. 'I don't see that as normal, grieving behaviour, Mrs Palmer. I think it shows something far more disturbed.'

Rose frowned. She leaned forward to study the two pieces of work. One was obviously Tally's hand; the other was different and did indeed look more like her son's. 'He could have done it before . . . before the accident,' she said hesitantly.

'The project wasn't set then. Mrs Palmer, I can't tell you what to do, I can only advise. I really do believe that Tally needs help and if you like I can arrange something for her.'

Rose was already shaking her head. She leaned forward earnestly. 'Tally hurts,' she said. 'We all do. People have different ways of grieving. When my grandmother died I still talked to her every night for weeks, but I got over it.' She stood up preparing to leave. 'All she needs is time and patience, Mrs Dean. Nothing more.'

Tally had no wish to hurt her mother but what Jack had told her was not something she could keep to herself. She turned things over in her mind, imagining the scene as Jack had presented it to her, and however she looked at it she could only think that her father was to blame. His actions had caused Jack to run and fear of what his father would do had caused Jack to fall. Tally knew that she had to say something. In her own mind she felt that she must confront her father and make him pay for his crime.

She finally cornered her father one night when he was in the kitchen poking in the fridge for beer.

'What's her name?'

He was bending over, peering into the refrigerator, and he glanced at Tally under his outstretched arm.

'What's whose name?'

'The woman you've been seeing? You were with her the day Zech fell. He saw you in the field down by the railway line.'

Her father straightened up, he was frowning at her.

'I don't know what you mean, Tally. Where did you get this daft idea from?'

He popped the ring pull on his beer and took a glass from the drainer, a nod to Rose who hated to see him drinking from the can.

'Zech told me.'

Her father stared at her for a moment and then turned away, closing the fridge door and then moving towards the dining room where her mother sat feeding baby Carl.

'Zech,' he said. 'Always bloody Zech.'

His voice was thick as though he had a cold and Tally wondered if he were about to cry.

'He told me,' she repeated. 'You saw him watching and thought he was spying on you. But he wasn't, Dad. He truly didn't know until you looked up at him. Then he got scared and tried to run away and you chased after him and then he fell.'

She saw her father's back stiffen. She could tell that what she had said to him struck home. That it was the truth no matter how much he should try to deny it. She moved around him, blocking his path to the dining room and leaning against the door so that he would have to physically move her out of the way if he wanted to get through.

'You killed him, Dad.'

Her father's face twisted with emotion and he clutched the beer can hard enough to compress the sides. Beer spilled out over his hand and on to the floor and his other hand gripped the glass until his knuckles turned white and the bones pressed against the skin.

'He knows you didn't meant to, Dad.' Tally didn't know if this was true but her father looked so pained she felt she must make the offering. 'He knows you didn't.'

'Your brother's dead,' her father said. 'Zech's bloody dead, Tally. When will you get that inside your thick little head?' His voice was raised now and so was the hand holding the glass. For a frightened moment she thought that he was going to strike her, but instead he smashed the glass into the wall beside the door. 'He's fucking dead and gone, Tally, he can't tell you a frigging thing. Dead, dead, fucking dead.'

He shouted the words, punctuating them by hammering what was left of the glass against the kitchen tiles. Blood ran down between his fingers where he had been deeply cut and as he moved his hand it splashed on to Tally's face and dress. She cried out, more startled by the wetness of the blood than by her father's outburst. She could hear her mother calling to them from the other room, hearing the raised voices and wondering what was wrong. Her father bent down, his face close to hers.

'Your mam told me what that teacher said.' He tapped his head with bloodied fingers, then straightened and called back to his wife that everything was all right. They'd just broken a glass and not to come through until he'd cleared it up. Tally stared at him, scared but not so scared that she was prepared to give up.

'Zech told me,' she asserted,' and I don't care if he is dead, he's still my brother and he didn't lie. You were with that woman and you chased him so he wouldn't tell.'

'There was no woman. There is no Zech.' He shook his hand as though trying to free the fragments of glass that pierced the palm and between his fingers. Blood splashed against the door and he cursed. 'Get out of here. Out while I clean up this mess. Go on.' He used his other hand to urge her through the door, spilling beer on a skirt that was already stained with his blood. Tally grasped the door handle and pulled the door open. As she did so, she said loud enough for her mother to hear, 'What are you going to tell Mum? That you weren't fucking someone else?'

She ran then, more shocked by her own use of a forbidden word than by anything else that had passed between them. Scared too because she knew her mother must have heard and it would not be like Rose just to let things lie.

And then Jack really did come back, Tally thought. He came back in the form of Jack Chalmers. A Jack who took her life away just as surely as Zechariah's had been taken away from him.

Thirty-Three

April

They arrived back at Naomi's flat from speaking to Rose around five o'clock to find a message from Patrick's father, Harry. Alec called him back, then put it on speakerphone so that Naomi could hear. Patrick, it seemed, had come home very excited. He swore that the man from the photofit, this Jack, had been hanging around outside the school. What should they do?

'Did anyone else see him?' Alec wanted to know. 'Harry, did he report this?'

'He went back in and told one of the teachers, yes. She came back out with Patrick and the man was still there but he took off when he saw Patrick wasn't on his own.'

'Did he say anything to Patrick? Approach him?'

'Fortunately, he didn't get the chance.'

'Harry, I'm not doubting him, but I don't see what interest Jack would have in Patrick.' He paused, wondering. Patrick often came over to do his homework at Naomi's. 'Unless he saw him at Naomi's place.'

'There's another possibility,' Harry told him. 'This Tally Palmer, she did that talk at the school and Patrick spoke to her afterwards. He mentioned Naomi. You know what Patrick's like, didn't even tell me about the talk never mind having spoken directly to the woman.' Harry was clearly miffed by this lack of communication, though Alec knew it had nothing to do with the way the two got along. Patrick just didn't mention things, unless he was talking to Naomi or Napoleon. Napoleon was a good listener. Alec himself had frequent and long conversations with the big black dog.

'I don't like this, Alec,' Harry was saying and Alec agreed quickly.

'I'll need to get a statement from him and I'll make arrangements with the school, maybe get a police liaison officer to go in for assembly. Look, Harry, I'm going to catch Dick Travers before he goes off duty, get the wheels in motion. I'll get someone over there to take Patrick's statement. I'll come myself if I can. Meantime, I'll send Naomi.'

'Thanks, Alec. I appreciate it.' The relief was evident in Harry's voice. 'We're at Mari's, Patrick came here after school and she had the sense to call me. I came straight home.'

'Of course he did,' Naomi smiled when he got off the phone. 'Poor old Harry, life just won't settle down for him, will it? First Helen and now this.' She reached for her coat. 'Drop me off on your way, will you Alec, I'll go now rather than ring a taxi.' She frowned. 'I'm worried,' she confided. 'First me and then Patrick. This Jack, he doesn't like people getting in his way.'

DCI Dick Travers had pulled out all the stops. He'd contacted the head teacher and got liaison officers in place to brief the teaching staff before the children arrived that morning. Officers and teachers were standing by with copies of the photofit compiled from the descriptions of the advice centre staff, and arrangements had been made that any pupil feeling the need to call their parents would have a teacher standing by to help them explain.

Patrick found himself the centre of attention and not liking it very much, the only compensation being that a girl he fancied who'd spent all term ignoring him, finally glanced his way.

The head teacher, Eileen Mathers, cast her most serious expression over the sea of expectant faces and told them about the incident reported last night.

'This man could be dangerous,' she said. 'We don't know why he was here outside our school, but Patrick Jones must be commended on his sensible actions. He did exactly the right thing in reporting it to a member of staff and his father then informed the police.'

She nodded across to Alec sitting next to her on the stage. 'Detective Inspector Friedman and his team want to know if any of you others spotted this man. If you've seen him before or if anything has happened either close to the school or on your journeys home that have given you case for concern. I'm sure they will emphasize, do not approach this man. Keep together and if you see him, report it immediately. You'll be given a number to contact should you have any worries on this score. I know, despite our rules –' she paused and fixed her charges with the beadiest of gazes – 'that many of you persist in bringing your mobile phones to school . . .'

A frisson that was almost a giggle, drifted through the room.

'This might be the one time when the infernal devices actually prove useful, but' – she raised her voice emphatically – 'they must still be kept switched off on school premises. I hope that's understood. Now, return to your tutor rooms. Any of you who feel you have something to say will be released by your tutors and allowed to come to my room for interview. A teacher will be present and I'm sure I can count on all of you to deal with this with maturity and restraint.'

She left the stage, Alec following. The soft buzz of conversation that had broken out the moment she had turned to go exploding into full scale hullabaloo as the hall doors closed.

'Maturity and restraint,' she said and laughed somewhat

mirthlessly. 'Some hope of that. You realize you'll have half the school queuing up to talk to your lot just so they can claim their five minutes of fame.'

Alec smiled and nodded. 'I realize,' he told her, 'but we've got to be seen to go through the motions just in case. I thought it was fifteen minutes of fame,' he added.

'Not in my school. You'll give them five each and no more.' She smiled properly at him. 'Play it my way, Inspector Friedman or believe me, you'll be here for days.'

By lunchtime, Alec was beginning to believe her as the queue snaked down the corridor, noisy and giggly – and that was just the boys. Alec was reminded of why he wasn't all that keen on teenagers.

Most were dealt with in much less than the five minutes. Many had come along as moral support for a friend – why was it that girls always had to do everything together, Alec wondered – and he was learning that one interview could often do away with three or four waiting in the queue.

Most thought they might have seen something. A few were genuinely scared. One or two actually had spotted Jack, standing across the road and watching the school gates, though they had assumed he was just waiting legitimately for one of the kids. The fact that they noticed him at all was down to him not being one of the regulars who stood there and Alec decided it was worth getting uniform out to talk to the parents at the end of the day. A regular collector of children was more likely than not to notice someone new. He'd almost discounted the parent thing, thinking that these kids were mainly old enough to take themselves home, but it emerged than some came quite a distance, out of catchment and off the regular bus routes.

The day's big breakthrough came just after lunch when one of the teachers called to him from down the hall.

'I've been trying to get a minute to talk to you all morning,' she said. 'Only with the chaos I'm minding another class along with my own and I didn't get the chance. I saw him before, you see, but it didn't register straight away.'

'Oh . . . Mrs . . .'

'Spencer, sorry, I should have said. 'It was on the day the photographer came in for careers week. Miss Palmer. She talked to my class and two others. I didn't get to hear all of it, which is a pity. She was very good, but anyway, I saw her drive off. She's got one of those little Mazdas, an mx5. I noticed it because I'd love one.' She grinned. 'Not really practical with kids, but, you know. Anyway, when I left a bit later on, her car was outside a shop. I know it was hers because she came out as I passed by. That man was waiting for her.'

'Waiting for her. You're sure?'

'Yes, leaning against her car. She spoke to him. I don't know, maybe he was making a nuisance of himself then as well. She didn't look too pleased.'

Alec thanked her, asked her to make sure she made a formal statement. Until then it had been in his mind that Patrick could have been mistaken. He'd known that he could not take the chance. That he had to, as he'd put it earlier, go through the motions, but the connection had seemed a little tenuous. This seemed to confirm the connection. If Jack had seen Tally talking to Patrick or if she'd mentioned him, if he'd also seen the boy entering Naomi's flat . . .

He'd better go back and talk to Miss Palmer again, Alec thought.

Thirty-Four

Naomi took her usual cab from the advice bureau the following afternoon. George having traded his three o'clock appointment with his brother, took her to Ingham Comprehensive to collect Patrick. This had been the arrangement since the previous week and the now notorious Jack sighting. They were not the only ones to be taking extra precautions. A mild, hardly restrained air of hysteria pervaded the school and the streets outside and, although Jack's threat had never been defined, the feeling had grown among the increased numbers of parents who clustered outside the gates waiting for their offspring that this man was a direct threat to their children.

Jack's face, or at least the police image of him, had been plastered all over the local papers for the past two nights. It had been shown on the local news and even made an appearance on a couple of the nationals, filling in on what had been a flat week, newswise. Things would die down, Naomi knew, but until they did the dedicated line DCI Travers had set up, would continue to be inundated by calls from anxious teens and worried parents demanding more police action.

Uniformed officers loitered outside the school gates each afternoon and staff watched for latecomers in the morning. At the present time, Ingham Comprehensive was, Naomi thought, the least likely place in Britain for Jack to show up.

'Ay, ay? What's up here,' George wondered as they rounded the corner into the street on to which the school gates opened. 'Some of your lot here, Nomi. Two patrol cars and a lot of shouting going on.' He pulled over at the side of the road and hopped out to help Naomi and Napoleon on to the pavement.

'What's happening, George?'

'Don't know, love. Looks as if they've arrested someone.'

'Jack?'

'Let's go have a look see.'

She took George's arm and held Napoleon close to her side. She could hear the shouts and almost feel the press of people before they even reached the outer ranks of the crowd.

There seemed to be some kind of an argument going on, but she couldn't make out what. Words crowded against each another, people yelling. An officer's voice trying to urge the crowd to disperse: 'Nothing to see here. Nothing to see,' and a man shouting, 'She's my kid sister for God's sake. I come down here to protect her from wankers like that and I get arrested for being him?'

The general shouting had now calmed and someone even laughed. The atmosphere seemed a little calmer.

'Naomi.' Patrick's voice now. He sounded slightly breathless. 'The police got called. One of the year seven kids, her brother came to fetch her home 'cause her mum couldn't. They thought he was Jack.'

'Did he look like Jack?'

'No. *I* don't think so anyway.' He sounded pleased with himself. 'I told them that. Anyway, he could prove who he was and Mrs Reed, the teacher . . . the year seven's form teacher,' he clarified, 'she knew him anyway.'

The crowd was breaking up now and the police were again remonstrating with someone. 'I'm sorry, sir, but if you'd just come into the school for a few minutes so we can make quite sure we've got to the bottom of this.'

'I've told you who I am. I've proved it to you. What more do you want? Blood?'

'Pity,' George commented. 'That was quite a bit of excitement. You set, Patrick?'

'Yeah, sure.' He sounded slightly disappointed as though he too thought it all quite exciting and was unwilling to let it go.

'What will happen now?' he asked, as he walked with Naomi and George back to the cab.

'They'll have an informal chat in school, I expect. Probably get the child's mother down just to confirm identity. He might have to make a statement and if he's lucky he'll get an apology.'

George laughed. 'How often does that happen?' he asked.

'It's not good, though,' Naomi commented. 'Things can so easily get out of hand, people get hurt.'

'They're saying he's a paedophile,' Patrick supplied.

Naomi rolled her eyes. 'Of course they are,' she said. She consoled herself with the thought that tomorrow was Friday, then two days of weekend. With luck, by Monday – two days away from the hothouse environment of a school full of teenagers and a street full of anxious parents – reason might prevail.

Alec had missed out on the fun. He was out at Pinsent talking to the Cranes. Tally's father's second wife had taken a little tracking down. Alec had wanted to speak to her since he and Naomi had been to see Rose. If their assumption and Tally's story were right, then Zech had disturbed their meeting on the day he had died. The father had chased him; Zech had died. Neither Naomi nor Alec could believe that the woman would not have been aware of that fact.

Information on Sarah Crane, who had been the second Mrs Palmer, came from Simon's notes. He had collected together all the reports that he could find on Richard Palmer's funeral and Naomi had commented on something the others had noted. No one ever called him by his name. Tally referred to him, when necessary, as 'my father', Rose did not use his name. It was as though by expunging this one word from their common usage they were also able to erase the man.

The Cranes were in the import export business. Antiques, stuff from India, rugs and so on that they sold direct to the interior design market. They had a small shop in Pinsent, a little way up the coast, but most of their trade was mail order. Sarah Crane had reverted to her maiden name for business purposes. Brother and sister looked very much alike. Short grey hair, slightly angular features and dark grey eyes. They were affluent but not ostentatious. The flat above the shop beautifully furnished, but kept simple and uncluttered. Had Alec been asked to guess on the basis of their respective homes, he would have placed these two as Tally Palmer's kin and not Rose.

'You're asking me to delve into long past history,' Sarah Crane told him. She wore a dark blue dress trimmed with a silver brooch, star shaped, pinned precisely on her shoulder. Slim, almost boyish, a major contrast to Rose. Alec briefly tried to imagine her, bedded down in the long grass with Tally's father. Skirt hitched up and legs wrapped around the man's back. He gave up, the image incongruous. But she had been younger then, he reminded himself. Younger and more foolish perhaps, carried away by the excitement, the almost childish thrill of it.

Did her brother know about their assignations au naturel? Somehow, Alec doubted that too.

'I would have thought it was something that might stick in your memory,' Alec told her. 'It was the day Zech Palmer died. You met his father on the embankment. Zech saw you.'

The brother, Stephen Crane, raised an eyebrow, but did not speak.

'I don't know what you're talking about.'

'The day Zech Palmer died,' Alec repeated patiently as he had in various guises for the past several minutes. 'I don't see how *you* could have wiped it from your mind or Richard Palmer from *his*. After all, he may have felt himself responsible for his son's death. I imagine that would take some living with.'

Sarah Crane fixed him with a look that was meant to either impale or silence. 'Richard suffered because of the death of his son, yes. He suffered because of that woman too and that crazy daughter of his, but how can you ever believe Zech died because of him?'

'I believe it,' Alec said simply, 'because the evidence points that way. And I believe you must have known too.'

'What can it matter now?' Stephen Crane demanded. 'Look, I know that Tally, the sister, she made certain accusations. She told her mother about Sarah and her father and certainly hastened the end of their marriage, but it was on the rocks anyway. Sarah and Richard had already made up their minds that they wanted to be together. Anyway, the poor man's long dead.'

Alec sighed. 'I'm not trying to make trouble for you or your family,' he said. 'This isn't about Zechariah, not directly, it's connected to another investigation and the implications of this other investigation affect the here and now. And I do need answers. I'm not prepared to take vague protestations. Ms Crane, if you don't talk to me off the record, as I'm giving you the opportunity to do, I will arrange for you to be brought in to the station to answer my questions.'

For a long time she stared at him, the distaste in her eyes enough to make most men writhe. Alec was not most men. He'd been on the receiving end of far worse, though her brother shifted awkwardly in his chair as though the look were aimed at him.

'I knew what she accused him of,' she said at last. 'That crazy child. Crazy mother though. What chance did she ever have? We were disturbed that day. We heard something. Richard got up and went to look. I heard him shout and then he took off after someone. That's all I know.'

'And it never occurred to you to put two and two together after that?' Alec questioned. 'You must have realized what went on after. That his father chased Jack and that Jack fell. Jack died.'

'Jack!' she interrupted. 'That's what *she* called him, wasn't it?'

She turned away from Alec, then got to her feet and walked stiffly from him as though she planned to leave.

'Sarah,' her brother spoke, his voice soft as though coaxing a child. 'Sarah, you must tell him, you know. What harm can be done now?'

Her shoulders trembled, the false rigidity breaking as emotion took hold. 'Yes,' she admitted, brokenly. 'I knew. I tried hard not to know, to pretend that none of this had happened.' She spun around, facing Alec once again but this time her eyes blazed with anger. 'What could I do about it? What the hell was I supposed to do? Go to the police? Tell them that Richard accidentally killed his son? That his son saw us fucking on the grass and ran off to tell his mother?'

'Was that what Richard thought?' Alec asked her.

She closed her eyes. 'I don't know what Richard thought,' she said. 'Only that he lived with it. That it came between us. That if he hadn't died when he did our marriage would have ended anyway. He believed he'd done wrong and that feeling grew and grew until it all but ate him alive. That boy of his was everywhere he ever looked. Haunting him, speaking to him in the night. Tormenting his dreams until the only way he could sleep was to dope himself with pills and booze.'

She hugged herself as though suddenly cold and turned away again, her head bowed but her body once again rigid with anger.

'I think you'd better go,' Stephen Crane said quietly and Alec nodded. He had what he had come for and felt tainted by the getting of it.

As Stephen Crane opened the door to let Alec out of the flat, he told him, 'I met her once, the little girl I mean. She'd been dragged along to the funeral by that mother of hers. I took the kiddies outside while all the fuss was going on and we talked. She was . . . an unusual little thing. I'm not surprised she made such a success of her life, despite everything.'

Alec nodded. 'Rose Palmer isn't crazy, you know. She admits herself that she might have been furious with her husband and frankly, the more I find out about what happened, the more I understand how she must have felt.'

Stephen Crane nodded, but Alec could tell he found his words incomprehensible. He had only that frozen moment. That one decisive image of Rose Palmer upon which to make his judgement, and the words of a stranger, years after that opinion had formed, were less than nothing.

When she was thirteen years old and her brother Carl was three, her father died. They heard about it through her father's solicitor the day before the funeral and her mother had spent hours phoning around to people who had once been their mutual friends, threatening and cajoling until she had found out where the funeral was being held.

'Should we be going?' Tally asked her. 'I mean, she *won't want us there.'*

'Who cares what she wants?' Rose had said. 'He's still your father and he's still the man I married. We've every right.'

Rose had calmed in the past year or so, rearing her

children unconventionally, but well enough and getting on with her life. News of the funeral seemed to have resurrected the hysteria that had characterized the first months after her husband had left. Tally said nothing more. She knew her mother well enough to be aware that little could prevent her now from carrying out her own will regardless of anyone else's feelings.

When Tally woke on the morning of the funeral her mother was already dressed. The black frock with its low back and short sleeves had been hanging in the wardrobe for the past five years and was perhaps a little tight, but her mother had squeezed into it. At Tally's tentative suggestion that it might not be altogether suitable, Rose had made it plain that she would not be taking it off.

'I've been waiting for an occasion since I bought it,' she said. 'This is it.'

Her hands and arms were covered in scratches and cuts. They looked red and raw like marks left by long clawed cats. Blood oozed from several of them and was brushed, unnoticed on to the dress leaving darker stains on the black lace fabric. 'I've been making that,' her mother said by way of explanation, motioning her head in the direction of the kitchen table.

'Oh Mum,' Tally said. 'I really don't think.' She fell silent, her mother's determined expression telling her not to waste her breath. 'That' proved to be a wreath of roses. Long stems cut from the rambler in the garden and twisted into a woven circle, the vicious thorns responsible for the bloody damage done to her mother's hands. Ivy and fresh flowers pillaged from the hanging baskets finished the decoration, wired in place, the end of the wire left long and bare. The ring was small, a parody of a crown rather than a funeral wreath and Tally shuddered as she thought what her mother might have in mind to do.

They got the taxi to St Luke's. Rose donned long black gloves to hide her hands. They came up past her elbows and she had adorned her wrists with bracelets of twisted beads.

She had rummaged in Tally's cupboard, finding clothes that she deemed as suitable. Black long-sleeved shirt and a skirt that Tally had outgrown the year before. It was dark, certainly, but it was far too short even for everyday, never mind a funeral. Tally, shy and uncertain at the best of times, felt cheap and painfully exposed. The taxi driver said nothing, but his look told Tally everything she didn't wish to know.

'Can't we just go home, Mum?'

'Not until I've seen him.'

'But he's dead, Mum.'

'Best thing for him. I just want to see.'

Tally sighed and said no more but concentrated her attention on little Carl, who, in the nature of small children, seemed to be taking everything in his stride. They sang nursery rhymes together and songs he had learnt at playgroup while their mother maintained a silence that was as profound as her appearance was absurd. Tally was afraid that her mother had lost it this time and wondered how she was going to sneak away long enough to phone for Aunt Bee to come and help.

The service had begun by the time they had arrived. Rose opened the heavy door and ushered the children inside, then let it slam loudly behind them.

'Mum!' Tally flushed scarlet. Every eye in the church had turned upon them. A man in a dark grey suit had been standing at the front giving some kind of address but he too fell silent as Rose led her children down the aisle and towards the altar.

Tally followed reluctantly, leading Carl by the hand. The church was filled with flowers. Lilies and deep-red roses. Their fragrance flooded her senses and she followed her mother more slowly as the scent of angels fogged her mind, washing away the embarrassment and fear of what her mother was about to do. Finally, she halted, watching in a dream as her mother continued her slow promenade towards the coffin.

'Look, Tally, look.'

Carl's high little voice broke into her thoughts. She looked to where the child was pointing. Somewhere at the front of the church she could hear a woman scream and a man lifted a child into his arms, turning to his neighbours to help with the woman before he hurried away, the child's face turned towards him so that he should not see.

Briefly, Tally wondered about the woman's cries but it was the child that Carl had pointed to and the child that now held Tally's eye.

She had known about her father's other son of course. Had lived through months of her mother's wailing when she discovered that barely a month separated Carl and this little boy in age. Tally could have picked the child out in any crowd. The eyes – clear and blue as her own where Carl's were brown – she had always thought of as her mother's legacy but it was clear now that they came from her father's genes. And the soft blond hair waving around the small face, a hint of copper in the curls, reminded her of Zech.

The man who held the boy paused where Tally stood. He hesitated, then shifted the boy on to his hip and gently took her arm.

'Best we go outside,' he said.

For a moment, Tally resisted, staring past him to where the woman screamed and her mother fought. She took a further hesitant step down the aisle. Her sleeve caught the lilies tied with white ribbon to the ends of the wooden pews. They spilt bright pollen that looked red as blood against the black sleeve of her shirt. She stared at it, then looked up and nodded gratefully at the man, thankful to be taken away. Away from her mother struggling with the vicar and the grey suited man and the other woman screaming and the congregation surging forward, overturning the tall pillars that supported the ornate floral displays, sending lilies and deep red roses spilling to the floor, crushing perfume beneath their feet.

Thirty-Five

When Tally was sixteen she fell in love properly for the first time. If she had thought that Miles had been her first passion then she soon realized that it had been mere infatuation. Adam was it and Tally had never been so happy. The only cloud on the horizon was Jack; he was so different now from the Jack that the child Tally had known that at times she hardly recognized him.

Jack would often disappear for days at a time, doing whatever it was he did – Tally rarely questioned him. Once or twice when she had been out with friends she had run into him. Always at the centre of a crowd, laughing, joking, charming those around him and it had become an unspoken rule that Tally did not acknowledge him at such times. Where Jack went death and sorrow had a habit of following, and Tally had long decided that Jack was not a safe person to know if she wanted to keep the police and grieving families from her door. And sometimes he would come to her at night, the way he had done when they both were children. Climbing in though her window late at night and slipping quietly into her bed. And she would taste his other life, the life of the stranger Jack. Taste the others on his lips. Feel them in the way he touched her. Be possessed of knowledge that she did not want, but did not know how to refuse. The slow scent of arousal, cloying in her nostrils, the feel of flesh melting against her own and thoughts draining into a mind so hungry it could never be filled.

'I like to share my life with you,' Jack told her. 'See these things as gifts, Tally, precious things.'

Once she had been in control of Jack, had nurtured him, counselled him, protected him, fought for him and cherished him until he had grown beyond her. Now, it was no longer a question of Tally letting go; it had long been a question of Tally escaping.

Not that she wanted to most of the time. Jack was still her closest friend and dearest ally, but in her heart of hearts she was forced to admit that she was frightened of him, when Jack was provoked or denied, trouble seemed sure to follow.

Tally was well aware that Jack worked best with the cover of secrecy and so, from the beginning of their relationship, she had been careful to keep Adam well in the public domain and so out of Jack's world. Jack would be jealous, she argued, and when Jack was jealous, bad things happened.

Adam was as unlike Miles as it was possible to be. Quiet and studious, though well capable of having fun. Open with his feelings and proud to be seen with her. He laughed easily and when he did his rather nondescript grey eyes gleamed and became beautiful. And, as importantly, Tally got along with his friends. Her skill with the camera took her to places that she would never otherwise have gained entry, and when Graham's band got its first gig, Tally was there to record the moment. When Phil Bryce, the eldest of Adam's group, ran his first half marathon, Tally was there at the finish line. Her pictures appeared in the college magazine and were plastered on the walls. For the first time in her life she was accepted; an insider and not made outcast by virtue of her difference.

When Adam first entered her life Tally's nights were full of nightmares. Jack was stalking him. Jack was reaching out for him with the tentacles of hatred that Tally imagined issued from his very soul. But as time passed and the days grew into weeks, Tally began to relax. Jack seemed so absorbed in his own world that Tally started to believe he had no interest in Adam at all and did not mind that someone else was taking over her life.

'I still love you, Jack,' she told him one evening as he lay beside her.

'Of course you do. I know that.' He smiled at her and reached out to stroke back a strand of hair. His hand was warm on her face and he lay his palm against her cheek, his thumb gently stroking over her lips. Tally rolled over on to her back and gazed up at the sky. They had wandered together into the fields behind her mother's house and lay down in the long grass as they had long ago when both were children and life seemed to stretch forever into the distance. Summer was here early, June days warmer than expected, though the forecast threatened rain before the week was through. Tally had finished her exams and, although she had found herself a summer job, she would be working the early shift and have her day returned to her by two. Adam would be leaving for university in the autumn, but they had a long season yet to enjoy and nothing was going to spoil it.

'You love him too, don't you?'

Tally, her limbs heavy with the sun and the brightness of the sky, turned her head reluctantly to look at Jack. 'Do you mind?'

'I mind. But I want you to be happy.'

'I am happy,' she smiled. 'You'd like him, Jack,' she said hopefully. 'I wish you two could meet.'

'And how would you explain me, Tally? This friend you like to keep at arms' length because he's not acceptable?'

Tally turned over again and leaned on her elbow regarding him with concern. 'Jack, people do things, make mistakes, act like complete wankers, but you can't make judgements about them on the strength of that. There's more. Always more to it and the stupid things you do when you're growing up are just that, part of growing up.'

'Generous of you to say so,' Jack told her sarcastically.

'Don't, Jack. I hate it when you're like this.' She sat up and gathered her arms around her knees, drawing away from him.

'Don't, Jack,' he mimicked.

She got up and walked a little away from him. The day seemed to have darkened. The light blue sky patched with indigo and the green of the fields fragmented by tears. Tally loved days like these, the calmness of the sky, so solidly and reliably blue and the golden yellow haze of distant hills.

'You're not Jack,' she said, her voice thick with unshed tears. 'Not like Zechariah at all. Not even like you were when I first met you. You're just someone who takes from other people. Takes lives and dreams and all the things that they might become if you left them alone. My Jack would never do that. You've turned into something else.' She turned around and glared at him, unable to keep the thought to herself any longer. 'You're cruel and you're twisted and I hate you, Jack. I hate what you've become.'

He was on his feet and his hands were on her arms, gripping tight enough to hurt. She pulled away from him but he wasn't about to let her go. 'You belong to me and I belong to you. Two heads, one soul, remember?'

'We were kids. That's all, just kids.'

'And that makes a difference? We're still here and we're still bound, for better or for worse. For always, Tally.' His mouth twisted into a sarcastic smile. 'Till death and more.'

He let her go and she stumbled away from him knowing that what he said was true.

'Go and play your games,' Jack shouted after her as she ran. 'Go and fuck your Adam and pretend that you're in

love and when you've finished, you'll still need me. I'm your guardian angel, girl. Archangel Jack.'

April

In the hospital, Simon read the papers. The photofit of Jack appeared on the front page of the *Ingham Courier*, Simon's paper, the one he'd written for when he'd first met Tally Palmer. He'd told Naomi that he'd never met Jack. Never seen him, but looking at this image he knew now that had not been the truth.

There had been a night at Tally's flat. It had been well after midnight when Simon woke and groped for his watch to check the time. Tally rolled over, murmuring something in her sleep.

Simon froze. The feeling that someone else was in the room. A shadow momentarily blocking the faint light that came through the bedroom door from the room beyond. The blinds had been left open and the city light, night-time yellow, filtered in.

Simon sat up, knowing who it was. 'Jack.'

The shadow in the doorway resolved itself briefly into a figure. A man, tall and muscular, though lightly built for all that, with dark curling hair. Simon leapt from the bed, snatching his jeans from the floor, clutching them in his hands as he moved towards the door. But the figure had vanished and Simon, grabbing hold of what little sense he had left, struggled into his jeans before storming into the main room and hitting the light.

There was no one there.

'Dreaming,' Simon muttered to himself. Then he froze. The door to Tally's flat stood wide open and, receding rapidly, Simon could hear, the sound of booted feet upon the stairs.

Thirty-Six

April

Tally paced back and forth in her apartment, her gaze fastened firmly to the polished hardwood floor. She was thinking about Simon – thoughts of Simon seemed to have occupied her mind more than any other subject lately. And she was thinking about Jack. What to do about Jack.

DI Alec Friedman was right. Jack had attacked Simon. Jack wanted Simon dead. Jack had wanted only to frighten Naomi – for now – and had no intention of doing actual harm. Had that been his intention Naomi would at the very least be occupying a bed in the same hospital as Simon. Maybe worse. Jack didn't get frightened, nothing scared him off once he'd set his mind to something and now, Tally knew, his intent was to keep Tally and, once and for all, be rid of Simon.

Trouble was, Tally had told the truth when Alec had interviewed her. She didn't know where Jack lived, didn't know about his other associates. Didn't know if he had other friends. She'd taken care *not* to know such things for so long now that it had become habit, second nature. Unchallenged until now.

And that was the difficulty, Tally acknowledged. She'd put this off for so long, managed to live her life around Jack's demands and somehow make allowances for Jack's actions; but she knew that she could no longer do this. Somehow, she had to free herself of Jack once and for all and somehow –

this, to Tally's mind an even bigger problem – she had to convince Simon that she still loved him. More than anything else. More than anything Tally had ever in her life desired, it was to have Simon back, and to do that, she must be rid of Jack.

Tally had chased this conundrum around and around in her head for the last few hours and before that for days, and she had come to no conclusion. Had she been able to tell Alec what he wanted to know, then, she told herself, she would have done so. Though the thought of betraying Jack in this way bit into her stomach like acid eating away at her insides. Her main reason for not knowing about Jack, Tally was honest enough to admit to herself, was so that she could not betray him. A tacit understanding between them. An unspoken deal made so long ago that Tally could no longer remember a time when this had not been so.

Tally halted and turned to look out of the wall of windows across the town. The sky had cleared a little. The morning rain had been blown away by a strong wind coming off the sea and driving the weather inland.

Making up her mind, she grabbed her bag and coat from the bedroom and ran out into the chill of the afternoon. A straggle of journalists still kept guard at the entrance to the car park. A lone, uniformed officer keeping company, stamping his feet in unison with their shivers. They fired questions at her as she jumped the low wall on the far side away from them and ran around the corner before they'd had time to realize that she was gone. She ducked down a side alley, taking a short cut between two factories, on to the main road. The hospital was a twenty-minute walk away. Tally walked fast, looking only straight ahead.

Naomi and Patrick were out too. They'd taken Napoleon on to the beach and Naomi stood, listening to the boy's laughter and the dog's excited yelps and barks as they played with Napoleon's favourite yellow frisbee.

It was good, she thought, to enjoy such normality. Many of their Saturday afternoons were spent this way, often finishing with a half-hour in the beach arcades – Napoleon back on his harness, his status as a guide dog allowing him to go inside. In her sighted days, Naomi had loved arcade games, especially the pointless shoot 'em ups, and Patrick had persuaded her to try them again. Patrick, Naomi reflected, had a touching faith in her that she could do anything.

In this case, he'd been right. Firing at random, or under Patrick's excited instruction – right a bit, man with big gun at four o'clock, left a bit now – Naomi recaptured much of her earlier fun. They usually ended up giggling uncontrollably and Naomi had visions of one day being asked to leave because they created too much mayhem.

It was getting chilly on the beach and she could hear the tide coming in. The sound of waves crashing on shingle definitely closer than it had been an hour ago. She was about to suggest they cut the beach and make for the warmth of the arcade when Patrick came running up and she could tell at once that something was very wrong.

'Patrick?'

'Jack, he's on the promenade.'

'Jack? Are you certain?'

'Sure I am. He's watching us.'

Naomi groped in her pocket for the phone. 'I'll call Alec.'

'OK, but he's moving now. Nomi, we should follow him.'

'Follow him!' She felt for the A on her phone and pressed, holding it in. She had Alec on fast dial. 'We can't follow him, Patrick, he's . . . Alec, it's Naomi.' Quickly, she filled him in.

'He's coming and he's sending a patrol car,' she told Patrick as she rang off.

'That's good, but Nomi, he's moving away fast. We've got to see where he goes.'

Naomi thought hard. Alec would be furious. Not something that bothered her on its own, but to involve Patrick . . .

The boy was on his knees fixing Napoleon's harness in place. He took Naomi's hand and folded it around the taped metal. 'Nomi, we don't have a choice,' he said. 'Come on.'

He took her arm, setting the pace, leading her as rapidly as he could back up the beach towards the steps.

'OK, OK, where is he? Tell me what's going on.'

'He's walking fast. Towards the funfair. There's a lot of people on the prom, so that's slowing him down. Lots of families and such.'

'Good. Any sign of Alec or the car?'

She felt him turn his head, scanning both ways along the narrow road that ran parallel to the promenade. 'Nothing yet. Can you go any faster?'

'Only if you want me to fall flat on my face.'

'What if I . . . ?'

She gripped his hand tightly against her side. 'Don't even think about it. What the hell was he doing here anyway?' she wondered.

'You think he followed us from your place?'

'I don't know.' She shivered slightly at the thought of Jack watching her, hoping Patrick would take her reaction simply as sudden chill; knowing he was far too perceptive for that. She felt him squeeze her arm reassuringly.

'I didn't see him before,' Patrick said. 'But I wasn't looking. I just didn't think.' He sounded so self-reproachful that Naomi almost laughed aloud. Patrick saw himself as being solely responsible for her when they were out together.

'Ah, there's the police car.'

'Good.' He let go of Naomi's arm and she heard him

running up the beach, feet crunching across the pebbles. She heard him shout to the uniformed officers who'd pulled up on the promenade, Napoleon leading her at a steadier pace towards the steps.

Then Patrick was beside her once again. 'They're following him,' he told Naomi, 'but I can't see where he's gone. They'll not catch him now,' he added glumly. 'Pity we couldn't have got after him ourselves.'

Naomi bit her lip, thinking fast. 'It's not right,' she said. 'Why would he be here? Why show himself? Patrick, did he look worried when he realized you'd noticed him?'

He shook his head. 'No, just kept staring at me. I ran over to you and when I looked back he was still there. He didn't move until we did.'

'What's he playing at?' Naomi wondered.

'Dunno. Here's Alec.'

Patrick left her again, running excitedly to Alec and recounting the incident.

'You both all right?' Alec asked.

'We're fine,' Naomi reassured him. 'It's a public place, I can't think he'd do much while we're out here.'

The uniformed officers had returned. They'd lost Jack. By now, something of a crowd had gathered, Naomi could hear their voices, speculating, buzzing with mild excitement that seeing two uniformed policemen tearing along the promenade would naturally excite.

'Bugger,' Alec muttered. 'I hoped . . . Never mind, chief thing is the two of you are OK.' He paused, glancing at his watch. 'I'll get them to take you home,' he said. 'Sorry, Nomi, but you called me in the middle of a meeting. I've got to go.'

'On a Saturday?' Patrick questioned.

''Fraid so.'

'We don't need a lift,' Naomi told him. 'I'd sooner walk.'

'Naomi . . . This man's dangerous, you know that. I want—'

'Alec, I won't be wrapped up in cotton wool. Patrick and I are walking into town, we'll be on a public street and then we'll be inside some very public shops. I'll get a taxi back, if it makes you feel better.'

'None of this makes me feel better,' Alec told her angrily. 'Naomi . . .'

'Please, Alec. Get back to your meeting. We'll be all right.'

'How did Jack know where to find you?' Alec continued. 'What the hell's he playing at?'

Naomi shrugged. 'His own game,' she said.

When Alec had gone and the patrol car departed, they walked slowly along the promenade, Naomi deep in thought and Patrick waiting impatiently for her to speak.

'You know,' she said at last, 'Jack wanted us to see him, Jack wanted us to react. It's as if he was diverting our attention from something. From whatever he plans to do next.'

'Like what?' Patrick asked. 'You think he might want to finish Simon? Maybe he's gone to the hospital?'

Naomi thought about it and then shook her head. 'Tally,' she said at last. 'Maybe I was wrong. Maybe he's drawing our attention to things, not diverting us. Tally's place is closer. Fifteen minutes away, maybe. Patrick, there's a taxi rank somewhere around here, can you get us to it?'

'Sure,' he said. 'But I don't get it, Naomi. Why would he *want* us to know where he was going?'

Naomi shrugged. 'He must know this is coming to a head,' she said quietly. 'Maybe . . . maybe he wants an audience? Patrick, I don't get it either, but he's heading for Tally's flat. I'm sure.'

Thirty-Seven

'Simon?' she stood in the doorway, uncertain of her welcome. She'd been relieved to find Simon alone, dreading having to run the gamut of the close guardianship Lillian and Samuel had positioned around their son.

'Tally, what . . . what are you doing here?'

He didn't sound angry, only curious. Tally was glad of that. Lord knows, she thought, he has every right to throw me out.

'I wanted to see you. I tried to come before, but they wouldn't let me in.'

'I didn't know,' he said uncertainly.

'Would you have wanted to see me?'

He hesitated. 'I don't know that either,' he said at last. 'Tally –' he eased himself into a more upright position – 'does Jack know you're here?'

The expression in his voice chilled her as he mentioned Jack and Tally looked away, biting her lip. She shook her head. 'I've not seen Jack,' she said. 'Not since . . .' She turned back to look at him. 'I didn't know what he planned, Simon, I didn't even know he was there! Simon, I had nothing to do with this, you know that, don't you?'

Tears began to fall and she looked away again, wiping them with the back of her hand.

Simon watched her, not knowing what to say. Her pain cut him as sharply as the knife had done, but he could think of no words of comfort. He'd pictured her coming to see him so many times. Wondered what he'd say to her. How he'd react to the sight and the presence of Tally Palmer, the woman he'd loved, the one he still . . .

Did he love her? Simon realized abruptly that he no longer knew for sure.

'Simon?' Tally was asking.

'I don't know what to say to you,' he said quietly. 'Tally, we can't let things go on and we can't go back to the way it was. You live in Jack's shadow. Jack almost killed me and much as I've tried not to think badly of you because of that, I can't separate the two things any more. You and Jack, you're part of the same deal. Part of the same being somehow, and I don't want to be caught up in that any more.'

'I still love you,' Tally argued. 'I still feel the same way. Simon, can't you . . . ?'

'Can't I what? Tally, I've been lying here trying to think, to figure out just what it is I feel for you, and I can't say any more. Take Jack out of the picture, for good, and maybe we could have something, but how can you even ask while he's still out there, just waiting to have another go.'

He waited, but she said nothing. At last Simon asked, 'Have you told the police where to find him?'

'I don't know where to find him.'

'I can't believe that, Tally. How can I possibly believe that?'

'It's the truth!' she told him, her eyes momentarily blazing with anger. Then, more softly: 'It *is* the truth, Simon. I don't know where to find Jack. He always came to me. It's always been that way.'

She turned from him and headed for the door, moving slowly, her shoulders hunched, waiting, Simon knew, for him to call her back. He opened his mouth to speak her name, but then could not find it in himself to speak. He was scared, Simon acknowledged. He'd looked death in the face and seen the empty, most painful parts of himself reflected there. He needed distance from Tally, from the insane triangle. Distance even from himself and his feelings for this woman before he could possibly call Tally back and say, let's try again.

She let the doors swing closed and he could hear her footsteps clicking across the polished floor . . . and he knew that Jack had won.

Thirty-Eight

Jack stood across the street from Tally's apartment block, shadowed from sight by the corner of a disused factory building. Like Tally's apartment block, this was yet another conversion, not yet complete but due to be given over to exclusive loft-style homes.

From his vantage point, Jack could see the front entrance to the block and the car park. Around the entrance to the car park a small knot of people had gathered. He'd been there a few days before and the assembly had been considerably larger, stimulated by the media connection between Tally Palmer and the jumped up little journo Jack had stabbed. As the story had failed to develop further with Tally making no statements and the police refusing to comment – and Simon failing to die – interest in the story had waned. Those left, less than a handful, were locals. Cold and uncomfortable, stamping feet and huddling together against the March wind. Even as he watched, two of them gave in and went off to sit in a car that was parked nearby. Jack didn't blame them, it was bloody freezing.

Jack prepared to move. He knew the code for the outer door and was pretty sure he could cross the car park without attracting attention to himself – or at least, not until it was too late.

But then, he spotted her, walking with her head bowed back towards home.

Tally.

He knew at once that she had been to see Simon. He could think of no other reason why Tally would have ventured out. Jack's anger flared.

Tally had intended to walk back the way she'd come, cut back between the buildings and then run across the car park. Had she done this, Jack would have met her out there on the street.

As it was, she was too preoccupied by Simon's last words to remember where she was meant to go and as she rounded the corner and saw the remaining reporters standing, chatting to the uniformed policeman, it was too late to withdraw and backtrack.

Taking a deep breath, Tally bowed her head and quickened her pace, determined to barge her way between them, relying on the police officer to prevent them from blocking her way.

'Miss Palmer, can we have a statement, Miss Palmer?'

'Have you visited Simon Emmet, Miss Palmer?'

'I've got nothing to tell you!'

She ran the remaining few yards to the door, the officer on duty arguing with the reporters and delaying them. Then, there was another figure, someone approaching at a run and leaping the low wall. He came at her from the side and as Tally turned to face this new threat, thinking it to be another journalist, she realized that it was Jack.

Tally swung around and keyed in the door code, pushed inside through the slowly opening doors, tried hard to force them closed again before the running figure reached her. But Jack was too fast. He shouldered his way through.

'Get out of here, Jack.'

'Why should I, Tally? I've come to see you. Time we decided on things, once and for all.'

'Decided? What things?'

'Oh, things like Tally Palmer and Simon Emmet. Tally and Jack. Which do you want it to be, Tally? And I should think carefully before you answer. There's a whole lot riding on it.'

It had, Naomi reckoned, probably taken them longer to find a taxi than it had for the driver to bring them here. She paid him off at the corner of the street and felt for the button on her watch. Ten past three, the tinny voice told her. Ten past three on a Saturday afternoon in the middle of March.

'Something's going on,' Patrick announced.

'What?'

'There's a policeman and four others, journalists, I think. One's got a camera. They're all talking into mobiles. The policeman looks annoyed.'

'What does he look like? I might know him.'

'Squarish, oldish, grey hair . . .'

'Oldish?'

'Well, you know. Forty or so. About Alec's age, I guess.'

Naomi laughed. 'OK, take me over, we'll see what we can find out.'

It didn't take too much figuring out. From the phone conversations, one-sided though they were, it was clear that Tally Palmer had returned to her apartment block – returned from where? Naomi wondered – and that Jack Chalmers, suspect in the attempted murder of Simon Emmet, had charged through the door after her. Neither had come out again.

'Naomi?' A voice she recognized spoke her name. 'What brings you here?'

'Hello, Fred,' she said. She guessed from Patrick's description that the officer in charge was Fred Thompson. Fred was a nice man. A good officer, but with a burning lack of ambition that had kept him in uniform all these years. 'What's the score then?'

'Um . . .' He led her a few paces away, almost tripping

over Napoleon. 'Oh, sorry, mate.' He bent to ruffle the dog's ears. 'Not much I can tell you, you've not just overheard. Jack Chalmers showed up, came hurtling across the road and into the car park like he was going for a record. Miss Palmer had just opened the doors. Next thing we know, he's got inside. We ran over, but the two of them were halfway up the stairs by then. She saw me and tried to pull free but he wasn't about to let go.'

'And you don't have the key code.'

'Don't have it and wouldn't have used it if I had, Naomi. We've been warned, if spotted, report but don't confront. Just call for back-up.' His laugh was self-deprecating. 'I've got two years to go to retirement, I don't plan on playing the hero in the meantime. Anyway, what the hell are you doing here?'

'We came to see Tally,' Naomi lied.

'Oh? Didn't know you were acquainted.'

'At school together,' she elaborated. 'I know it's been difficult for her to get news of Simon Emmet. I thought she'd like an update.' She turned towards where she thought Patrick was. 'This is a friend of mine,' she added. 'Patrick Jones.'

'Jones . . . the boy that reported seeing Jack outside his school,' Fred noted. 'Up to your neck in this, aren't you?' he observed, archly. 'Alec know you're here, does he?'

'He does now,' Patrick announced ominously as Alec's Mondeo, accompanied by two marked cars, lights flashing, pulled up to the kerb.

'Ah,' Fred mused. 'I'll leave you to it then. Best of luck.'

'Yeah, thanks,' Patrick muttered under his breath.

'That bad?' Naomi asked him.

'I should say so.'

Alec slammed the car door and strode to where they stood.

'What are you two doing here?' Alec demanded. 'Naomi! What the hell are you playing at?'

He broke off and lowered his voice, aware of the interested audience they had. 'Patrick, get yourself and Naomi into my car. Stay there.'

Two more patrol cars arrived, stopping with a screech of brakes at the kerbside.

'Fred,' Alec ordered. 'Get everyone back across the road. I want boundaries established here and traffic re-routed.'

Reluctantly, Naomi allowed Patrick to lead her to the car. It could have been worse, she thought stoically. He could have bundled them into a patrol car and ordered them home. At least this way they were still on the spot and Naomi felt an overwhelming desire to be where the action was. To have been pushed away, right away, would have been unbearable.

But it wouldn't do, she admitted uncomfortably. She was no longer DI Naomi Blake, with rights and privileges that allowed her access to information and investigations. She was Naomi Blake, private citizen. Civilian. Blind civilian, at that.

Just for a moment the reality of her situation hurt so much that she thought she might cry. She swallowed hard and held her breath, curbing the frustration, the bitterness and anger that still bubbled to the surface from time to time despite her best efforts.

'You OK, Naomi?' Patrick looked at her anxiously.

Too perceptive by half, she thought irritably. Then she clamped down hard on her irritation as well and managed a smile. 'I'm OK,' she told him. 'Just . . .'

'Yeah. I know.' He reached out and clasped her hand briefly in a gesture that was so like his father's, Naomi wanted to cry all over again, the more so since she knew that Patrick's words were not merely that. He really did understand the way she felt.

'I've got to get a hobby,' she laughed weakly. 'Stop fiddling about in Alec's affairs.'

'Um, I don't think this was just Alec's affair,' Patrick defended. 'Simon came to both of you.' He paused as though considering something. 'What hobby anyway?'

'Don't know. I'd have to think about it.'

'May as well start now,' Patrick told her. 'Don't think we've anything better to do. Here,' he added, rummaging about in his pockets. 'I've got chocolate. Want to share?'

Naomi laughed. 'The panacea for all ills,' she said.

'Yeah, right,' Patrick replied. 'It's fruit and nut.'

Alec marched back to his car and rummaged in the glove compartment.

'Looking for something?' Naomi asked heavily.

'Tally Palmer's number,' he replied sharply. 'Damn.'

She handed him her mobile. 'You'll have to find it,' she said. 'I don't have it on fast dial. Surprised you didn't program it into yours.'

Alec took the phone from her without a word and left them.

'He's really mad,' Patrick observed.

Naomi sighed. 'Guess he's got cause the way he sees it,' she said. 'Just sometimes, I wish he'd act less like a father and more like . . .' She shrugged, wondering if such confidences were appropriate for sharing with a fifteen-year-old boy. 'Harry's not going to be best pleased either,' she added. 'Seems I get you into trouble every time. He'll be saying I'm a bad influence.'

'Oh, I don't know,' Patrick observed. 'He was the one took the day off to help you.' He wriggled uncomfortably, trying to position himself around Napoleon, who'd decided he was going to share the back seat and had his nose down, snuffling for crumbs of chocolate they might have missed.

'Dad likes you a lot,' Patrick hinted and Naomi felt a sudden pang of guilt, knowing that her conflict with Alec gave Harry encouragement that she was not certain she wanted to give. Her relationship with Alec was a strong one, she was sure of that. He had been her bedrock when she'd first been injured and been finding it hard to come to terms with her new status. But, as she'd slowly achieved more and more independence, their relationship had strained and creaked at times as Alec tried hard to come to terms with this changing woman Naomi herself barely recognized at times.

Across the street, Fred was penning in the journalists and the crowd of onlookers attracted by the police action. He'd purloined cones and barriers from the building work going on in the factory conversion across the way and was erecting makeshift defences, helped by a couple of the workers. Uniformed officers had taken up position in the car park, two more were busy diverting traffic past the building. Alec scanned though the numbers in Naomi's phone and found Tally Palmer's.

Inside Tally's apartment Jack had become agitated. He paced the wooden floor as Tally had done earlier, pausing occasionally to look from the window at the police and sightseers gathering below.

'How could you even think they wouldn't see you? Jack, you come racing in here liked some masked avenger, and you expect no one to notice?' She laughed harshly. 'You're losing your touch, Jack. Thought you'd show a little more finesse.'

He swung about so sharply she had no time to react. He hit her, flat palmed to the side of her head and Tally fell, stunned.

'Finesse?' he challenged. 'What would you know about any of that? Finesse, pride, good sense. You showed any of those things lately, Tally? Or have you taken to behaving like a slut on heat?' He paused, watching her as she struggled back to her feet. 'Where did you go this afternoon?' he asked her. 'To see him, I suppose? Not dead then?'

'No, not dead,' Tally said thickly. 'You failed, Jack. And they're waiting for you outside. You won't get out.'

'For a woman who'd just been to see her so-called lover,' Jack observed, 'you didn't look so goddamned happy. What's the matter, Tally, he tell you to get lost?'

She looked away and Jack knew he'd struck home. 'He did, didn't he?' Jack laughed heartily. 'No staying power after all! Oh, poor little Tally, rejected by some nobody. Serves you right, Tally. You encourage these people, these nothing people, and they let you down soon as the going gets a little bit rocky.'

'Not like you, I suppose?' The side of her face hurt. Burned. Already beginning to swell. She could feel her left eye closing. But his comments about Simon hurt more, especially knowing the truth of them.

'Why did you do it, Jack?' Tally asked softly. 'You don't love me, you don't even care any more. You're not the Jack I used to know.'

'No,' he agreed. 'No, Tally, you're right there. I'm not and you know why? Because I grew up. Something you failed to do.'

In the kitchen, the phone began to ring.

'Not answering,' Alec said bitterly as Fred came back across the road. 'Any word on the negotiators yet? Or on the key holder?'

'I'll check on it,' Fred told him, heading off towards the nearest patrol car.

Alec scanned the building for signs of life. Neighbours who might be home. Was Jack armed? It seemed a fair bet that he carried a knife. No weapon had been recovered after the attack on Simon. Signalling to one of the uniformed officers to follow him, Alec walked swiftly to the main door, keeping close to the wall and out of sight should Jack be looking down from Tally's windows.

There were three others listed on the buzzers. The first gave no answer. The second sounded half asleep. 'What?'

'Mr . . .' – Alec tried to make out the name on the label – 'Seddons?'

'Yes, what? Look, I got in from work less than an hour ago. I'd just dropped off, so . . .'

'I'm sorry to disturb you, Mr Seddons. But this is the police.'

'Police? What?'

'Mr Seddons, if you'd buzz us through then I'll come up and explain.'

A reluctant muttering issued through the speaker, but the buzzer went and the door opened. Alec and the uniformed officer slipped inside. 'Second floor,' he said. 'The one below Tally's flat.'

'How much did you pay for this bloody place?' Jack demanded. 'And still no bloody cameras.'

He was peering down though Tally's blinds trying to see who had entered the building.

'They're fitting them next month,' Tally said heavily. 'When that other conversion's finished across the road, there'll be a monitoring station in their lobby. I seem to remember one of the things you liked about this place was that there were no cameras. Nothing to record the great Jack Chalmers coming to visit.'

He turned and looked sharply at her, his gaze scanning the marks he'd left on her face. 'You're bruising,' he said. 'Get a cold compress on that.' Then he turned back towards the window.

For a moment, Tally stared at him, then she headed for the kitchen, rummaged in a drawer for a linen glass cloth and rinsed it under the cold tap. She glanced about her, wondering what to do. In the next drawer, she kept her knives. Quietly, the sound concealed by the noise of running water, she slid the drawer open and looked inside. Kitchen utensils arranged in a fitted wooden tray, each in its place. Each immediately obvious should one be missing. And would she have the nerve to use it anyway? The nerve even to threaten Jack?

There was no way she could conceal anything large. In the end, she removed one small boning knife, its blade slender and flexible. Then she grabbed a second glass cloth from the drawer and dropped it over the empty space, knowing it wouldn't fool Jack for a second should he look. He was far too meticulous for that. Jack would notice anything even a little out of place as this would be so out of Tally's character.

Hastily, she wrung the cloth out and folded it, enclosing the knife inside and then lifting it to her face. Not a moment too soon. Jack came striding across to the kitchen door, his footsteps heavy and purposeful, shouting at her, wanting to know what the hell was taking her so long.

Tally stood guiltily beside the kitchen sink, holding the compress to her bruised face, willing him not to know.

Scowling, Jack glanced around the kitchen. 'Go,' he said, jerking his head towards the main room. Tally eased by him, and sat down on one of the large cream sofas. She dropped the compress from her cheek for an instant, taking the opportunity to slide the knife down the side of the seat cushions and praying that Jack would not find it. She dare not even think what he would do if he should. She'd never seen him this far from control, taking such risks, exposing himself this way.

It struck her suddenly that Jack had no intention of getting out of here unseen. That he had no intention of either of them getting out.

*   *   *

Alec was questioning Tally's neighbour. Shocked out of his sleep and now shocked into leaving his flat, Brian Seddons was throwing clothing into an overnight bag.

'No. Lower flat's empty,' he told Alec. 'They moved out a week ago and the new people haven't moved in yet. The first floor . . . Is there a match on at Pinsent this afternoon?'

Alec glanced at Fred, who nodded. 'Rugby, that would be,' Fred supplied.

'Yes, he's a big fan. Lives alone since his girlfriend walked out.'

'And you?'

'No. I'm married, but Janny's sister's just had a baby. She's staying for the weekend to help out. I'll head over there.'

'Leave a contact number and address,' Alec told him. 'We'll let you know when it's safe to return.'

'This bloke's dangerous then? Really dangerous?'

'Don't want to take chances,' Alec told him soothingly. 'Chances are it'll all be over in an hour or so. People get overwrought and do stupid things. When they've had time to cool off they're more reasonable.'

Fred's mobile rang. He listened. 'If you're ready, sir?' he asked, slipping it back in his pocket.

'Yes, of course.'

'Negotiator's been delayed,' Fred told Alec in an undertone as they followed Brian Seddons down the stairs.

'Typical,' Alec said. Not that he thought it would be much help, not with the likes of Jack, but it would be good to have someone else dealing. Alec felt suddenly too involved and too much out of his depth.

Jack came over to where Tally sat and eased the compress away from her face with a gesture that was almost tender. 'I never wanted to hurt you,' he said. 'But sometimes, love, sometimes you know how to push a man too far.'

The lobby door closed. Not a loud noise but Jack heard it. He was on his feet and at the window.

'Neighbour's leaving,' he said 'Got your friend Alec Friedman with him and we've quite an audience across the road. Come and see.'

'I don't want to see,' Tally told him heavily.

'I said come and see,' Jack told her flatly. Reluctantly, Tally got to her feet. Praying that the knife was still hidden. Not daring to look back.

Thirty-Nine

Naomi was bored. Her watch told her that it was now ten past four so only an hour had passed since they had first arrived. Patrick's commentary had helped to pass the time. He'd told her about Alec going into the flat and emerging later with a man and, to Patrick's eyes the most exciting, officers in body armour slipping back inside Tally's block.

'They'll get as close as they can without Jack hearing,' Naomi told him. 'Tally's landing, probably.' Then, there had been a whole load of nothing.

'Is it always this slow?' Patrick asked.

'I'm sure I could arrange for a lift home,' Naomi told him.

'No way! Alec's coming over,' he added.

Alec seemed to have calmed somewhat. He clambered into the front seat of the car, reached around to pet Napoleon who stuck his head between the seats and whined a bored greeting.

'I know, old son,' Alec sympathized. 'You'd rather be back on the beach.'

He sighed. 'I'm handing over to Dick Travers soon as he arrives.'

'You're stepping down.'

'I've talked to Dick. We always knew this might be a possibility. My involvement's been too personal all along. Now the media interest is going to increase, Dick doesn't feel we should risk some smart lawyer pushing the point should anything go wrong. And I'm not sorry,' he added. 'Frankly, the last thing I need right now is to sit here playing the waiting game.'

'That doesn't sound like you,' Naomi said.

'Doesn't it? Naomi, frankly, I've had enough of Tally Palmer and Jack and even Simon.' He leaned back and rubbed his eyes wearily. 'Patrick, I'm going to take you home as soon as I've been relieved and then Naomi and I are going out.'

'Out?' Naomi demanded.

'Meal, cinema if you like. Frankly, I don't care. You call the shots. My only rule is we don't talk shop.'

Naomi didn't get the chance to reply. Fred was tapping urgently on the window. Alec opened the car door and slid out.

'What's up?' they heard him say.

'Something's wrong,' Fred told him. 'The officers we've got on the landing, they reckon they can hear sounds of a struggle and a woman crying.'

'It would be so easy, Tally,' Jack was saying. He pressed the little plastic container into her hands. 'Take them with wine. You've got wine in the kitchen. It will all be over in minutes and then nothing can touch us any more.'

'You're crazy, Jack!' She threw the container back at him. 'Suicide pacts are for romantic novels, Jack, not the real world. I don't want to die.'

Jack stood stock-still looking at her. She could not read his expression. His face closed and calm.

'Jack . . . what happened to us, Jack?'

'Nothing, Tally. Nothing happened to *us*.'

'Let's get out of here, Jack. I'll tell them you were with me that night. That you were at the gallery and couldn't possibly have attacked Simon.'

'And they'll believe you, I suppose.'

'I'd swear to it Jack.'

'Despite the fact that no one else at the gallery saw me. Tally, you've got fifty people who'd swear they never set eyes on me. Your word against theirs. I don't think so.'

'I've got money, Jack. I'll hire the best—'

He grabbed her, taking her by the shoulders and shaking her hard. 'You just don't get it, do you? This is the end of the line for us, Tally.' He kissed her, mouth hard against hers, holding her even tighter as she tried to pull away.

'I love you,' he said finally. 'You've known that, always. And I'm not about to let you go.'

'This isn't about love, Jack. It's about possession. Always has been. You! You don't know how to love!'

She struggled free of him and dropped down as Jack hit out at her again. The blow missed her head but caught her shoulder and she cried out in pain.

'That's what you do when you love someone,' she yelled at him. 'Hurt them. Destroy them. Wipe out anything else they might want or need or love. That's what you do, is it Jack? Well, I don't want you any more. I don't want any of it. And yes, before you ask, I do want Simon. Simon Emmet is worth a hundred of you. A thousand!'

He advanced on her again and Tally scuttled back out of his reach. The back of her shins hit the edge of the sofa and as Jack dived on her, Tally fell back, her hand sliding down the side of the cushions, fingers closing on the handle of the knife.

'I can live without you, Jack.' Tally told him and the knife plunged deep.

Alec had run up the stairs, Fred and two other officers following.

'Well?'

'They've gone quiet, sir. Shouting and arguing and then, suddenly, nothing.'

Alec hammered on the door. 'Tally. Tally Palmer, can you hear me?'

Should have waited for the negotiator, Alec thought. Should have . . . Something told him there wasn't time to wait. He put his ear to the door and listened. The door was heavy, solid wood and he could hear only faint sounds as though someone paced slowly across the wooden floor. 'Tally? Jack?' He stepped back. 'Break it down.'

It took three attempts, then the frame gave with a loud crack and the door swung wide.

'Sir?'

Alec stepped across the threshold and stared in shock.

Tally had pushed Jack off her and on to the floor. He sprawled there, knife still between his ribs, blood pooling thick and glossy on the polished floor. He did not move, though Alec, looking closely, could discern the shallowest of breaths and his left hand twitched as though reaching for something he could not quite grasp. His eyes followed Tally.

One door in the long run of cupboards stood wide open. Tally had taken her camera from the case and now she circled Jack, framing each shot with infinite care. Trying, now she had the chance again, to capture that fleeting but decisive moment of transition; the picture she could not take at Momolo.

Epilogue

It was, Naomi thought, a strange assortment of people who attended Jack Chalmers' funeral. Individuals who had never met Jack but whose lives had been changed beyond measure because of him.

Tally had stabbed Jack Chalmers half a dozen times and pathology said that several of the wounds had been inflicted as he lay on the ground already losing blood. She had, it seemed, wanted to be sure he was dying, but this would make any self-defence plea very hard for a jury to swallow.

Naomi was sorry for that. A small part of her wished that Tally had struck only the once. Maybe twice if Jack had not been disabled by the first blow, but not so many times. Alec had seen her since her arrest. She refused to take the easy option of diminished responsibility and her lawyer was in despair.

'I knew exactly what I wanted to do,' she told Alec calmly at their last meeting. 'And frankly, I don't care any more. Jack is gone and that's all that matters.'

Naomi had come to the funeral almost on Tally's behalf, though she could not have explained why she felt that way, only that in some strange fashion she understood. Much as she might have wished it, Naomi realized that in Tally's position, she herself could not have ended it with just a single blow. Jack had possessed Tally's life. At first because she had allowed, even encouraged it. Then, because she had been a child afraid of being in trouble after the incident with Miles. Later, because she no longer knew how to exist without him and, like some self-fulfilling, Jack-induced prophecy, a little of her world ended each time she tried.

Adam, Jon O'Dowd, Simon. The roll-call was a solemn one and, Naomi wondered, how many others had there been who'd escaped with less, like Robert Principle. Tally must have felt herself cursed and Jack fed her dependency.

Lillian and Samuel had turned up unexpectedly. 'I want to see him gone,' Lillian had told her. Simon was home now and being fussed to death by his family.

Harry came, with Patrick; Harry having invested more than a stolen day in Jack. It had been a simple act of defiance, Naomi thought, but one which had overwhelming significance for this rather gentle, ineffectual man who knew what it was like to live in another's shadow. The shade of his dead sister had kept him from the sun too many years.

And Alec, of course, he came along with two of the officers who'd broken down the door that day. They'd come as official observers, and also, she felt, because they could still not believe what they had seen. This beautiful young woman, bending calmly to look into the eyes of her dying lover, then raising the camera and preserving that final image. Perhaps the most dramatic and startling she had ever captured in her entire career.

Alec had described the pictures to her – now part of the evidence from that day.

'They have a terrible beauty,' Alec said. 'And if I had my way, I'd burn them before they ever saw the light of day.'